MW01076067

THE
ALTAR
BOY

call Chantel
Sunday
Report a problem @ Apple.com

o Apple
1 800
692
7753

o Wall Street
800
568
7685

ALSO BY
THOMAS CLARK

Noah

The Storm

THE ALTAR BOY

A NOVEL BY

Thomas Clark

LUMINARE PRESS

WWW.LUMINAREPRESS.COM

The Altar Boy
Copyright © 2020 Thomas Clark

All rights reserved. This book or any portion thereof may not be reproduced or
used in any manner whatsoever without the express written permission of the
publisher, except for the use of brief quotations in a book review.

Printed in the United States of America

Cover Design: Clark Concepts, LLC

Luminare Press
442 Charnelton St.
Eugene, OR 97401
www.luminarepress.com

LCCN: 2020912211
ISBN: 978-1-64388-401-1

To

the countless good priests and nuns

who kept the promise they made

PART 1

FATHER KAVANAUGH

CHAPTER ONE

‑‑‑∞‑‑‑

When I turned five, Father Kavanaugh declared that it was a good thing I was old enough to start kindergarten and begin the process of becoming a God-fearing Catholic because—here he eyed me like I was a bug that had landed in the sugar bowl—he had detected unmistakable signs that the apple had not fallen far from the tree, and he was damned if he was going to allow me to become the spiritual degenerate my father had been. He did not have the time to keep an eye on me every second of the day, he continued, unfolding a napkin and placing it on his lap, and in any case, the whole purpose of him putting up with a convent full of nuns was to have people under him whose sole responsibility it was to herd problems like me onto the path to salvation and keep them there. So it was that in September of that year I began my Catholic education at St. Lawrence's Parochial Elementary School, an institution Fr. Kavanaugh controlled with an iron hand, the same way he controlled the Holy Name Society, the

Sodality, the CYO, and everything else connected with the parish.

I had no idea what apple had fallen where, and I didn't care. I was so excited about starting school that I could hardly stand still. Five days a week I was going to be free to flee the confines of our backyard, as big and wildly overgrown as it was, and become part of the running, hollering horde that, since my earliest memories, I had spied on through the hedge that separated our property from St. Lawrence's playground.

As much as anything about my first day of school, I remember the sunny disposition of the young nun, Sister Patricia Ann, who gathered us together on the blacktop and did her gentle best to organize us for our first trip into the school. With kindness and patience that I had never before experienced from an adult dressed in black, she showed us how to line up by twos, moving all the girls to the front of the line and all the boys to the back.

"That's wonderful," she said at last. "I can tell that you're all going to do very, very well in kindergarten. Now everyone take the hand of the person next to you."

The skinny boy who tentatively reached for my hand had curly, black hair and a very large nose. His name, I was to learn, was Vincent Rinaldi. He was extremely nervous that morning, and he remained nervous all the way through the seventh grade when my school days at St. Lawrence's came to an abrupt end. As he took my hand, he whispered that he had to go to the bathroom. I didn't know what to whisper back.

"That's it. Very, very good. Now everybody follow me," Sr. Patricia Ann said in a voice just loud enough to be heard in the back of the line where my partner was having a great deal of trouble standing still.

A red-haired girl broke ranks and sprinted, wailing at the top of her lungs, toward a woman in the small gallery of parents who had assembled to witness the big day. Sr. Patricia Ann smiled in the direction of the girl's embarrassed mother, mouthed words that made the mother smile back, then turned to lead us toward what would come to seem like an eternity in Catholic school. My own mother wasn't among the group of parents who were present to watch us that day, and it had never occurred to me that she would be. If the hedge along our property line had not been so overgrown, she could have watched the proceedings through the kitchen window behind which I knew she would be ironing clothes while saying the rosary to herself. At that stage of my life, I assumed that all mothers prayed while they ironed, prayed while they dusted, and prayed while sweeping the floor, their lips moving silently, their eyes closing from time to time while they almost imperceptibly shook their heads.

Wearing a brand-new white shirt and corduroy pants so stiff that moving my legs generated a strange scuffing sound, and with Vincent Rinaldi hanging onto my hand so tightly that I could no longer feel my fingers, we followed Sr. Patricia Ann through St. Lawrence's School's ornately arched entrance and down the wide hallway stairs to the basement where the kindergarten was located. The room she led us into was a huge rectangular space with pale-green walls and high windows along one side of the room through which the legs of the older kids who were still on the playground could be seen.

Sr. Patricia Ann smelled like Ivory Soap and, like a magician, could produce a pitch pipe from behind her starched, white chest bib or fish a pair of scissors from the bottomless pockets of her flowing, black habit. Unlike my mother, she seemed happy. She smiled and read our nametags and told us how much we were going to enjoy our year in kindergarten. Looking back on those days, I can only assume that she was new to St. Lawrence's and that the older nuns had decided not to dampen her enthusiasm by telling her about the ogre who ruled the parish.

While we hunched over the long green tables at which she had assigned us seats, Sr. Patricia Ann dragged the piano bench over to the window wall so she could reach high enough to water the sweet potato vines whose heart-shaped leaves spilled in a neat purple tangle from coffee cans lining the sill. She was busy at this task when the classroom door flew open and Fr. Kavanaugh burst in, his unsmiling eyes sweeping the room.

"What are these children doing, Sister?" he demanded as he stalked between tables that were no higher than his knees.

"They're cutting fall leaves out of construction paper, Father," she replied uncertainly while struggling to climb down from the piano bench without spilling water all over the floor. "We're going to decorate the classroom with them."

My classmates immediately stopped cutting out leaves, their eyes darting nervously from Sr. Patricia Ann to Fr. Kavanaugh. My scissors kept working away. By that age, his grizzly bear size, his booming voice, and his constant rage had become as much a part of my life as the house I lived in.

"Making classroom decorations may be a suitable activity for the public kindergarten down the street, but we have more important things to do here at St. Lawrence's!" He was angry, but then I had rarely seen him when he wasn't angry. I finished my leaf and held it up for Sr. Patricia Ann to see. She stared at me, horrified.

"The next time I visit this classroom, I expect each and every one of these children to know both the Our Father and the Hail Mary by heart." Fr. Kavanaugh's voice had grown ominously quiet, each word aimed at Sr. Patricia Ann with the thrust of a giant finger. Before he left, his eyes found me and narrowed, transmitting the usual warning that if I knew what was good for me, I'd better not do anything to make him mad, advice I had already learned was useless, since everything I did made him mad.

The kindergarten door slammed so hard behind him that a picture of the Blessed Mother tumbled off the wall and crashed to the floor. Somebody started to cry, and then somebody else started to cry, and pretty soon half the kids in the class were crying. Phillip Harrison raised his hand to tell Sr. Patricia Ann that Vinnie Rinaldi had peed his pants and that it was making a puddle under his seat. Sr. Patricia Ann closed her eyes, made the sign of the cross, and told us to keep cutting out our leaves. She led Vinnie, sounding like a duck as he sobbed through his big nose, out into the hallway. A few minutes later, Mr. Shifflet came in with his mop and cleaned the floor, and for the rest of the week, we practiced the Our Father, the Hail Mary, *and* the Glory Be and learned how to stand up and say "Good morning, Fr. Kavanaugh" as soon as we saw him come through door. After we had practiced it a hundred times, our greeting sounded like a little song.

CHAPTER TWO

He waltzed through our kitchen door every night. Never once knocking. Acting like he owned the place. Acting like he owned us. He didn't greet my mother, and my mother, busy at the stove, rarely said anything to him. I, on the other hand, had learned the hard way to immediately stop whatever I was doing and acknowledge Fr. Kavanaugh's arrival. He did not require that I stand up if I was already sitting at the kitchen table, but he fully expected me to say "Good evening, Father" distinctly and without mumbling. He invariably gave me an inspector general's once-over as he pulled back the chair at the head of the table and sat heavily, unfolding the *Washington Evening Star,* which he expected to be waiting for him, and creasing it open to the crossword puzzle. At least once a week he brought over his dirty laundry, stuffed into an army-green duffel bag, and casually tossed it down the stairs to the cellar where the next morning huge black pants, black socks, and black Roman-collar shirts would swirl around in the washing machine with our own things. I thought nothing of it. It was the way we lived. When I was younger, I assumed that it was perfectly normal to have a priest in the kitchen, an enormous one at that, who growled nightly about people he called "Begging Bettys" and "Helpless Harrys," members of the parish who had made the mistake of coming to the rectory that day to ask for help. "As helpless as the day they were born," he lamented with a shake of his head, twisting lead into the point of his gold pencil.

As he worked the puzzle, he grumbled about the weaknesses of his flock, shooting impatient glances toward the stove where my mother was scurrying to get dinner onto the table. Like his Sunday sermons, his listing of their faults started with the sins of the flesh, a failing that, according to him, afflicted every adult in the parish. "And you know exactly what I'm talking about, Rose Marie," he said to my mother's back, omitting the details I would have given anything to know more about.

He regularly recited the names of parishioners who had come to Mass late the previous Sunday, a transgression he considered no less flagrant than the Seven Deadly Sins. One Sunday, he had stopped Mass right in the middle of the Creed, his sudden silence freezing the packed church into absolute stillness. Turning to face the congregation, he had bellowed that there would be a brief intermission while the Doyle family took their seats. Mrs. Doyle, who had an army of little kids and whose husband never came to church with her, was so embarrassed that she began crying into a Kleenex.

The list of things that made him mad was apparently endless: President Eisenhower; altar boys who forgot to fill the cruets or light the altar candles; Catholics who sent their children to public school when they should have been paying tuition at St. Lawrence's; his two assistant priests, Fr. Fowler and Fr. Ellenberger, who he claimed didn't have the brains of a horsefly between them but whose main weakness, it occurred to me years later, was the fact that they were nice to people.

Worst of all were the "Fallen-Aways": baptized Catholics who no longer practiced their religion. In Fr. Kavanaugh's ranking of sinners, Fallen-Aways were worse than blasphemers and heretics. My late father had been a Fallen-Away. That fact had been thrown in my mother's face countless times by Fr. Kavanaugh or, more accurately, at her back as she scurried from the refrigerator to the stove, preparing his dinner. While Dennis Ignatius Flynn, whose name Fr. Kavanaugh could not utter without shaking his head, had clearly demonstrated by his fatal preference for golf over Sunday Mass that the Catholic religion meant nothing to him, he was by no means the only member of St. Lawrence's parish who had plunged to the bottom of the barrel of sinners.

"Did you know that Mr. Nolan who owns Madison Ford is a Catholic?"

Lowering his grizzly bear head, Fr. Kavanaugh studied the crossword puzzle for a minute, waiting for my mother to answer. He wasn't a patient man. His questions were not meant to be rhetorical. He cleared his throat and asked the question again, this time loud enough to make her turn quickly from the stove and admit nervously that she had never seen Mr. Nolan at Mass.

"And you never will. Rich as Rockefeller he is, divorced from the mother of his children, and living in sin with that shameless woman who used to be his bookkeeper. A harlot if ever one walked this earth."

My mother glanced quickly in my direction, unintentionally confirming that *harlot* was a dirty word, one I intended to look up in the big Webster's dictionary in the living room the minute I had the chance.

"That man had the gall to look me in the eye today at Miller's Drug Store and bid me good morning. Just as free and easy as you please. For the life of me I don't know what a man like that is thinking. With God as my witness, I don't. The eternal fire of hell is what he should be thinking about." Fr. Kavanaugh licked the point of his pencil and filled in a word. "Baptized, confirmed, and headed to hell in a handbasket that man is."

Encounters with sinners put Fr. Kavanaugh in a mood worse than the one he obviously awoke in every day. He glared at me, seeking some fault he had overlooked and, apparently finding none, raised the back of his hand in my direction anyway, a warning, perhaps, to stay away from harlots, whatever they were.

How many kids in the parish grew up like that? How many of my classmates at St. Lawrence's ever saw Fr. Kavanaugh without his Roman collar on or at the table in the summertime in his Fruit of the Loom undershirt or knew that their pastor had a Marine Corps tattoo on his thick left arm? How many of them knew about the gun he kept in the drawer of the money-counting desk in the church basement, a souvenir from his days as a Marine chaplain, that he often made clear to me he would not hesitate for one second to use on anyone stupid enough to try to rob the Sunday collection money? The answer was zero. Not one of them. But because I had never known any other way of life, I assumed that there was nothing out of the ordinary about the way we lived.

There were people in the parish who felt otherwise, a reality I encountered for the first time after I started school at St. Lawrence's. I must have been in at least the first grade, because the incident occurred in the school cafeteria, and when we were in kindergarten, we ate lunch in our class-room. The two girls in line behind me, Diane Rosario and Theresa Callahan, were a year older than me. They were talking about something that was making them giggle their heads off. When I turned around to ask them what was so funny, they put their hands to their mouths and tried to make straight faces. Finally one of them, Diane Rosario, managed to control herself long enough to ask me if Fr. Kavanaugh really lived in our house.

I said no.

Theresa Callahan said yes he did. Her mother said he did, lots of people knew he did, and her mother said it wasn't right.

I didn't know what to say. *What* wasn't right?

That day when I got home from school, I told my mother that Theresa Callahan's mother thought Fr. Kavanaugh lived with us. I'll never forget the way she looked at me when I said that. She appeared shocked, then frightened, then tried to laugh but managed only to make a strange nervous sound. Finally, after a couple of false starts, she wiped her hands on her apron and said: "I'm sure Mrs. Callahan was simply referring to the fact that Fr. Kavanaugh has dinner with us frequently. After all, the church is right next door." She studied me uncertainly, hoping, I can see now, that I was satisfied with her answer. I was, but only because, at that point of my life, I was an idiot.

CHAPTER THREE

Like scattered blackbirds, Mr. McDevitt's curses sailed over the tall hedge whose impossible assignment it was to separate his busy gasoline station from a genteel world that survived only in my mother's mind. To a small child, lurking like a spider in the corner of our wide porch, the words were every bit as mysterious as Fr. Kavanaugh's Latin. They were aimed at tires that wouldn't come off their rims, cars that wouldn't start, and, with a particular passion, at his son Butchie, whose aversion to work seemed to drive Mr. McDevitt crazy.

Though most of the rules that governed my life had been handed down by Fr. Kavanaugh, the "Thou Shalt Not Set Foot On The Gas Station Property" commandment had been imposed by my mother. "Satan works through people like the McDevitts," she reminded me often. "You are too young to understand that right now, but it is the truth. You must stay away from them, or their sinfulness will spread to you like a germ."

Mr. McDevitt knew Satan? This was fascinating news. Being an idiot, I began to wonder if the devil ever showed up at the gas station to see how things were going. Since my mother's commandment made no mention of spying on the enemy encampment, I began slipping off the porch and watching for the devil through the tangled branches of the hedge. I never did see him, but I came to know every detail of Mr. McDevitt's gas station from the pattern of its white porcelain enamel walls to the details of its two dark-green garage doors. I studied the way Mr. McDevitt squeezed under Fords and Buicks on his back and groped for the tools that lay at his side, and I watched Butchie sneak behind the building to smoke cigarettes. Peeking over my shoulder for signs of my mother, I practiced the casual way Butchie raised a finger to the sky when his father yelled for him to take care of cars at the gasoline pumps. Didn't Butchie know the fourth commandment made it a sin to disobey his father? Were the commandments only for Catholics? If so, how old did I have to be to quit being a Catholic?

"Russell Flynn, get inside this minute!" my mother yelled the second she discovered what I was doing. "What would your grandparents think if they looked down from heaven and saw you spying on those evil people?"

By grandparents, she meant the Cornells, her parents, the only grandparents ever mentioned in our house. Their picture was in the living room next to the fireplace with two smaller pictures: the one I loved of my father in his army uniform, holding a baby that was me, and the one of my mother when she was so pretty I had trouble believing it was really her. She dusted those pictures every day, often sitting down on the sofa with them and becoming lost in a spell that the world within the silver frames cast upon her.

In that world, my grandfather stands ramrod straight in a fully buttoned suit and a flat-brimmed straw hat. My grandmother stands beside him, attired in a full-length, white dress, protected from a long-ago summer sun by a wide bonnet obscuring in shadow everything above the bright tip of her nose. She is smiling a smile that made me certain I would have liked her. It is a smile my own mother never wore. Cradled easily in my grandmother's crossed arms is a tennis racket that, according to my mother, she brandished with great skill. Behind the two of them, surrounded by a high metal fence interlaced with a wildly flowering vine, is the tennis court where, I was often informed, my grandmother played tennis on Sunday afternoons with a group of women who had attended Trinity College with her.

"The first private tennis court ever constructed in Madison County," my mother glowed a hundred times. "Your grandfather had it constructed just for my mother. He loved her so much." Her voice invariably faltered when she added the part about the way my grandfather loved my grandmother. Sometimes I thought she was going to cry.

Beyond the tennis court, a meticulously maintained lawn embellished with well-tended rose gardens rolled like a carpet down to what is now Thirty-Eighth Avenue. It was hard for me to imagine what living in our house would have been like without McDevitt's gasoline station sitting almost exactly where the tennis court had been, without the constant noise, the coming and going of the cars, and without the oval sign that, at night, bathed the walls and ceiling of my bedroom in a strange green light.

While, to her dying day, my mother blamed herself for the existence of McDevitt's gasoline station on the south side of our house, the presence of St. Lawrence's church and, eventually, the rectory, the convent, and the grade school on the north side of our house was entirely due to the generosity of her father, Theodore Andrew Cornell, the founder and sole owner of the largest insurance agency in Washington, D. C. His prestigious list of clients included the Potomac Electric Power Company, the *Times-Herald* newspaper, The Hecht Company department stores, and the Archdiocese of Washington. The yellowing obituary that my mother preserved like a pressed rose between the pages of his worn Daily Missal noted that he had been known among his peers as a brilliant businessman who invested with "uncanny success" in the stock market and in downtown Washington real estate.

In 1916, the year before my mother was born, my grandfather made the momentous decision to move with my grandmother from their townhouse near Thomas Circle in Washington to the fresh air and leafy splendor of rural Maryland. He purchased a peach orchard eight miles northeast of the District of Columbia line from a man named Dixon Chandler, hired a well-known residential architect from Philadelphia, and constructed what for years was apparently the most imposing home in suburban Maryland, a textbook example of the Victorian style whose wide screened porch, embellished with scrolled gingerbread and dusty-green lattice work, faced an unpaved country lane that would eventually become Prospect Street, one of the busiest thoroughfares in Harrisville.

My grandfather was perfectly content with his new surroundings until shortly after he purchased a 1917 Oldsmobile touring convertible, a luxuriously appointed mechanical marvel that became his pride and joy. As my mother told the story, my Grandfather Cornell became increasingly concerned about the toll that bouncing over five miles of rutted roads between his new house and the nearest Catholic church was taking on the Olds. After one especially rough and mud-splattered trip, my grandfather, apparently as practical as he was religious and rich, decided to donate what remained of the peach orchard on the north side of the house—eleven and one-half acres in total—to the Archdiocese of Washington for, in the language of the deed, "the construction of a new church and rectory and such additional structures eventually deemed necessary by the Archdiocese for the propagation of the Catholic Faith in Harrisville, Maryland." In all fairness to my grandfather, he had no way of knowing that by placing his signature on such a document, he had set in motion a chain of events that would one day cause his only daughter to lose touch with reality and compel his only grandson to commit what was undoubtedly the most appalling sin in the history of the parish, if not the entire Archdiocese.

By the time I was old enough to begin recording memories, the house my grandfather built no longer reigned supreme at the crest of a grassy knoll, surrounded by acres of rabbit woods and abandoned peach trees. While it was still among the largest in town, it was no longer a candidate for the annual Harrisville house tour. Not only was it in disrepair, it was wedged so tightly between St. Lawrence's Church and McDevitt's Gasoline Station that a circus elephant, had one wandered into the neighborhood, could not have walked through either of our side yards without holding its breath. In a futile attempt to preserve a sense of residential dignity, privet hedges had been planted along both sides of what remained of the original property, first when the church was constructed and, years later, when my mother sold the land on the opposite side of the house to the Mason Dixon Oil Company that, in turn, built the gasoline station and leased it to Mr. McDevitt.

Those two hedges never had a chance. The fortress-like presence of St. Lawrence's Catholic Church ignored them totally as its walls soared skyward, monopolizing the view from both the downstairs and upstairs windows on the north side of our house. Measured to the tip of the golden cross atop the bell tower, St. Lawrence's was easily the tallest structure in Harrisville. "Taller by sixty-three feet than that monstrosity on Gallatin Street that the Methodists are prone to crow about," Fr. Kavanaugh declared at least once a week as though the height of its place of worship verified the superiority of the Catholic Church.

On summer evenings, the heavenly strains of the choir practicing "Panis Angelicus" and "Holy Queen Enthroned Above" drifted through our open kitchen windows, and on Sunday mornings, Fr. Kavanaugh's unheavenly condemnations of our fellow parishioners rattled the pots of African violets crowding our kitchen windowsills. From the opposite side of the house, we were bombarded daily not only by Mr. McDevitt's amazing arsenal of obscenities but also by the racket of power tools and the constant clanging of the gasoline pump bell.

"That John McDevitt is the most disgusting man I have ever met in my life," my mother declared almost nightly, staring at the gas station sign through the curtains above the kitchen sink. "What must my good parents think when they look down from heaven and see the likes of him and his horrible son inhabiting what was once the most beautiful yard in Harrisville?" She wrung out the dishrag with which she had been wiping a pan and draped it neatly over the neck of the faucet. "They will never forgive me for selling that lovely property to an oil company."

"Don't be a fool, woman," Fr. Kavanaugh bellowed without looking up from his crossword puzzle. "What choice did you have after that parasite you chose to marry squandered every cent your good parents left you?"

A rare flash of color reddened my mother's face.

"A sensible woman would be down on her knees every night thanking Almighty God for striking the man dead before he cost her the very house she was born in!"

"Dennis was not a strong person."

21

"I do not care to hear the man's name! A baptized and confirmed Catholic playing golf on a Sunday morning when it was his sacred duty to be at Mass!" Fr. Kavanaugh twisted the point back into his gold pencil and tossed the folded newspaper onto the vacant chair to his right. "Don't waste a single Hail Mary on him, Rose Marie! God Almighty struck him dead as a warning to others who would dare defile the Sabbath! The man made his sinful choices, and he will pay for those choices through all eternity."

My mother crossed the kitchen and slid the platter of pot roast onto the table, the dinner we were required to have every Wednesday night, because, as Fr. Kavanaugh constantly reminded us, it was the meal his saintly mother served on Wednesdays when he was a boy in Wilkes-Barre, Pennsylvania, just as she served meat loaf on Mondays and chicken cutlets on Thursdays.

"It's entirely possible that Dennis was able to make an Act of Contrition in his final seconds," my mother half-whispered, slumping into her chair.

"The sinner did no such thing, and you know it! The man is where he belongs, and it is a waste of breath to deny that simple fact!"

My mother stared into her napkin as Fr. Kavanaugh growled the words of grace, after which he helped himself to enough pot roast and buttered carrots to stuff a grizzly bear. "Smells almost as good as the pot roast my dear departed mother used to make." My mother's face tightened into what she meant to be a smile. Fr. Kavanaugh pushed the steaming platter across the table and gave me the nightly once-over, searching for the smallest lapse in posture, neatness, or facial expression that would give him reason to raise the back of his enormous left hand. In a reflex of self-preservation, I flinched in anticipation of being belted and saw the flicker of a smile that appeared on his face whenever I did.

CHAPTER FOUR

My classmates' reactions to encounters with Fr. Kavanaugh varied from stunned silence to peeing in their pants or worse. Neither they nor our teachers, the nuns, knew when or where our feared pastor was going to appear, a situation creating an atmosphere at St. Lawrence's that registered somewhere between tension and terror. On top of that, because Fr. Kavanaugh knew my name and frequently demanded to know how I was doing with my schoolwork, the other kids regarded me with suspicion. They were reluctant to sit near me at lunchtime or pick me when choosing sides for a game of tag on the playground. It seemed like I was never going to make any friends when, thanks to Fr. Kavanaugh's uncontrollable temper, my life and Butchie McDevitt's life collided.

The difference between Butchie McDevitt and the kids at St. Lawrence's could not be exaggerated. They didn't cuss. Butchie was an expert. They didn't smoke. Butchie stole Chesterfields from his father every chance he got and smoked them behind the gas station. No one at St. Lawrence's had a tattoo. Butchie had two, one on each shoulder that he had drawn with a blue ballpoint pen. They were supposed to be spiders but could have easily been mistaken for crabs or possibly even turtles. Nevertheless, there they were, clearly visible below the rolled-up sleeves of his tee shirt.

The events that brought us together began one evening when Fr. Kavanaugh showed up at our house in a particularly foul mood. He stomped in, dropped heavily into his chair, and slapped a piece of paper onto the kitchen table. Someone in the parish had had the audacity to mail an anonymous letter to the rectory accusing Fr. Kavanaugh of being the most insensitive Catholic priest they had ever encountered. With his eyes narrowed to slits and his enormous hands shaking, he read the letter once again to himself. "Not even the intestinal fortitude to sign their name!" he fumed, turning the single page over, apparently searching its blank backside for clues to the sender's identity. "Weasels and weaklings. God help me, Rose Marie," he complained to my mother. "That is what the Catholic laity has become! Nothing but weasels and weaklings!"

It was the word *weasels* that did it. That very day, our first grade teacher, Sr. Gertrude, had read us a story called *Willy the Weasel*. As she read, she held up the book and showed us pictures of Willy and his friends. Programmed with the knowledge that weasels were furry little things with pointed noses and long necks, my six-year-old imagination kicked into gear, generating a picture of hundreds of pointy-nosed weasels streaming into St. Lawrence's church, genuflecting and making little signs of the cross with their furry paws. The image was so unexpected and silly that I laughed out loud, spraying the table with half-chewed chunks of my dinner. One second my mouth was full of green beans, and the next second it wasn't. One second Fr. Kavanaugh was staring at me in enraged disbelief, and the next second, I was sprawled on the kitchen floor with fireworks exploding in my head.

It took four harrowing trips to the dentist to have my chipped front teeth repaired, and each time, my mother repeated to the dentist and his receptionist the same lie about me falling out of the sycamore tree in our backyard, embellishing the tale each visit with details such as the number of times she had warned me about the dangers of tree climbing and how I was lucky I hadn't broken my neck. After the last visit, instead of turning on Jefferson Street and driving home, she continued down Baltimore Avenue.

"Where are we going?" I mumbled through half-numbed lips.

She didn't answer my question, probably because driving a car made her more nervous than usual. We passed the old stone armory and the vacant lot where the Chinese restaurant had burned down before turning into the Pep Boys parking lot.

"What are we doing here?" I asked, completely puzzled.

She got out of the car, and I followed.

The inside of Pep Boys smelled like car tires. My mother looked around, ignoring a man who asked if he could help her, and headed for a long display of bicycles parked diagonally along the back wall. The man and I followed.

"Which one do you want?"

I was slow to comprehend. "I don't have all day, Russell. Which bicycle do you want?"

At first I was confused, and then, as the meaning of her question sunk in, I was flabbergasted. The highlights of my previous Christmas had been unwrapping a plaid winter coat and an illustrated book about the lives of the saints. Dizzy with disbelief, I started at one end of the line, intending to examine every one of the bicycles in minute detail. My mother had no intention of standing for such foolishness, impatiently informing me that if I didn't make up my mind in two minutes, we were leaving. The one I picked was a maroon Schwinn with chrome fenders and a thumb-operated bell on the handlebar. As the man was maneuvering it into the backseat of the car, my mother informed him that the bike was a reward for me being so good at the dentist. I knew that was a bunch of baloney, because before she even started the car, she made me promise in the name of Jesus that I would never tell a soul about what Fr. Kavanaugh had done. She could have saved the money she had just spent on the new Schwinn, because Fr. Kavanaugh had already described in scary detail the things that would happen to me if I ever said one word about it.

None of that mattered to me. I had a brand-new two-wheeler, and from the minute we got back home until it was too dark to see, I did nothing but ride it, stare at it, and wipe it with a Windex-soaked rag.

The next morning, it was gone.

Butchie McDevitt, as I was to learn, did not possess the brains of a squirrel. If he had, before he started parading around the neighborhood on a stolen bike, he would have done something to disguise it like painting it another color or removing the chrome fenders. He did nothing. As I sat on the front porch steps, blubbering like a baby, Butchie pedaled the bicycle of my dreams up the sidewalk and brought it to a stop right in front of our house. I stared in disbelief as he grinned and thumbed the handlebar bell.

"Hey, Peckerhead, how do you like my new bike?"

I ran into the house, screaming that Butchie McDevitt was riding my stolen bike. My mother's eyes narrowed, she grabbed me by the hand, and the two of us marched next door to the gas station, pushing through the hedge to save time. To my amazement, she dragged me right into Mr. McDevitt's office, a cluttered, oil-smelling space with an assortment of naked-lady calendars decorating its cinder block walls.

"Well, I'll be damned, Mrs. Flynn," Mr. McDevitt said, looking up from an auto parts catalog through which he had been tracing a grease-blackened finger. "To what earthshaking event do I owe this honor?"

"Never you mind the crude sarcasm, Mr. McDevitt. That son of yours has stolen Russell's bicycle!"

"No shit. Are you sure?"

My mother gasped; any expression stronger than *damn*

affected her like an electric shock. "I am quite sure," she replied, regaining most of her composure. "He is riding it up and down Prospect Street as bold as brass."

"Bold as brass, no shit?"

Before my mother could manage another gasp, Mr. McDevitt walked to the door and bellowed at the top of his lungs, "Butchie, get your ass in here!"

Mr. McDevitt sat back down, grinning. I closed my eyes, trying not to look at the naked-lady calendar on the wall behind him, fully aware that looking at dirty pictures was a sin. A second later, I opened them again. "We've Got What You Need," the words below the naked lady said. "Wilson Auto Parts, Bladensburg, Maryland." I couldn't see the part between the naked lady's legs, but I could see everything else. I knew I was breaking the commandments, but I couldn't help myself. I kept looking.

"Butchie, don't make me come out there and get you!" Mr. McDevitt yelled at the open door.

A few seconds later, Butchie appeared. As soon as he saw my mother and me, he blurted out that he had found the bike in the woods behind the gas station and was only riding it around so he could find out who it belonged to.

"Get over here."

Butchie knew what was coming, but my mother and I didn't. Mr. McDevitt stood up and slapped him so hard that Butchie flew backwards against a pea-green filing cabinet.

Apparently forgetting the many things she had witnessed Fr. Kavanaugh do to me, my mother froze and clamped her hand over her mouth.

"Anything else I can do for you today, Mrs. Flynn?" Mr. McDevitt asked, already back to tracing a dirty finger through the pages of his catalog.

My mother grabbed my arm and yanked me toward the door, abruptly separating my bulging eyes from the first pair of breasts I had ever seen, not counting the ones in the *National Geographic* magazines at the library.

CHAPTER FIVE

"These bottles represent your souls, children." Sr. Eleanor Rose stopped abruptly and glared at Gerald Brown, who was rolling his pencil down the sloped top of his desk, trying to catch it before it hit his lap, a game he played by the hour. She made him change places with Susan Rollins, who sat in the front row. Gerald protested, promising he would stop playing with his pencil, but Sr. Eleanor Rose made him do it anyway.

When my classmates and I reached the second grade, we were deemed by the Catholic Church to have reached the age of reason, meaning that, in the eyes of the Church, we were old enough to be held accountable for our sins. The emphasis in religion class shifted from memorizing basic catechism questions like "Who Is God?" and "Why Did God Make Us?" to feverish preparations for our first confession and first communion. For the third day in a row, Sr. Eleanor Rose was drawing milk bottles on the blackboard.

"Please pay strict attention," she ordered, putting the finishing touches on her neatly constructed illustration. "As I told you yesterday, this lesson is extremely important." She pointed at the milk bottle with a long piece of chalk. "When we are born, we already have original sin on our souls." She drew a very neat O in the middle of the milk bottle. "Why is that?" she asked, turning to face the class.

A forest of hands flew up, most of them belonging to girls eager to demonstrate how smart they were. "Sister, Sister!" they hissed frantically.

I knew the answer. I knew we were born with original sin on our souls because Adam and Eve took the apple from a snake that was actually the devil and got kicked out of the Garden of Eden when they ate it. One thing that happened was that they were all of a sudden embarrassed about not wearing any clothes, and another thing was that God told them that because of what they had done, everyone who was born after that day was going to have original sin on their souls. There was a picture of them slinking out of Eden in our religion book, but Eve's hair was so long that you couldn't see anything.

"That's right," Sr. Eleanor Rose was saying, "because of Adam and Eve, and how is original sin removed from our souls?"

Most of the girls in the class went nuts again, eager as a bunch of beavers to explain that original sin was washed away when we were baptized, which got me to thinking that Butchie and Mr. McDevitt probably still had original sin on their souls, because it was hard to imagine that either one of them had ever been inside a church, let alone been baptized. I glanced out the classroom window in the direction of the gas station. I wanted to see Butchie again. I wanted to be close to someone with original sin to see if I could tell if there was anything different about them. The problem was that my mother had forbidden me to ever set foot on the gas station property again and warned me that she would tell Fr. Kavanaugh if I did.

By the time I started paying attention again, Sr. Eleanor Rose had moved on to the difference between venial sins and mortal sins and was drawing a new milk bottle on the blackboard. This time she made it about two feet high so the kids in the back of the room could see it better.

"When we are in the state of grace, our milk bottle is completely full, like this." Using the side of her chalk, she shaded the entire bottle white. "There are two kinds of grace, actual and sanctifying, but you will not be getting into that until the fourth grade. For now, we will just say that grace is a beautiful gift from God that we get when we are doing His will." She scanned the classroom to make sure everyone was paying attention. "Grace is the gift of God that helps us be good people. When our soul is like this,"—she tapped on the chalk-filled milk bottle with the point of her chalk—"it means that we are friends of God and have been doing His will. Does everyone understand that?"

Nobody said they didn't understand what a full milk bottle meant, not even the dumb kids, probably because she had talked about the same thing for two weeks. Everybody, except probably Gerald Brown, who never paid attention, knew she was going to tell us next that when we committed venial sins, some but not all of the grace disappeared from the bottle. With the corner of an eraser she carefully rubbed out a few inches of chalk and turned back around to face us. "Now if we commit another sin, what happens?"

Joanne Harper said out loud, "More grace comes out of the bottle!"

"Raise your hand and wait to be called on before you speak, Miss Harper!" Sr. Eleanor Rose scolded, causing Joanne to deflate like a punctured balloon.

Margaret Turner, whose hand was waving furiously, was called on just before her arm became disconnected from her shoulder. "More grace comes out of the bottle!"

Sr. Eleanor Rose erased more milk from the bottle for each time its make-believe owner committed another venial sin until there was not enough left at the bottom of the bottle to use on a small bowl of cereal. She stood back, studying the smudged but mostly black soul, and shook her head. "A soul like this makes God very sad and makes the devil very happy, children." When she blessed herself, most of the girls and a few of the boys did the same thing.

For the rest of the week, she repeated the difference between venial sins, like disobeying your parents or forgetting to say your night prayers, and mortal sins, like murdering someone or going to holy communion when you weren't in the state of grace. The big difference was that when you committed venial sins, only a little bit of grace went out of your soul, but when you committed a mortal sin, every last drop of grace disappeared. To emphasize this point, Sr. Eleanor Rose obliterated the chalk milk bottle with two dramatic swipes of the eraser. I could tell that she meant to do it in one try but she missed one corner of the bottle the first time.

"I don't mean to frighten you, children, but you have reached the age of reason, and you are now old enough to understand that if you die with a single mortal sin on your soul, you will be condemned to the fires of hell for eternity." She closed her eyes and shook her head. "And, if that happens, all the prayers of your mother and your father or your aunts and uncles and your brothers and sisters here on earth will be in vain."

Victoria Vescusso immediately burst into tears.

"Victoria, child, what is the matter?" Sr. Eleanor Rose asked, squeezing into the narrow aisle between the desks.

"Is being mean to a chicken a mortal sin?" Victoria wailed.

Sr. Eleanor Rose stopped halfway to Victoria's desk. "What on earth do you mean?"

Victoria was crying so hard that she had difficulty answering. What I thought I heard her say was that a chicken had been chasing her in her grandfather's backyard, and she threw some mud at it. Everybody heard her howl that she didn't want to go to hell.

Victoria's outburst opened the floodgates. Marsha Berry wanted to know if stepping on bugs was a sin. Michael Scott asked if throwing a firecracker at your sister was a venial sin or a mortal sin, and Vinnie Rinaldi raised his hand to ask if forgetting to kiss his mother good night was against the commandments.

Gerald Brown, who rarely showed interest in anything, seemed mesmerized by the subject of mortal sin. He wanted to know what a person's soul would look like if they chopped somebody's head off or put rat poison in their food. Sr. Eleanor Rose told him that she wasn't going to dwell on things so terrible, because no one who went to Catholic school would ever commit such sins. Gerald was undeterred and pleaded for her to draw a picture on the blackboard of what Adolf Hitler's soul looked like when he died. Sr. Eleanor Rose told everyone to put their hands back down. "It makes no difference whether a person eats a hot dog on Friday or does horrible things to other people," she explained. "A mortal sin is a mortal sin, and there is no chance of that person attaining eternal salvation unless they make a good confession or say an Act of Contrition before they die."

I didn't understand how it would be fair for somebody who ate a hot dog on Friday, even if they did it on purpose, to end up in the same boat with Adolf Hitler. That may well have been the first time I had a problem with something I heard in religion class. It certainly wasn't the last.

Sr. Eleanor Rose asked if anyone had a sensible question, placing a great deal of emphasis on the word *sensible*. Even though I had spent a great deal of time wondering if looking at Mr. McDevitt's naked-lady calendars was a mortal sin or a venial sin, I didn't raise my hand, mainly because I wasn't sure what would happen if a second grader said *naked* out loud in a Catholic school. I decided again that there was no way out of it; I was going to have to tell about looking at Mr. McDevitt's calendars when I made my first confession. If I didn't and made my first communion the next day with a black sin like that on my soul, I would probably get struck dead on the way back to my pew. The best I could hope for was that the priest in the confessional wouldn't recognize my voice, and to increase the odds of that happening, I had been practicing speaking with a Chinese accent like a detective I had seen at the movies.

CHAPTER SIX

Mr. McDevitt was shoulder-deep under the hood of a green Plymouth station wagon, cursing at a carburetor, when I slipped into the garage. After several failed attempts to get his attention by clearing my throat, I took a deep breath and was about to tap him on the back when my eyes discovered the calendar hanging over his tool-cluttered workbench. At that point of my life, all I knew about boobs was that if you thought about them on purpose, much less looked at them, you were guilty of sinning against the sixth commandment and would go straight to hell if you had a heart attack or got run over by a bus before you had a chance to say an Act of Contrition. I couldn't help myself. Never had I seen a sight like the one that now met my eyes. The redheaded woman on the calendar was kneeling on a blue-and-white blanket that had been spread out in a field of long, green grass. She was holding a can of motor oil in her hands and smiling at it like it was her favorite thing in the world. That wasn't the amazing part. The thing that froze me in open-mouthed wonder was that her boobs hung almost down to her belly button. Until that moment I had no idea they came that big. Reluctant to abandon such an incredible sight but wilting before a growing fear that bigger boobs meant bigger sins, I shut my eyes and began reciting the Act of Contrition, reaching the part about dreading the pains of hell before Mr. McDevitt poked me on the shoulder.

"Does your mother know you're over here?"

I jumped about two feet.

Mr. McDevitt stared down at me, one eye closed against the smoke from the cigarette in the corner of his mouth while he wiped his hands on a grease-stained rag. I had trouble getting my mouth to work.

"Your bike disappear again?" he asked, tossing the rag onto the workbench.

I shook my head.

"Your mother send you over to borrow a cup of sugar?"

I shook my head again.

He took the cigarette out of his mouth and snapped away some ashes. "I'm all out of guesses. What the hell are you doing over here?"

After a few more tries, my mouth began to work, and I asked him if Butchie was around.

"His sorry ass better be. He's supposed to be cleaning the men's room."

That's where I found him, sitting on the painted concrete floor in the semidarkness, reading a *Superman* comic book. "Hey Peckerhead," he said, looking up. "What the fuck are you doing over here?"

I shrugged. The space was cramped and smelly. A web of cracks formed a triangular shape in the mirror over the small, stained sink. Next to the mirror, bolted to the wall, there was a scratched-up orange contraption with decals plastered to it. I approached it carefully. On one of the decals there was a picture of a guy wearing a giant cowboy hat with the words "Big Tex" stitched into it. He was winking and smiling. Another decal said "25 Cents" in big, black numbers, and next to it, there was a slot with the orange paint around it worn down to the bare metal. From his seat on the floor, Butchie grinned at me, flicking his eyebrows up and down. Not wanting to seem stupid, I flicked my eyebrows back at him.

I had absolutely no idea what I was looking at. As I edged closer, I saw that there were messages scratched into the orange paint. One said "Agnes knows what you like." The only Agnes I knew was Agnes McDermott, who was in the second grade with me and whose nose was always running. The mystery deepened. Whatever was inside this thing had something to do with sin, I could tell that by the look on Big Tex's face, not just sin but sin that was in an entirely different league from looking at big-boob calendars. All I had to do was put a quarter in the slot, and I would find out what it was. Images of Sr. Eleanor Rose's milk bottle souls flashed into my mind. I wasn't sure how much grace was in mine, but I knew it was all about to disappear. Taking a deep breath, I mapped out a plan. I would put a quarter in the slot, see what came out, then instantly say an Act of Contrition, a course of action that would kill two birds with one stone: I would find out what Big Tex was grinning about, but I wouldn't go to hell if I got struck dead before I made my first confession with the rest of the second grade. I fished in my pocket for a quarter, but all I found was a dime and some stuck-together Wild Cherry Lifesavers. I asked Butchie if he had a quarter.

He leapt from the floor and wedged himself between the orange machine and me, his arms outstretched. "You trying to get your ass arrested?"

I was dumbfounded. "Arrested!"

Butchie stole a glance at the broken mirror as if it he suspected there was a spy behind it. He dropped his voice to a whisper.

"Didn't you see that bell over my old man's workbench?"

I shook my head.

"Course not. That's because it looks like a regular old electrical box." His whispered words smelled like cigarettes. "My old man told me it's a special rubber machine bell that he ordered all the way from Mexico. It goes off the second anybody drops a quarter in the slot."

Butchie eyed the mirror again and pulled me to one side. Lowering his voice even more, he admitted that he had never heard it ring himself, but his father had ears like a dog and could hear it clear as day. "Whenever he does," Butchie continued breathlessly, "he runs outside to see if the person coming out of the men's room is old enough to use rubbers. If they ain't, my old man calls the cops."

Old enough to use rubbers? I was pondering the meaning of those mysterious words when somewhere beyond the men's room door, the two-tone chime of a bell sounded, and I froze.

"Don't piss in your pants, Peckerhead. That's only the gas pump bell." Butchie shook his head as he slid back down onto the floor and reopened the comic book. "I swear to God you don't know shit from Shinola."

He had just resumed mouthing comic book words to himself when Mr. McDevitt hollered loud enough to be heard through the wall that if Butchie didn't want his head to get shoved into the men's room toilet, he better get his ass out to the gas pumps. Butchie cussed quietly, raised his middle finger in the direction of his father's voice, and reluctantly pushed himself to his feet.

A long, red convertible with a folded white top waited at the gas pumps, the music that blared from its radio seeming to shake the air. Two guys in the front seat were laughing like crazy about something while two girls in the back seat held little mirrors in front of their faces, combing their hair. They all wore sunglasses.

"You old enough to pump gas?" the guy behind the steering wheel yelled above the music when Butchie strolled up to the car. The girls laughed like that was the funniest thing they had ever heard.

"We're out of gas," Butchie told him, spitting on the ground.

"What?"

"No gas."

"What the hell kind of gas station is this?"

Butchie, maybe ten years old at that time, shrugged his shoulders and spat again. The guy in the driver's seat couldn't see it, but this one hit the bottom of his car door and slid slowly to the ground. He stared at Butchie, and Butchie stared back at him. Behind his back, Butchie wiggled his middle finger. For a minute, it was like the guy in the car didn't know what to do. His face grew redder and redder. "Well, fuck you, you little punk!" he exploded, tromping on the gas pedal and roaring out of the gas station, tires squealing and dust flying.

"Are you really out of gas?" I asked, watching the red convertible swerve into Prospect Street and run through a red light at Thirty-Eighth Avenue.

"Fuck no. We got a million gallons," Butchie answered, heading back toward the men's room and his *Superman* comic book.

"What if your father finds out?"

"Finds out what?"

"Finds out you told that guy you were out of gas."

"How the fuck is he going to know?"

My understanding of what the word *fuck* meant was limited to a vague concept of something done in the dark by men and women who smoked cigarettes and drank cocktails. The kind of degenerates I pictured didn't go to Mass, and if they did, they certainly didn't go to communion. People like that fascinated me. They didn't seem to be the least bit worried about what their souls would look like if drawn on the blackboard by Sr. Eleanor Rose. They didn't seem the least bit worried about the eternal fires of hell, a place hotter than a frying pan but where sinners never turned into ashes and therefore burned forever, crying out day and night for the smallest drop of water, relief that not even their mothers and fathers, looking down on them from heaven, were allowed to give them. How could anybody not worry about a fate so horrible? I worried about committing sins all the time. I worried about my mind wandering at Mass, about forgetting to say my night prayers, and about being struck dead in the middle of thinking about naked-lady calendars.

This latest contemplation of the hopelessness of living a sin-free life was interrupted by the sight of an agitated Mr. McDevitt emerging from his office, slapping an envelope against the back of his hand.

"Where the hell did Butchie go?" he barked.

Unable to find my voice, I gestured toward the men's room door. I thought he was going to yell for Butchie to bring him the gasoline money, an event I didn't have any interest in staying around to witness, but he didn't. He just shook his head and turned his attention to the envelope, ripping it open with a screwdriver he had taken from his back pocket. His eyes moved back and forth over the single sheet of paper he had unfolded. They closed for a second, then reopened and repeated the process. "Fucking bitch," he snarled. "Her and her fucking lawyer." He folded the paper back into the envelope and stuffed it into his shirt pocket.

I wasn't sure if I should say goodbye or just leave. I began edging in the direction of our house.

"Looks like you're going to have to find somebody else to lead you astray, kid."

I stopped and looked up at him. I had no idea what he was talking about.

The sun slid from behind a billowing cloud and set the cross atop St. Lawrence's steeple on fire. I was never sure if events like that were signs from God, but just to be sure, I made the sign of the cross and recited another Act of Contrition. Two more sins had been added to the already lengthy list I had compiled for my first confession: I had disobeyed my mother by sneaking over to the gas station while she was working at the St. Vincent de Paul Society, and I had once again taken pleasure in the sight of Mr. McDevitt's naked-lady calendars. It wasn't clear to me if listening to the word *fuck* without holding my ears was a sin, but there was no way I could ask about that in religion class without being expelled.

CHAPTER SEVEN

"You ever seen a real naked woman?" Butchie asked me a few days before he disappeared.

"Not that many," I lied.

"Liar," he replied, giving up on the shriveled cigarette butt he had been trying to light and throwing it into a patch of knee-high weeds behind the gas station.

All I could do was shrug.

"I saw my first one when I was six," he casually informed me.

My shock at such a revelation obviously showed.

"Maybe I was seven," Butchie amended.

"Where?"

"Some lady over in Bladensburg when we lived there. Old lady with wrinkly tits. Saw her through her bedroom window."

With the sleeves of his dirty T-shirt rolled up above his thin shoulders, he proceeded to tell me that he saw lots of naked women at night when he went around looking in windows. "I seen Sue Butler in her underpants last week."

"Who?"

"Sue Butler, the coolest girl at Harrisville Junior High. Seen her last night. Little teeny tits. She must wear falsies to school." He sat up straight and rolled up one of his pants legs. "Got these goddamn scratches from some rose bushes in her backyard."

A year earlier, when I was in the first grade, we had been informed that there was always an angel sitting on our right shoulder reminding us to obey the commandments and a devil sitting on the left one, trying his best to get us to commit sins. According to the picture in a book that Sr. Gertrude held up for us to see, they were both approximately the size of parrots. As I listened with growing interest to Butchie, the devil said nothing. The angel, on the other hand, was having a fit, reminding me in no uncertain terms that I already had more sins to tell at my first confession than any kid in the history of St. Lawrence's parish and that looking at Sue Butler's teeny tits, through a window or any other way, would be one more thing I would have to describe out loud to a priest who might very well recognize my voice. After mulling the situation over for a couple of seconds, I swiped at my right shoulder like I was shooing away a wasp. "Do you peek in windows every night?"

Butchie thought for a minute. "Not when it rains." He fished another cigarette butt from the front pocket of his dirty jeans and did his best to straighten it out. "I do it mostly on Wednesday nights when my old man is at the Moose playing poker."

It was only Monday, but I looked up at the sky anyway. There wasn't a rain cloud in sight.

Butchie struck a match and attempted to light the remains of a cigarette barely longer than the tip of his nose. "If you got the guts, you can come with me."

Ignoring the distant protests of a screaming angel and having no clue how I was going to sneak out of the house without my mother hearing me, I nodded.

"Midnight," Butchie said, getting to his feet. "Right here behind the building."

I nodded again.

Before Wednesday came around again, Butchie was gone. Because I could only sneak over to the gas station when Fr. Kavanaugh's big Chrysler was gone from behind the church at the same time that my mother was working at the St. Vincent de Paul store, a few days went by before I got a chance to ask where he was. Mr. McDevitt was stretched out underneath a car when I got there. The first time I asked him where Butchie was, he asked me to slide him a wrench that was on the floor next to my feet. I waited a minute then asked him again.

"Got no idea where they took him," he finally answered.

Getting down on my hands and knees so I could see under the car, I asked Mr. McDevitt where *who* took him, but he didn't say anything else.

I was unwilling to give up. When I made it back to the

gas station again, Mr. McDevitt was sitting at the desk in his cramped office, drinking a beer with his heavy work shoes propped on his battered desk. He didn't say anything when I slipped in, still looking over my shoulder to make sure a big, black car I had seen on Prospect Street wasn't Fr. Kavanaugh's. Mr. McDevitt leaned back in his chair until his head was almost touching the wall.

"Did Butchie come back?" I asked.

He drained the rest of the beer, tossed the can in the general direction of a trashcan in the corner of the room, and shook his head. "Nope." That was all he said until I picked up the empty beer and dropped it into the trashcan. He said thanks, burped, and told me to beat it.

The next time I snuck into his garage, he was sitting in the driver's seat of an orange Chevrolet taxicab, racing the engine, then cocking his ear to listen for something when he took his foot off the accelerator. "Hear that?" he asked me as he raced the engine again.

I didn't know what he meant. A deaf person would have heard the racket he was making. "Did Butchie come back?" I asked when the garage was quiet again.

He looked at me with both hands gripping the steering wheel. "Look, kid, do me a big favor, go home and stay there. You hear me? The last thing I need right now is trouble with your uptight mother." He slipped out of the taxi and bent over the front fender, tugging hard at something with both hands. "Trouble with one woman is enough for any man," he informed me without looking away from whatever he was trying to do. "One woman and her fucking lawyer!"

He straightened up and turned around, holding what looked like a black cup with a bunch of long wires attached to it. "Distributor cap," he said, turning it over and looking inside the cup part. "All pitted to hell." He threw the whole thing into a big oil drum filled with junk and went into a storage room crammed with boxes of parts. I followed him. "Distributor cap, distributor cap," he mumbled, scanning the shelves. He almost tripped over me when he turned around. "Come on, goddamn it, get your ass back over to your house."

He was almost as tall as Fr. Kavanaugh, but for some reason, he didn't scare me the way Fr. Kavanaugh did. I could tell he wasn't mean that way, but when I asked him if he had called the police or the FBI about Butchie disappearing, he pointed what I assumed was a new distributor cap in the direction of our house and told me to move my ass before he gave it a good kick.

With Butchie gone, my chances of seeing Sue Butler in her underpants went up in smoke, leaving me with nothing to do except go to school and spend time hoping that Fr. Kavanaugh would stop dreaming up jobs for me to take care of over at the church, an objective that seemed increasingly important to him. I prayed secretly for Butchie's safe return when we said the rosary in class despite the fact that we were supposed to be praying for the Russians to be converted so they wouldn't drop the H-bomb on us. Three times a week we practiced taking shelter under our desks in case the rosaries didn't work, drills that continued even after Thomas Alford raised his hand and told Sr. Eleanor Rose that what we were doing was a complete waste of time. His father, he announced importantly, was an army officer at Fort Meade and had told him that if the Russians ever dropped the H-bomb anywhere near Washington, every one of us would end up looking like charcoal briquettes, a statement that reduced most of the girls in class to babbling idiots and caused Vinnie Rinaldi to pee in his pants for the first time since kindergarten.

Something else happened about this time that had nothing to do with Butchie disappearing or the Russians turning us into charcoal briquettes with H-bombs. It was weird and confusing at the time, but because I was so young, I was not able to grasp the significance of the series of events that started when I came downstairs in the morning and I told my mother I was too sick to go to school.

She seemed so startled by what I said that she had trouble placing her coffee cup back in the saucer. She glanced up nervously up at the clock and then out the kitchen window in the direction of the church.

"You can't miss school," she told me uncertainly.

"We don't have any tests today."

"That doesn't matter," she insisted. "School is very important!"

"But I haven't been absent all year," I argued, feeling vaguely like I was going to throw up. I had already turned around and started back toward the stairs when she informed me, surprisingly and emphatically, that I was going to school.

I made it through the morning, but by the time my class marched into the cafeteria at lunchtime, I was feeling so bad that I told Sr. Thomas Johanna, who was on duty, that I was too sick to eat anything. It may not have been a matter for confession to miss a meal, but in the old nun's book, it was obviously a sign of human weakness. "You will feel perfectly fine after a good lunch, Mr. Flynn," she informed me, steering me firmly by the shoulders into the serving line and ordering me to put a bowl of spaghetti and meatballs on my tray, along with a piece of bread, a small carton of milk, and a jiggling dish of green Jell-O in which fruit cocktail had been suspended. "The starving children in China would praise God for such a wonderful meal," she lectured as she followed me to the second grade table where she stood over me and pointed insistently at the food piled on my tray.

I threw up. I mean, I really threw up, spewing spaghetti and at least one meatball across the table where John Hudson and Raymond Jennings, in clean, white shirts and blue clip-on neckties, were much too slow to duck.

Kids who threw up at St. Lawrence's were treated with roughly the same sympathy with which lepers were treated in the holy movies they showed us the first Tuesday of every month in the school auditorium. After being cast out of the cafeteria, I managed to stagger across the playground and push through the hedge into our backyard before dropping to my knees and throwing up again.

When I found the kitchen door inexplicably locked, I peered through the window. A basket filled with washed clothes sat on the floor next to the ironing board. The iron was plugged in, but my mother wasn't in sight. I stumbled off the porch and crawled through a clump of tangled azaleas to the basement window from which I could see the washing machine. There was no sign of my mother. After throwing up in the azaleas, I crawled back onto the porch and peered into the kitchen again. This time, I spotted Fr. Kavanaugh's black jacket draped across a chair and saw his Roman collar on the table.

I was much too sick to wonder why Fr. Kavanaugh was at our house in the middle of the day. After pounding on the door until I was too weak to lift my arms, I gave up and slumped onto the porch where I slept until the rumble of Fr. Kavanaugh's voice woke me up.

"What you are doing is in accordance with God's plan! I've explained that to you a hundred times!"

After a long silence, my mother said something too faint to understand.

"That's because you were not intended to be taught anything about it in school, in church, or anywhere else for that matter! There was no need for you to know about such complex matters until you became one of the chosen ones. Almighty God has reserved a special place in heaven for women like yourself, Rose Marie."

Once more there was a silence followed by words too quiet to be understood.

Fr. Kavanaugh thundered in response. "You are no such

thing! You are the comforter of a man of God. Why do you think God took your husband from you? Why do you think Almighty God, in His divine wisdom, placed you on this earth right next door to my church?" My mother's next words were cut short, Fr. Kavanaugh's reply vibrating the door. "I do not care to hear any more about it!"

His chair scraped against the floor as he left the table, and a second later, the door flew open, mashing me against the wall. Fr. Kavanaugh stomped down the porch steps and toward the gap in the hedge that had been forged by his never-ending trips. My mother followed him onto the porch, bawling at the top of her lungs that she was sorry. She watched him disappear through the hedge then slowly turned back toward the house. When she saw me, she turned absolutely white.

"What are you doing home?" she wailed.

"I'm sick," I managed to reply. I didn't expect my mother to hug me or take me upstairs and make sure I got out of my stinking clothes and into a hot bathtub. I'm not even sure I realized at that point of my life that mothers did things like that, but the last thing I expected her to do was to scream in my face. "Don't you ever come home again in the middle of the day like this! Don't you dare!"

I was bewildered. When other kids got sick in school, they went to Sr. Superior's office and waited for their mother or father to come and pick them up. My mother didn't even have to do that; all she had to do was leave the back door unlocked. I didn't have a clue why she was so angry, but I was much too sick to think about it.

It was late the next afternoon before I was well enough to come back downstairs, and when I did, my mother didn't ask me how I felt or want to know what I had done with my dirty clothes. All she wanted to know was exactly how long I had been out on the back porch and precisely what I had heard. She must have asked me those same questions ten times, seizing me by the shoulders and staring into my eyes. Even at that age, my instincts warned me to play dumb, and in any case, the meaning of what I had seen and heard would not dawn on me for a very long time.

CHAPTER EIGHT

———⊷∞⊶———

Before leading us into church to make our first confession, Sr. Eleanor Rose closed her eyes and folded her hands, fingertips to fingertips, and held them close to the starched, white bib that marked the Sisters of Notre Dame. "Children, this is a momentous week in your journey to becoming soldiers of Christ. As long as I live I will never forget my own first confession."

I was afraid that I would never forget mine either but for what I assumed were entirely different reasons. What kind of things could Sr. Eleanor Rose have possibly had to tell in confession when she was seven years old? Spending a nickel on a Popsicle instead of putting the money in the poor box? Accidentally getting some jelly on a holy card she was looking at while eating breakfast? I could confess things like that without even batting an eye. They weren't even real sins. Mine were. They were whoppers that had kept me awake at night wrestling unsuccessfully for a good way to rephrase the words *naked-lady calendars* without actually lying which, we had been informed, would constitute a bad confession and make us ineligible to make our first communion on Sunday. "Thank goodness that at your age such a terrible occurrence is beyond the realm of possibility," Sr. Eleanor Rose had assured us with a benevolent smile.

Only the helpless realization that I had no place to go, no place to eat, and only thirty-five cents in my pocket prevented me from breaking out of line and running for it as we were herded like a flock of petrified sheep across the parking lot and into the cavernous gloom of St. Lawrence's Church. I was lost in thought, wondering what it would be like to disappear the way Butchie McDevitt had, traveling with the circus or riding railroad cars with a gang of merry hobos, or whatever Butchie was doing, with no school to worry about, no homework to do, no stiff, white shirt and clip-on necktie to torture him daily. The pros and cons of being me versus being Butchie had yet to completely play out in my mind when I sensed the panic that had seized my classmates. As their wondering eyes adjusted to the darkness, it had become clear that green lights were glowing above only two of the four confessionals: Fr. Fowler's and Fr. Kavanaugh's. Like panicked rats, the entire class broke ranks and bolted toward Fr. Fowler's confessional, creating a single line that stretched all the way past the baptismal font in the rear of the church. With the quickness of a cat, Sr. Eleanor Rose sprang into action. Leaving the girls in the safety of Fr. Fowler's line, she snared boys by the collar and dragged them two at a time across the church to where Fr. Kavanaugh lurked inside his confessional like a bear in a cave. Jeffery Huff, the smallest boy in our class, dove under a pew and, as far as I could tell, never resurfaced. I jockeyed for a spot in the back of Fr. Kavanaugh's line, engaging in a free-for-all that raged until Sr. Eleanor Rose resorted to twisting ears. When order was restored, Vinnie Rinaldi, who had ended up at the front of the line, responded to the hopelessness of his plight by releasing a series of pathetic whimpers that fluttered high into the arched vaults above our heads like a flock of small birds desperate to escape.

While Sr. Eleanor Rose prowled the aisle like a prison guard, our line inched along, one reluctant penitent after another pushing aside the heavy velvet curtain and entering the scary confines of a confessional for the first time in his young life. From time to time, muffled growls erupted from Fr. Kavanagh's compartment, causing the entire line to stagger two or three steps backwards. With the inevitability of death itself, my turn came when an ashen-faced Lawrence McCarthy exited the confessional, and Sr. Eleanor Rose prodded me in the ribs. Kneeling in absolute darkness, I was aware of barely audible murmurs from the far side of the confessional that ignited explosive responses from Fr. Kavanaugh. Helplessly, I awaited my fate, painfully aware that the sins I was about to confess were not only the worst either priest would hear today but probably the worst ever confessed by a second grader in the history of St. Lawrence's parish. I had looked at Mr. McDevitt's naked-lady calendars ten times—that was the number I had settled on—not only looked at them but attempted, with total disregard for my immortal soul, to memorize every sinful detail. While the murmurs from the far side of the confessional dragged on, accompanied now by what sounded like sobbing, I pinned my hopes for survival on the fact that inspired by Charlie Chan, the Chinese detective I had seen at the movies, I had worked hard to perfect my Chinese accent. In the safety of my bedroom or hidden in the small jungle of ancient peach trees deep in our overgrown backyard, I had honed the recitation of my damning sin to the point where it came out sounding like "I rook at woman wiff big broobs tren times." Even if Fr. Kavanaugh managed to understand what I said, there was no way he would know it was me.

That finely crafted scheme evaporated the second the confessional window slid open, filling the perforated plastic screen in front of my nose with the shadowy silhouette of Fr. Kavanaugh's enormous head. My brain went numb. All I could focus on was the fact that I would give my right arm, both arms, even both arms and one eye, to trade places with any one of my classmates whose sins, I was confident, amounted to no more than allowing their minds to wander during Mass or throwing mud at their grandfather's chickens. If my legs had been working, I would have jumped up and fled, bursting past a startled Sr. Eleanor Rose and my awe-struck classmates, sprinting up the aisle and through the massive oak doors, bounding down the worn granite stairs and running across Prospect Street, ready to hop on the first bus to come along and ride as far as thirty-five cents would take me.

"Well?" Fr. Kavanaugh bellowed loud enough to be heard on the far side of the church. "Let's go! I haven't got all day!"

Ignoring a sudden urge to pee, I blurted out the words that had been drilled into our heads in religion class. "Bless me, Father, for I have sinned. This is my first confession."

Horror struck like a lightning bolt. I had forgotten all about speaking with a Chinese accent. Fr. Kavanaugh already knew who I was. If I told him about the naked-lady calendars, not to mention my sinful desire to put a quarter in the scratched, orange machine with a Big Tex decal in the gasoline station men's room, he would no doubt scream, "You did what?" so loud that every head in the church would turn in the direction of this very confessional. His giant fist would come crashing through the plastic screen as he grabbed me by the throat and strangled me. There was only one thing to do: lie. Make a bad confession. Commit another grievous sin that would pile on top of my other sins and make me the biggest second grade sinner in the history of the Archdiocese of Washington.

Reasoning that anything was better than being strangled in a confessional, I declared that I had disobeyed my mother 134 times, the number I had settled on during the numerous examinations of conscience we had been urged to make during the past couple of weeks, and that I had gone to bed without saying my night prayers eighty-four times. Because I was speaking so fast and those sins had only taken up a few seconds, I made up another sin on the spot and threw it into the pile. "I was mean to a cat three times." I didn't even know any cats.

There was a silence during which I was sure Fr. Kavanaugh could hear my heart pounding.

"Is that all?" he finally snarled.

"Yes, Father," I lied, committing yet another sin.

The silence that followed made me so nervous that I was about to make up another sin when I remembered that when we were finished telling our sins, we were supposed to say "these are all the sins I can remember. I am truly sorry for them."

Fr. Kavanaugh mumbled away in Latin, made the sign of the cross with a shadowy hand, and told me to say five Hail Marys and five Our Fathers. The window closed halfway then jerked opened again. "Mr. Flynn, the next time you disobey your mother, I will slap you silly."

I staggered out of the confessional with more sins on my soul than I had gone in with. There was no point in saying my penance, but since Sr. Eleanor Rose was watching me like a hawk, I knelt down in a pew in front of the statue of the Blessed Mother, resigned to the fact that someday I would be in hell with people like Mr. Nolan, the Ford dealer, and Attila the Hun.

CHAPTER NINE

⎯⎯⎯∞∞∞⎯⎯⎯

The next morning at nine o'clock sharp, the second grade girls, white veils bobby-pinned to their hair and bouquets of yard flowers clutched in twisted tinfoil, began the parade into the packed church. As at our many practices, the girls had been lined up from shortest to tallest with the notable exception that Martha Wigglesworth, by far the shortest girl in our class but much too dumb to lead the way, had been relegated to the rear.

When the line reached the front of the church, the girls genuflected two by two and slipped into the pews on the Blessed Mother's side of the church. Delirious parents whispered desperately for their kids to look at them so they could snap pictures that had no chance of turning out because of Fr. Kavanaugh's inflexible rule against the use of flashbulbs in church. High in the balcony, Mrs. Enright played "Bring Flowers of the Rarest" on the gigantic pipe organ that my Grandfather Cornell had donated to the parish when the church was built. My mother, who was extremely proud of that fact, may have been somewhere in the church, but it was much more likely that she had stayed home with the headache she had gotten the night before when Fr. Kavanaugh told her at the dinner table that she was starting to look old. He was there, of course, glaring down at everybody from the altar while Fr. Fowler and Fr. Ellenberger stood nervously at his side.

Next down the aisle came an eighth grade altar boy carrying a pole topped by a fake dove with real white feathers that was supposed to be the Holy Ghost. A carefully measured gap separated the Holy Ghost from us, the first communion boys, only one of whom, I was certain, harbored a soul as black as a lump of coal. Everything else about me was brilliant white: white shirt, white clip-on necktie, white short pants with a white belt, white knee socks, and white shoes so new that they refused to bend like feet. Progressing one shoe-squeaking step at a time to the front of the church, we genuflected two at a time, almost as neatly as the girls had, and filed into the pews in front of the life-size statue of Saint Lawrence. When we were done, there were exactly eight boys to a row, the successful conclusion of a maneuver that had been practiced a million times.

Amazingly, I survived the walk down the aisle. No lightning bolt fried me to a crisp; no Angel of Death, gold sword flashing in the morning sun, came crashing through a stained glass window to lop off my head. My heart rate was beginning to return to normal when I raised my eyes and noticed the statue of Saint Lawrence skewering me with its plaster eyes. In his right hand, he grasped the iron grill on which, we all knew, the Romans had roasted him alive. Maybe God meant for me to see that grill. Maybe that was His final warning. I suddenly had to pee, but Sr. Eleanor Rose had instructed us to do that before we got to the church. "Don't even think about raising your hand after we get inside," she had warned in a tone reserved for her most serious edicts, "because you are not leaving your pew! Does everyone understand that?" I pressed my knees together and hoped for the best.

As the last notes from Mrs. Enright's organ drifted into the carved arches high above our heads, Sr. Eleanor Rose clapped sharply, and we sat down like trained performers. In the packed rows behind us, hundreds of parents and grandparents cleared their throats in unison. The urge to flee resurfaced, causing me to forget that I had to pee. From the corner of my eye, I calculated the distance from where I was sitting to the aisle. Vinnie Rinaldi was on one side of me, fidgeting with his white necktie. Gerald Brown was on the other side, attempting to fold the five-dollar bill that had been a first Holy Communion present from his grandmother into the shape of an airplane. Beyond each of them, other white-clad classmates unwittingly blocked my path to freedom. My eyes darted around the church like those of a trapped animal. On both sides of the nave, biblical characters imbedded in the stained glass windows scrutinized my every move. The unexpected realization that my grandfather had also donated the money for these windows piled one more worry on top of everything else: what if he and my grandmother really could look down from heaven the way my mother thought they could? If it was possible for them to see that their beautiful gardens and the first private tennis court in the history of Madison County had been obliterated by the construction of Mr. McDevitt's gasoline station, then without a doubt, they were at this very moment craning their necks to see if it was true that their only grandson was about to make his first Holy Communion with mortal sins on his soul, a transgression so unimaginable that it had probably never happened in the history of the Catholic Church. I had just recognized the first signs of nausea when, from the foot of the altar, Fr. Kavanaugh boomed the words, "In nomine Patris, et Filii, et Spíritus Sancti." Mass had begun. I might as well have been clinging to a log heading down the river toward Niagara Falls.

Catholic Mass is a ritual of standing, sitting, standing again, kneeling, and then sitting and standing some more. By the end of second grade, we knew when to do what. We stood up while Fr. Kavanaugh read the gospel in Latin with his back turned to us, and we sat down when he came down the altar steps and made his way over to the pulpit. As he cleared his throat into the microphone, I glanced at the statue of Saint Lawrence and could have sworn that, almost too fast for the human eye to catch, he had flicked his plaster eyes ominously at the gridiron he was holding, an instrument of torture as horrible as any in history. His message was clear. I didn't know whether to flee or throw up right where I was. Fr. Kavanaugh cleared his throat a second time and waited impatiently until every man, woman, and child in the church was absolutely still. Gerald Brown, who couldn't sit still if his life depended on it, began walking his fingers crablike across the space between us and pinching me in the thigh. He didn't stop until I grabbed his hand and whispered that I was going to beat the crap out of him after Mass if he didn't quit it. Threatening a classmate in church had to be at least a venial sin, but to a sinner like me, being mean to Gerald Brown was like the residents of Sodom and Gomorrah forgetting to say their night prayers.

Fr. Kavanaugh began his sermon in such an agitated state that his face turned beet red in seconds. He bellowed that he found it unbelievable that every single grown-up sitting in front of him had once dressed in white like all of us and marched into church to make their first Holy Communion.

"Look what you have turned into! Just take a look at yourselves!" He pounded his fist on the pulpit so hard that the big leather missal from which he had read the gospel crashed to the floor. He didn't even look down. "Sinners!" he screamed. "Sinful of mind and sinful of body! Sinful by omission and sinful by commission!"

Somewhere in the rear of the church, a baby started crying. Vinnie Rinaldi closed his eyes and started saying Hail Marys, prayers he probably thought he was saying to himself but wasn't. Unlike the statue of Saint Lawrence, which I could swear still had its eyes on me, the statue of the Blessed Mother on the far side of the pulpit remained frozen in plaster, giving no indication that she heard Vinnie's prayers or that she was the least bit interested in Fr.

Kavanaugh's tirade. I couldn't remember if my Grandfather Cornell had paid for the Blessed Mother statue the way he had paid for the organ and the stained glass windows, but if he had, he had certainly gotten his money's worth. She was as beautiful as Snow White with this really nice smile and was wearing a pretty blue robe on top of a white gown with lines of gold decoration around the neck. I couldn't see the bottom of the statue from where I was sitting, but I knew from all the times that Fr. Kavanaugh had made me clean up the flowers that people were always leaving in front of her that the Blessed Mother was standing on a snake with her bare feet. In my opinion, that plaster snake was the neatest thing in the entire church. It was supposed to be the devil and had this fat head with little teeny eyes and a mouth that was stuck open so you could see its long, curved teeth and skinny, maroon tongue. One afternoon, I had just worked up the nerve to stick my finger in the snake's mouth when Fr. Kavanaugh spotted me from the sacristy door and hollered that I had exactly two seconds to get back to work if I knew what was good for me. I was still thinking about the plaster snake when Fr. Kavanaugh's tirade turned to sins of the flesh, words that always grabbed my attention.

"Each and every one of you adults know exactly what I am talking about!" he roared, thumping his beefy hand on the pulpit. "I sit in my confessional every single Saturday afternoon and hear your disgusting admissions! Sinners! Sinners, every last one of you! Look me in the eye and tell me that you are not!" He waited. Behind us, the baby cried

67

harder, throats cleared, and pews creaked as the grown-ups stirred uneasily. Vinnie Rinaldi, who knew no more about what Fr. Kavanaugh was talking about than the rest of us, started mumbling another Hail Mary. By the way he was counting on his fingers, I could tell that he was working his way through the rosary.

My mind wandered again when it became clear that Fr. Kavanaugh was not going to reveal any more details about sins of the flesh than he usually did. Out of the blue, I had this wonderful vision of the Blessed Mother coming alive, grabbing the snake she was standing on, and hurling it at Fr. Kavanaugh. It might have been the neatest thought I had ever had. In my mind, I saw everyone in the church screaming like they were at a horror movie. I saw the snake wrapping itself around Fr. Kavanaugh and sinking its curved teeth into his thick neck. I wondered if Fr. Fowler or Fr. Ellenberger would do anything to help him or if Mr. Higgins, the usher who had had his arm shot off in the war by the Germans, would run up to the pulpit to try to save him with the arm the Germans missed. Before I could get far enough for Fr. Kavanaugh to keel over dead, Vinnie Rinaldi cut a fart gross enough to make Gerald Brown pretend like he was passing out.

The daydream evaporated. There was no snake around Fr. Kavanaugh's neck, and if there had been, he probably would have smashed it to death with the same fat fist with which he was trying to pound the pulpit to smithereens. He lifted the fist slowly, turned it into a pointing finger, and aimed it at our white-clad first communion class.

"I dare say," he bellowed like a bullhorn, "I dare say that these offspring of yours, this fidgeting flock of"—he seemed to search for a word that he could not find and settled for "creatures" — "these creatures will someday follow you down the same disgusting path into the eternal abyss!" Fr. Kavanaugh waved a blessing over a shell-shocked flock of parents and grandparents, who must have thought that they had misunderstood him, and stomped back to the altar.

When it was time for my row to stand and parade up the aisle to receive communion, I followed along like a lemming. Kneeling at the altar rail, I closed my eyes and stuck out my tongue, hoping that if God were going to strike me dead it would be quick and painless. High in the balcony, the choir sang "Panis Angelicus," totally unaware that parish history, not to mention archdiocesan history, had just been made. A baptized second grader, attired in white from head to toe, had just trumped his bad confession with a bad communion. Back in the pew, while my classmates were no doubt praying for God to bless their parents or make them taller or give them a pony, I prayed that He wouldn't make me go blind or wither my arm for what I had done.

CHAPTER TEN

———∞∞∞———

In order to avoid extinction at the hands of Fr. Kavanaugh, I had no choice but to go on pretending that I was a good Catholic, a role that required allowing myself to be dragged over to church by my mother every Saturday afternoon to go to confession. For her, these trips were an unchanging ritual. Kneeling in front of the Blessed Mother's statue to examine her conscience, she covered her face with her hands and seemed to slip into another world. Inevitably her shoulders began to shake, and I knew she was crying. At that time, before I had figured it all out, I found it impossible to understand how a woman who said rosaries to herself all day long and constantly fingered the Miraculous Medal pinned to her apron could possibly commit sins appalling enough to make her cry.

She always got in Fr. Kavanaugh's confessional line, something that very few people who were not senile or new to the parish ever did. I never did, not even to lie to him, which is all I ever did in confession. I got in Fr.

Fowler's or Fr. Ellenberger's line and told them about things like disobeying my mother or falling asleep before finishing my night prayers but leaving out serious stuff like wondering what girls looked like in their underpants. What difference did it make? I was going to hell anyway for making bad confessions and bad communions that had started with the first ones and been adding up ever since. I could say Hail Marys until the beads fell off my rosary, I could be nice to old people and animals until the end of time, and I could put millions of dollars into the collection for pagan babies, and I would still go to hell. When I died, all Saint Peter would have to do was find my name in his big book, run a finger down to where it said first confession and first communion, and it would be all over. He wouldn't yell at me and go nuts like Fr. Kavanaugh would, at least when I pictured my arrival at the gates of heaven, he never did. I pictured him shaking his head sadly and nodding at some big angels who would take me by the arms and throw me down a giant sliding board, and that would be that.

It was going to be terrible down there, I knew that, with all the heat and smoke and devils running around jabbing at people with pitchforks. On the other hand, I would get a chance to meet my father, and that thought made the whole idea a lot less scary. Because of all the people who had been sent there since hell was invented, it might take a while to find him, but because I spent so much time looking at the picture of him in the living room, I knew I would recognize him when I did.

That photograph was my favorite thing in the world. In it, my father was all alone with me, sitting on some wide stone steps in front of a very large fountain, the kind of fountain where water flows like a sheet of glass over the edge of a big basin that statues of naked people are holding high above their heads. In the background, there was a wide street busy with cars and taxicabs and, in the distance, a very large classical structure that, thinking about it in later years as I often did, I realized was Union Station in downtown Washington. It was a Sunday afternoon; I don't why I am sure of that, but I am, and even though the photograph was in black and white, I was also sure that the sky was deep blue, and the taxicabs in the busy street were bright yellow.

My father, a bright smile lighting his deeply tanned face, was as handsome as a movie star. The sleeves of his army uniform were rolled up far enough for me to see that his arms were every bit as muscular as Fr. Kavanaugh's. My favorite part about the picture, the part that always made me feel strong and safe, was that in his left arm he was cradling me like a football. I was just a baby with teeny, teeny feet, squinting blindly against the sun in a funny white hat. With his right hand, a hand as big as Fr. Kavanaugh's, my father was pointing at me like he was saying "Hey, look what I found!" He wasn't just smiling; he was on the verge of laughing.

Some girl in my class said that babies were too young to really love anyone, but I didn't believe her. I know I already loved my father the day that picture was taken, and I know that he loved me, and I also knew that if he had not died when I was still a baby, my father would have knocked Fr. Kavanaugh on his fat ass if he ever caught him treating me the way he always did. I loved thinking about that. Sometimes at the dinner table, I got this vision of Fr. Kavanaugh with a bloody nose, sprawled on our kitchen floor in his shiny black pants and white Fruit of the Loom undershirt, and that thought would make me so happy that once my face must have lit up without me knowing it, and Fr. Kavanaugh demanded to know what I was smiling about. When I lied and told him I wasn't smiling about anything, he said that only imbeciles smiled about nothing, and the next time he caught me doing it, he would knock me off my chair, which he was always looking for some reason to do anyway.

I wanted my father to be alive more than I ever wanted anything. I wanted him to live in our house and play golf on Sunday mornings whenever he felt like it and for him to tell Fr. Kavanaugh to stay out of our house if he knew what was good for him. I wanted to ask him if I could go to public school and if I could stop being a Catholic, because all that being one did was make me worry about going to hell. I wondered if he would mind the gas station being next door the way my mother did. I wondered a lot of things about him. I wondered if he cussed. I wondered if he would let me play with Butchie, and as much as anything, I wondered if he could make my mother smile.

She knew how to smile; the picture of her in the living room proved it. It was on that same shelf in the living room with the one of my father holding me like a football and the one of my Grandfather and Grandmother Cornell standing next to their tennis court. I would have never known it was my mother if I hadn't asked her so many times that she finally told me it was.

"It was all so long ago," she had added almost to herself, taking the picture from my hands and returning it carefully to its place in the small nest of photographs between a bowl of wooden fruit and two silver candlesticks that we never used.

I remember being stunned. The young woman in the photograph was as beautiful as my father had been handsome. She was sitting on a stone bench near a birdbath and a bed of tall flowers. Far behind her, I could see what I knew was the corner of our screened porch and, beyond that, the high fence surrounding the tennis court. She was far prettier than any of the mothers who drove my classmates to school in the morning and picked them up again in the afternoon. She was wearing lipstick, and there was a bracelet on one of her wrists that flashed a crisscross sparkle back at a bright sun. The most surprising thing to me was that, unlike the mother I knew, she looked so happy, not tired and worried the way she always looked now. Her smile was not just one of those smiles you make when somebody takes your picture but a special kind of smile that makes a person's eyes smile too.

It's entirely possible that my mother may have hugged me or tucked me into bed and done other nice things when I was too young to remember, but it didn't seem like things like that counted unless a person could remember them and know what they felt like. She was never mean to me the way Fr. Kavanaugh was mean to me. It was just that she never acted like I was anything special to her. She never seemed to be proud of anything I did. When I brought home a report card with nothing on it except As and maybe one B, or a book report with a gold star and the word "Excellent!" spelled out in perfect nun handwriting, all I remember her doing was looking at me the funny way she always did and wiping her hands on her apron. At some point, I stopped showing her the things I had done. I stopped trying to tell her about things that happened in school or giving her reminders about parent-teacher meetings. There didn't seem to be any point.

One day, I pushed a pile of old magazines out of the way and sat down on the coffee table to look at the picture of me and my father. I knew my father would have wanted to see the things I brought home from school. I knew he would have asked me my spelling words at night and checked my arithmetic answers instead of saying he was too tired. Once I had a dream in which I actually slipped into the picture and settled into my father's strong arms. He smiled at me, and when my mother came along and sat down with us on the steps in front of that big fountain, he made her laugh. The three of us started being a family all over again, only this time my father didn't have a heart attack, and my mother didn't stop smiling and laughing and wearing lipstick. It was the best dream I ever had. I was thinking about that dream when Fr. Kavanaugh snatched the picture of my father out of my hands.

"I told your mother to get rid of this!" he thundered as he held the silver frame in his shaking hands. "I told her to rid this house of all signs of this sinner!" His face was red, and spit was flying out of his mouth. Before I knew what was going on, he raised the picture high above his head and hurled it onto the tile hearth in front of the fireplace. The glass shattered, and the picture and a piece of gray cardboard that was behind it slid halfway out of the silver frame.

"Damn that man! Damn his black soul to hell! Damn his drinking, and his gambling, and his sinful indifference toward Holy Mother the Church!" He grabbed what was left of the picture and was about to smash it again when a jagged piece of glass sliced into his finger. "Goddamn it!" he screamed. "Goddamn it to hell!"

My mother hurried into the living room. "What is it, Father?" she asked, wiping her hands on a dish towel. Fr. Kavanaugh sucked blood from his cut finger and yelled for her to get back into the kitchen.

"Take this!" he shouted at me. I was too shocked to move. "Take it," he demanded, shoving the smashed picture at me. "Now tear it to pieces!"

I slipped the photograph out of the silver frame as carefully as I could, showering the hearth with shards of glass.

"You heard me! Tear it to pieces!"

I didn't want to do anything to it. I wanted to keep it and look at it forever.

"Did you hear me? I will not permit you or your mother to gaze upon the face of a man who is burning in hell!"

With my hands shaking and my eyes filled with tears, I

tore the picture in to pieces. I tried not to tear my father's face or the little face of me when I was a baby. I wanted to slip them into my pocket and sneak them up to my bedroom after Fr. Kavanaugh left.

It was a plan that didn't work. Fr. Kavanaugh made me drop the torn pieces into the fireplace. He struck a match. The pieces browned, blackened, and curled into nothingness. As I watched in horror, my father's bright smile turned to dust.

That day, in that high-ceilinged old living room that had once, no doubt, echoed with the laughter and polite small talk of my Grandparents Cornell entertaining the first parishioners of St. Lawrence's Church, I learned that hatred, real hatred, was much more than a word. I learned that it was a living, pulsing thing with heat and weight and jagged edges, and I carried that feeling inside me until the night Fr. Kavanaugh's sorry life came to an end.

Chapter Eleven

———⦿———

"Lay-tiff-fee-cot! Lay-tiff-fee-cot! What in the name of Holy Mother the Church is so difficult about that!" Fr. Kavanaugh's beefy hand slammed down on the kitchen table, rattling the china my mother was hurriedly removing. "Ad Deum qui LAETIFICAT juventutem meum! Say it again!"

The misery of memorizing Latin began for me in the fourth grade, a full year before boys at St. Lawrence's were permitted to join the altar boys and at least a thousand years before I would have become one if I had any choice in the matter.

I recited the strange words endlessly while Fr. Kavanaugh scratched at his crossword puzzle. I had a lot of homework to do. Sr. Elizabeth Boniface, my teacher that year, had given us a mimeographed list of spelling words to memorize and practice using in sentences. She had also assigned all the problems on page twenty-eight of our arithmetic book except for number seventeen, which she said was over our heads. If I ever got done practicing Latin, I was going to work on number seventeen until I got it. I knew for sure that a few of the smart girls in our class would try to do it just to show how smart they were, but I also knew that girls weren't good at arithmetic, so unless they cheated and got their fathers to help them, I had a good chance of being the only one in the class to get it right.

"Introibo ad altare Dei," Fr. Kavanaugh boomed. Those were the first words a priest said at Mass, and when he did, the altar boys serving Mass were supposed to say, "Ad Deum qui laetificat juventutem meum," which I did. It must have come out better this time, because Fr. Kavanaugh's only reaction was to fold up his newspaper and clear his throat.

"Rose Marie," he said, pointing the rolled-up newspaper at me, "you may remember that I once caught this young man venerating—and that was the very word that came to my mind as I watched him—*venerating* a photograph of his late father, a photograph that had no more business in a Christian home than a likeness of Satan himself."

My mother made eye contact with Fr. Kavanaugh but quickly looked away. In all the time that that picture of my father had been missing, I had never heard her say a word about it.

Fr. Kavanaugh slapped the newspaper on the table hard enough to kill an armadillo. "I will state once more, as I have stated a hundred times before, the man you foolishly married was a worthless sinner, and with God Almighty as my witness, I will not permit this young man to follow in his father's unholy footsteps."

79

I expected him to say the thing about the apple not falling far from the tree, having figured out that I was the apple and my father had been the tree. He didn't, probably because he loved meatloaf and that was the dinner my mother had placed on the table. He slid the steaming platter across the table and sliced a big hunk off the end. My mother hung the potholders on a hook next to the refrigerator and took her seat. "When will Russell begin serving Mass?" she asked, steering the conversation away from my father, a subject that always made her too nervous to eat.

"As soon as he knows his Latin backwards and forwards unlike the hopeless flock of numbskulls that Fr. Fowler pronounces fit to serve."

For the simple reason that no one in his right mind would volunteer to become an altar boy if they knew Fr. Kavanaugh was going to train them, Fr. Fowler had been given the job of training the new boys. Unfortunately for me, there was to be one exception.

"Before you go to bed tonight, print out the entire Confiteor ten times in your copybook." Fr. Kavanaugh slid the laminated Latin response card toward me, tapping a finger on it ominously. "And print it very, very neatly."

The Confiteor might not have been the hardest Latin response in the Mass to pronounce—it didn't hold a candle to the verbal minefield known as the Suscipiat—but it was the longest, and I didn't have time to print it out once, much less ten times. Responding to some basic instinct that causes children to turn to a parent when they are in need of help, I looked at my mother, forgetting in my desperation that she had never shown the least inclination to protect her young, meaning me, and, in fact, exhibited a strong tendency at moments like this to remember that she had clothes to put in the dryer or laundry to fold.

When she saw me looking at her, she placed her fork carefully on her plate and, to my astonishment, reminded Fr. Kavanaugh that I usually did my homework after dinner. The words were barely out of her mouth before Fr. Kavanaugh held up his hand like a traffic cop. "There is no reason in this world, Rose Marie, why young Mr. Flynn here could not have done his homework this afternoon after school."

My mother could have rallied to my defense right there. She was fully aware that Monday was my afternoon to clean the church. School ended at 2:50, and by 3:00 sharp, Fr. Kavanaugh expected to find me on my hands and knees searching under pews for lost gloves and balled-up Kleenexes, a job that Mr. Shifflet, the janitor, was apparently no longer agile enough to do. As if that weren't enough for somebody my age to do when all he could think about was eating a peanut butter and jelly sandwich, I was expected to check all five racks of votive candles and replace the burned-out ones with extras, a job that required lugging a box of new candles up from the church basement on what had to be the steepest set of stairs in Harrisville if the outside stairs behind the church weren't.

My mother knew all of this. She not only knew about the jobs I had to do on Mondays, she was fully aware of the tasks Fr. Kavanaugh had dreamed up for me to do on

Tuesdays and Wednesdays and on every other afternoon of the week, jobs that kept me from joining the Cub Scouts, trying out for the St. Lawrence's Midgets baseball team, or doing anything else that normal kids did after school. She took a breath, her lips started to move, and for a second, I believed I was about to witness a miracle.

"Enough!" Fr. Kavanaugh bellowed before she had a chance to say a word. "I know what I am doing!" He glared at the bowl of peas until my mother handed it to him. "I know whose sinful blood is coursing through this young man's veins!" He scooped a pile of peas onto his plate. His narrowed eyes fixed on me, burning holes halfway through my skull. "It is just possible, Rose Marie, just possible mind you, that I might yet save this unfortunate product of your misguided union with such a man from the untold horrors of hell."

Before I was out of grade school, I would hear my mother scream and yell at Fr. Kavanaugh. I would hear her call him a phony and a liar with a vehemence that must have caused her pale face to burn red and every vein in her thin neck to throb into view. Unfortunately for me, that day was still some time off. All my mother did on this particular night was pick up her fork and stir the mashed potatoes on her plate in little circles.

By the time I was done printing out the Confiteor ten times, my eyes were spinning, and my brain was numb. I didn't do a lick of homework. I didn't work on the new spelling words, and I didn't do a single arithmetic problem. Worst of all, a girl in my class named Patricia Delsey did arithmetic problem number seventeen and got it right. When I whispered across the aisle that I knew her father had helped her, she totally ignored me.

CHAPTER TWELVE

By the time I was in the fifth grade, the number of jobs Fr. Kavanaugh expected me to do after school had mushroomed. Not only was I providing janitorial services at the church, I was washing and waxing his Chrysler New Yorker, helping him count the collection money, and doing odd jobs at the rectory. The latter included cleaning his personal office, a wood-paneled sanctuary into which the housekeeper, Mrs. Conover, was not allowed to take one step, an apparent application of another one of Fr. Kavanaugh's beliefs: the more rules the better.

"Where have you been?" he growled one afternoon when I arrived five minutes late.

"I had to go to the bathroom." That was my standard excuse, and it was usually a lie, but this day it had been technically true, even though the main reason I had raced home after school was that I was starving and needed to grab a handful of Fig Newtons to stuff in my mouth as I ran back out the door and over to the rectory.

He picked an envelope from the pile of mail on his desk, glowered at it, and dropped it unopened into the tin wastebasket at his side. "See those books?"

I saw them: a million of them lined floor-to-ceiling shelves covering an entire wall of the office. In front of the shelves sat a rickety stepladder, no doubt left there by Mr. Shifflet who, I had become convinced, did no chore that was lousy enough to be left for me.

"I want those books dusted, every last one of them. Pull them out, wipe them clean, and return each one to its original location. Start at the top and work down. Get busy." Fr. Kavanaugh was already scowling at the next piece of mail before he finished barking the order.

From the bottom of the ladder, I surveyed a Mount Everest of books: fat ones, skinny ones, books with leather covers, books with Latin names on the spines, and a ton of books that weren't books at all but pamphlets jammed between real books. It was going to take all afternoon to dust them, an afternoon when everyone else who had spent the day in school was outside enjoying the sun that slanted through the venetian blinds and splashed onto Fr. Kavanaugh's office floor. They were riding bikes. They were climbing trees. They were roller skating and playing catch. There was only one reason why fun things like that were missing from my life. I stared at his massive head, at his enormous neck, at the big hands that held a letter he was reading. It was the first time I remember actually wishing he was dead. There was no doubt in my mind that it was a sin to wish your pastor was dead, but to someone who had been piling up sins since the second grade, what difference could one more step away from the pathway to heaven possibly make?

"Do I have to get up?" he roared.

I scrambled up the ladder.

"Start at the top, and work left to right. Use that feather duster hanging on the side of the ladder." He didn't even look up from the mail; he just barked orders. *Bark, bark, bark.* I had a sudden urge to tell him *Bark, bark, bark yourself.* I would be dead two seconds after I opened my mouth, but it was a lot of fun to think about.

I had never seen Fr. Kavanaugh reading any of these books: *The Gospels of Saint John, The Lives of the Early Saints, The Imitation of Christ.* I studied one of the book covers, wondering for the millionth time if Jesus had really looked like the pictures of him. He always looked so nice, a lot like Fr. Fowler with a beard and a halo. It was hard to imagine Jesus screaming and yelling from the pulpit every Sunday and stopping in the middle of whatever he was yelling about to stare down some poor old lady who was trying to sneak into a pew late. Inside there was a picture of The Last Supper. Some of the apostles were talking to each other, and some of them were talking to Jesus. No one was giving anyone a dirty look. No one was banging their fist on the table like Fr. Kavanaugh would have been doing.

"Get working! Do you hear me! You're not leaving this rectory until every single one of those books is dusted!"

I slid the book back into its slot, trying to remember if Jesus ever yelled at anyone in the Gospels or the Epistles. Maybe He did when He threw the money-changers out of the temple; I couldn't remember for sure. In any case, I didn't know what money changers were, so it was hard to know if they were worth yelling at.

There was a ton of dust on the tops of the books, especially the ones on the highest shelves. Some of it was so thick that it looked like gray fur. The fastest way to wipe them off was to do it without climbing down off the ladder; just slide them out, dust them off, and push them back into place. I got busy, clinging to the hope that if I worked fast enough there might be time to play outside for a little while before it got dark. I didn't notice Fr. Kavanaugh's first few coughs. I'm not even sure I noticed it when he started gagging, and it wasn't until he went berserk that I realized that the dust I was brushing off the books was cascading all over him and all over his desk and all over the pile of mail he was trying to read. He screamed and he yelled and he jumped up and yanked me off the ladder. If the phone on his desk hadn't started ringing, he probably would have shaken me to death.

"Kavanaugh!" he growled into the phone, glaring at me. He didn't care if it was the pope calling or some poor person who needed a priest to run right over and administer Extreme Unction to their dying mother—that's the way he always answered the rectory telephone. "Kavanaugh! "

"Who?"

Dropping back into his chair, he clamped the phone between his shoulder and his thick neck and snatched another envelope from the mail pile. He grunted into the phone a couple of times while unfolding and scanning a letter that appeared to be three or four pages long. Before he got to the third page, he wadded it into a tight ball and dropped it into the wastebasket.

"Just what common concerns are you referring to?"

His enormous, black shoes thudded onto the desk as he leaned far back in his chair. He removed his reading glasses and massaged the bridge of his nose. He grunted some more and stared up at the ceiling.

"I get enough of that from the archdiocese office."

The springs in the base of swivel the chair groaned as he sat up straight. "No, I don't think so."

His fingers drummed heavily on the edge of the desk. "No reason that I can see."

His face was turning red. I could tell he was on the verge of getting mad.

"No need for that at all. Good day to you sir!" He slammed the receiver into the cradle. "God help us and save us," he muttered, snatching the next envelope and slicing it open before he remembered about me. "And you better get back to work before I throw you through that window you keep looking at!"

I did. I had learned long ago to take everything he said literally.

"I wouldn't have believed it if I hadn't heard it with my own ears," Fr. Kavanaugh repeated, more to himself than to my mother who was trying her best to get dinner onto the table. His eyes returned to the crossword puzzle but only for a second. He stood abruptly, scraping the legs of his chair nosily against the linoleum. "Does that man actually believe those other churches are comparable in any way to the Holy Catholic Church?"

My mother said nothing. She had already made the mistake of suggesting that the Lutheran pastor who had telephoned Fr. Kavanaugh that afternoon was simply trying to be friendly. Folding a potholder into her hand, she opened the oven door to check the chicken potpie.

Fr. Kavanaugh stalked to the kitchen door and stared out into the evening. "The man wants to form a committee, a *council* I believe he called it, a *council* comprised of the pastors of all the churches in Harrisville." It was the second time in the fifteen minutes since he had arrived at our house that Fr. Kavanaugh had gone off on the subject of that afternoon's phone call, and both times he had become too agitated to remain at the table.

"He informed me that he had already obtained the enthusiastic—*enthusiastic,* mind you—support of the pastors of Christ Episcopal Church and the Harrisville Presbyterian Church and was waiting for the pastor of Emmanuel Baptist to return from a bible conference in Atlanta." He shook his head. "May the saints preserve us!"

He returned to the table and sat down heavily. "The next thing you know he will be asking the rabbi of that new synagogue on Adelphi Road to join his little group." After muttering something unintelligible about Jews, his eyes returned to the crossword puzzle. Thinking that the storm had subsided, my mother slipped the potpie onto the table and crept back to the stove to retrieve the rolls.

"The nerve of the man!" Fr. Kavanaugh exploded, swatting the folded newspaper halfway across the room. "To think that the pastor of a Roman Catholic Church, an ordained priest of God, would be interested in participating in such poppycock!" Wisps of steam curled from his plate as Fr. Kavanaugh helped himself to half the potpie and reached across the table for a roll. "You know as well as I do, Rose Marie, that the whole lot of them will be in for a shock when the gates of heaven slam in their sadly misguided faces!"

Chapter Thirteen

It might have just been a coincidence, but in a school ruled by Fr. Kavanaugh, that wasn't very likely. The overwhelming odds were that he had issued a directive to the convent the very night of his call from the Lutheran pastor, ordering every nun under his command to nip in the bud any and all doubts that might exist in the minds of their students about the Catholic Church being the one true church of God.

Sr. Julie Bernadine, our fifth grade teacher, didn't seem to know exactly how to begin. She hesitatingly explained that Protestants were very well-meaning, that they believed in God, and that many of them lived good lives. She looked out the window. She straightened some papers on her desk that were already perfectly neat. After fiddling with the oversized rosary attached to her habit, it appeared that she had been blessed with an idea. "How many of you children actually know a Protestant?"

There was some hesitation, no doubt produced by the

suspicion that she had asked a trick question. Finally, a few hands went up.

"Yes. Carmella."

"We live next door to the Wagners. They go to the Lutheran church."

"And do you like them? Are they nice neighbors?"

"Oh yes. Mr. Wagner has three beehives in his backyard, and he gives us real honey."

"Very good. And you, Maureen?"

"My babysitter, Noreen, sings in the choir at Christ Episcopal."

"Is she nice?"

"She is. She shows me the pictures in her wallet while my parents are at the movies."

A look of concern clouded Sr. Julie Bernadine's face. "What kind of pictures are they?"

"One is of her grandmother sitting on her porch in Ohio with a cat on her lap, and two are of the rabbit Noreen got for Easter last year that her dog ate."

Despite the mixed reactions to Maureen Hogan's description of the Easter rabbit's fate—the girls horrified, the boys hungry for details—Sr. Julie Bernadine seemed pleased by the responses so far.

"Yes, Vinnie? You had your hand up."

Vinnie Rinaldi slid out of his desk and stood fidgeting in the aisle. A piece of Scotch tape was stuck to the seat of his corduroy pants, but he didn't know it.

"We live next door to the Shepherds who go to the Lutheran church or the Methodist church or something. I forget. My father doesn't like them because they buy their shoes at Sears."

"I'm sure your father doesn't actually dislike them, Vinnie. He probably just wishes they purchased their shoes at his shoe store."

"He really doesn't like them," Vinnie insisted. "He won't even let Mr. Shepherd borrow our lawnmower."

It was obvious that Sr. Julie Bernadine didn't care for Vinnie's contribution to the discussion. She told him to sit down, and when he started to tell us about the Shepherds' two sons beating him up, she ordered him to sit down, addressing him sternly as *Mister* Rinaldi. "So you see, children," she concluded, ignoring Vinnie's input, "Many Protestants are perfectly nice people. The problem, unfortunately, is that being a nice person is not enough in God's eyes." There was an unmistakable shadow of sadness in her words. "In order to enter into the Kingdom of Heaven, a person must be baptized. Not just baptized but baptized in the Catholic Church the way all of you were baptized."

"Will they all go to hell?" an alarmed Eugene Foster called out from the back of the room.

Ignoring Eugene's flagrant breach of the *Never Speak Without Raising Your Hand First* rule, Sr. Julie Bernadine replied thoughtfully, "Not necessarily."

"Oh yes they will!" Vinnie Rinaldi declared, jumping excitedly back into the aisle. "My father told Mr. Shepherd to go to hell last Saturday, and when I asked what it meant when Mr. Shepherd waved his finger at him, my father said it meant he was going to hell for sure."

"Sit down, Mister Rinaldi!"

The lesson about non-Catholics went on for two more days, even taking the first fifteen minutes away from geography class on Thursday. Sr. Julie Bernadine did her best to make us understand that some people, even people who died with no mortal sins on their souls, would not be allowed into heaven. "In fact," she added sadly, "those unfortunate souls will not even be allowed into purgatory."

In large nun penmanship, she wrote the word UNBAP-TIZED on the blackboard. Tapping on each letter with a stick of chalk, she described the three categories of unbaptized people. First were people like natives in the jungle who, because they had never even seen a missionary priest or had ignored them—or worse—were never baptized. Even boys who rarely paid attention in class wanted to know what she meant by *or worse*, but she ignored their frantically waving arms and moved on. The next category included little babies who died before they had a chance to be baptized. They went to limbo with the natives. I counted five girls who started crying when Sr. Julie Bernadine told us about the babies, and they were just the ones I could see from where I was sitting. Sr. Julie Bernadine did her best to calm everybody down by explaining that God was good and kind and would make sure the babies were very happy in limbo. The final people on the UNBAPTIZED list were people who had no excuse for not being baptized except that they were just plain lazy—*lax* was the actual word she used. The most people like that could hope for was to spend eternity in limbo with all the natives and little babies.

"Now," Sr. Julie Bernadine said, erasing the blackboard, "we come to the important question of our Protestant friends." She looked up at the crucifix centered above the blackboard, closed her eyes for a second, and took a deep breath. "This may be a little advanced for fifth graders, but it has been determined that every student in this school should receive instruction on this matter." She closed her eyes again as though she was rehearsing the words she was about to say.

"The Protestant religions have forms of baptism." She closed her eyes again and concentrated with her lips moving before continuing. "Even though their baptisms are not the same as the Sacrament of Baptism that you received when you were babies, a lot of our Protestant friends believe their baptisms are real." She removed a book from the top of the neat stack on her desk and opened it to a page she had marked with a holy card. "You will not get to this question until you are in the eighth grade, but Sr. Superior has given me permission to read to you what *The Baltimore Catechism* has to say on this subject." She cleared her throat. "The question is 'how can persons who are not members of the Catholic Church be saved?' Vincent Rinaldi, please pay attention!"

Vinnie, who could only sit still for two minutes at a time, had torn a page from his spiral notebook and begun folding it into the shape of what appeared to be a boat, totally unaware that his efforts were accompanied by an excellent imitation of an outboard engine.

"To repeat, class," Sr. Julie Bernadine resumed, "how can persons who are not members of the Catholic Church be saved? Let me read the answer as spelled out for us in *The Baltimore Catechism*: 'Persons who are not members of the Catholic Church can be saved if, through no fault of their own, they do not know that the Catholic church is the true Church, but they love God and try to do His will, for in this way they are connected with the Church by desire.'"

I wondered how long it had been since Fr. Kavanaugh had read *The Baltimore Catechism*, because if I understood what I had just heard, there was a boatload of Protestants who had a better chance of getting into heaven than he did. Some of the smart girls were madly waving their hands in the air, dying to ask questions or say things that they thought would make everybody else think they knew a lot. Sr. Julie Bernadine ignored them. "Take out our geography books and turn to chapter 6, where we will begin our study of Peru," she told us.

CHAPTER FOURTEEN

Among Fr. Kavanaugh's endless edicts was one stipulating that each year right after the Christmas holidays, Sr. Superior was required to submit to him the names of all fifth grade boys who she deemed worthy to begin altar boy training. From his dinner table ravings, it was clear to me that not a single boy whose name appeared on those lists would have made the grade when he was young, but because he needed altar boys for five Masses every Sunday and two Masses every weekday, not to mention novenas, funerals, and weddings, he was forced to go easy on the number of names he rejected.

On at least one occasion, he unfolded Sr. Superior's neatly typed list on our kitchen table and enumerated the character flaws and mental weaknesses of each boy whose name had been submitted. An eavesdropper would have thought he was dissecting the roster of a reform school or insane asylum. "May the good Lord preserve us, Rose Marie," he lamented to my mother as he refolded the list and turned his attention to the crossword puzzle. "If this is the best we can do, God preserve us all."

I never made that list for the simple reason that by the time I was in the fifth grade, I was already an altar boy. I knew my Latin backwards and forwards, sideways and upside down, having endured countless nights standing against the refrigerator while Fr. Kavanaugh, like a one-man firing squad, fired Latin at me and expected a properly pronounced response within two seconds. Unlike my classmates who would be patiently instructed by Fr. Fowler about when to switch the missal from one side of the altar to the other and the proper time to retrieve the cruets, I learned such things the hard way: serving daily Mass at six o'clock in the morning, lightly attended services when Fr. Kavanaugh was free to cuff me upside the head for making a mistake without any detectable reaction from the sleepy parishioners present.

One of the first Sunday Masses I ever served was especially notable because it coincided with the arrival of The French Lady, an event undoubtedly imbedded in the memories of everyone present that particular October morning.

To be precise, it was not morning, it was noon, and noon Mass, despite the fact that it was always celebrated by Fr. Kavanaugh, was packed every week, a phenomenon most likely attributable to the fundamental human tendency to sleep as late as possible on the weekend. The price for such a luxury was being subjected to Fr. Kavanaugh's inevitable butt-numbing tirades in which, week after week, he hammered home his favorite theme, which asserted that most if not all of those who occupied the pews of St. Lawrence's on any given Sunday had as much chance of passing through the gates of heaven as a snowball had of surviving in a frying pan.

As was customary at noon Mass, Mr. Higgins and Mr. McCloskey, blue usher ribbons pinned to their lapels, patrolled the side aisles, squeezing late arrivals into seats invisible to the untrained eye. One-armed Mr. Duda manned his customary position in the center aisle, waving insistently with the arm that didn't get shot off in the war for the people standing in the back to come forward and fill the sparsely occupied front pews, seats that were much too close to Fr. Kavanaugh for anybody with good sense.

I was serving Mass by myself that day, a circumstance brought about by the fact that Fr. Kavanaugh had forcibly removed the other altar boy from the sacristy for wearing sneakers instead of polished leather shoes, a flagrant violation of the Altar Boy Code, a set of commandments that, while not chiseled in stone, was in fact framed and hung on the sacristy wall.

> You WILL arrive fifteen minutes before Mass.
> You WILL immediately fix the cruets and light the altar candles.
> Your cassock and surplus WILL be clean and ironed.
> Your shoes WILL be polished.
> Your hair WILL be neatly cut and combed.
> You WILL speak softly while in the sacristy.
> You WILL visit the restroom before Mass starts.

You WILL NOT cough or sniffle while on the altar. You WILL NOT chew gum while on church grounds. You WILL extinguish the altar candles and return the cruets to their proper place in the sacristy immediately following Mass.

The words WILL and WILL NOT were capitalized and printed in red. All altar boys were required to know these rules by heart, and while sneakers weren't specifically mentioned, it was the polishing rule, not to mention the white shoelaces and the white patch with the blue star on each ankle, that produced the same effect on Fr. Kavanaugh that a red flag does on a bull. Since the altar boy who had pulled such a dangerous stunt that morning was an eighth grader who obviously knew better, it was my guess that he had done it on purpose to avoid serving Mass on such a beautiful fall day.

Even though the sneaker incident had put him in a worse mood than usual, the Mass proceeded surprisingly smoothly, a delicate situation I did my best to maintain by attempting to pronounce my Latin as precisely as a seminarian. Approximately halfway through Mass, the congregation stood noisily as Fr. Kavanaugh prepared to read the gospel in English. After glaring in the direction of a young child who had started howling at the sound of his ominous voice, Fr. Kavanaugh thumbed quick crosses on his forehead, lips, and chest, clutched the gilt-edged missal in his enormous hands, and began. "A reading from the Gospel according to Saint John," he boomed. He hurried through

Saint John's telling of a man who begged Jesus to cure his son who was about to die as well as the part where, after a little bit of back and forth, Jesus went ahead and did it. In their sermons at the other Masses that day, Fr. Fowler and Fr. Ellenberger would, in all probability, preach sermons about the fact that such a wonderful thing happened only because the man in the gospel truly believed Jesus could do it, and then they might have made the point that if all of us have the same kind of faith in God, really good things can happen to us too.

Liturgical silliness of that nature was meaningless to Fr. Kavanaugh. In his opinion, there was absolutely no hope of saving the souls the Archdiocese of Washington had entrusted to his care. He knew the terrible evil that lived in their hearts. He knew the forbidden pleasures they would return to when they left church that morning. He knew they would come creeping back to confession the following Saturday afternoon, searching for the right words to cushion their embarrassment and disguise the disgusting nature of their secret lives. The number of people in the parish without mortal sin on their souls, he repeatedly bellyached to my mother, would fit easily into a single row of pews, and most of them would be senile degenerates who had abandoned sinning only because they had grown too old to wallow in the pleasures of the flesh. Each and every Sunday he would use the pulpit to attack their sinful ways, he swore repeatedly to her, and come down on them with all his might. Sunday after Sunday he would rub their noses in the filth that filled their lives. It would do no good, he declared over and over, but by God, he would do it anyway.

This particular Sunday, he lit into them the second their butts hit the pews. "Go home, each and every one of you, and take a good look in the mirror!" he bellowed. "Don't stop at the bakery! Don't stop at the drugstore to pick up your Sunday newspaper! Go straight home and look at yourself in the mirror!"

The congregation stirred like frightened sheep, knowing from experience that whatever was coming next would not be good. Fr. Kavanaugh took off his glasses and wiped them with a white handkerchief he produced from under his chasuble. "You heard me. Take a look in the mirror, and see the face of a sinner who is destined to spend eternity in hell!"

The words were barely out of his mouth, the startled gasps of the condemned congregation still resonating, when the massive oak door at the rear of the church swung open. People in nearby pews, welcoming any manner of distraction, turned to look, and when they did, they continued to look. With a muffled creak, the door swung closed. More heads turned, curious to see the fool who would dare interrupt a Fr. Kavanaugh sermon.

The tall woman who was the focus of their attention could have cared less. One after another, she removed her long, leather gloves, stuffed them into a beaded purse, and snapped it shut. She was dressed entirely in black as she would be at every noon Mass she attended from that Sunday on. Mr. Duda, his empty sleeve pinned into the pocket of his suit coat, approached her carefully and whispered something, nodding toward empty seats in the rear corner of the church. The wide brim of the woman's hat shook slowly in response as she started down the center aisle, the click of her high-heeled shoes echoing sharply in the dead silence of the church.

Along with everyone else, I waited for Fr. Kavanaugh to explode. He had humiliated entire families for coming into Mass during the epistle, much less in the middle of his sermon. His fingers drummed the edges of the pulpit as the lady in black strutted to the front of the church; once or twice, his mouth started to open, but he said nothing. There was no explosion; absent was the barrage of ridicule the people of St. Lawrence's had come to expect in such circumstances. To everyone's surprise, all Fr. Kavanaugh did was watch like the rest of us. At the front of the church, The French Lady, as she would come to be known on the school playground, genuflected, blessed herself, and slid into the front pew next to the flabbergasted Fallon sisters, two unmarried parishioners in their late eighties if not their early nineties.

To my amazement, and undoubtedly to the amazement of every person present that morning, Fr. Kavanaugh seemed unsure what to do. With every eye in the church fixed expectantly on him, he cleared his throat with a growl, often the first warning of an angry eruption. He narrowed his eyes and attempted to aim one of his death-beam stares at the audacious newcomer. It didn't work. The French Lady smiled back at him and nodded with her big hat, granting him permission, it appeared to me, to continue with whatever he had been talking about.

It took Fr. Kavanaugh a few sentences to get rolling again, but even when he did, the air had gone out of the business about everyone going home and looking in the mirror so they could see what a person who was going to hell looked like. He tried his best to tap the bottomless pit of anger he carried around in his big gut, but he had no success. Totally missing was his special gift for making babies cry and grown people squirm in their seats. The French Lady checked her fingernails and pinched a piece of lint from her sleeve, but for the most part, she simply sat next to the half-paralyzed Fallon sisters and looked up at him.

CHAPTER FIFTEEN

The first intelligence reports regarding The French Lady came from Leon Duda, whose previous popularity stemmed entirely from his willingness to describe in minute detail what the stub of his father's missing arm looked like. Leon delivered the *Washington Daily News* in Orchard Hills, a neighborhood devoid of anything remotely resembling a hill, located in the area behind St. Lawrence's church. The French Lady's real name was Mrs. DeSimone, and she had become one of Leon Duda's newspaper customers when she moved into the neighborhood. If there was a Mr. DeSimone, Leon had never seen him. These facts were interesting enough but left the boys surrounding him on the playground eager for more. Reluctant to give up the spotlight, Leon stunned every last one of us by whispering that the first time he went to her door to collect money for the paper, she had opened her purse, and right next to her cigarettes and lighter, he saw a pack of rubbers. He swore to God it was true.

In the weeks that followed, small herds of St. Lawrence's boys on bicycles cruised slowly past her house or hid behind parked cars across the street, hoping to catch a glimpse of her. Stories arose out of nowhere: she used to work at a nightclub in Baltimore; she had been divorced four times; she had been spotted coming out of Duffy's Liquor Land with a bag of booze so heavy she could hardly carry it.

She became a fixture at noon Mass at which she always arrived late, strutting like the Queen of Sheba, as Mrs. Enright put it to my mother, all the way up to the front of the church and taking her place right in front of the pulpit in a pew that, since the Fallon sisters had not been seen since her first appearance, she had all to herself. Noon Mass became more crowded than ever, its ranks peppered with parishioners who had previously surfaced exclusively at Christmas and Easter. Fr. Kavanaugh's sermons regained their old steam. In fact, if anything, they became even more scathing. On one occasion, he spotted Mr. Doyle sitting with poor Mrs. Doyle and their horde of kids and roared that if Mr. Doyle was going to start coming to church again, the least he could do was shave and wear a necktie. From all the way up on the altar where I was sitting, I could see Kathleen Doyle, who was in my class, turn red.

At the same time all of this was happening Fr. Kavanaugh started being meaner than ever to my mother. Every night at the dinner table, the things he said to her were worse than the night before. He told her she was getting old. He wanted to know why she didn't dress better for dinner and do something with her hair. It didn't seem to matter to him that she had spent all day washing and ironing his clothes and cooking the dinners his dear old mother used to cook for him back in Wilkes-Barre; as soon as he came busting through our back door, he started in on her. She was stunned and humiliated. I could tell. I really think the worst part for her was that he did all these things in front of me, and she had no idea what to do about it.

The more these things happened, the more I wished that if there really was a God in heaven, He would speak to me out of one of those bunches of white clouds that look like cowboy canyons and tell me I could choose one miracle and He would grant it, anything in the world. Cure all the sick people? Make the Russians be nice to everybody? Just name it. *No, God,* I would have answered as respectfully as possible, *I want my father to walk into our kitchen after all these years and, with his movie star looks and the big muscular arms I remembered from the picture I had been forced to tear up, grab Fr. Kavanaugh by his Roman collar, throw his big ass out into the yard, and beat the living hell out of him.* If God granted me that one wish, I would go to Mass every day for the rest of my life; I would go to confession and tell the truth; I would give half of all the money I ever made to the pagan babies fund. Once when I was praying for such a miracle, I almost promised that I would become a priest but caught myself in the nick of time.

It never happened, of course. The more Fr. Kavanaugh criticized my mother, the more her shoulders slumped. She looked at me out of the corner of her eyes, pushing the food on her plate with her fork and sipping coffee with a shaking hand. I didn't love my mother like I suspected other people loved their mothers, with hugs and kisses and warm memories of when they were little, but I hated seeing her hurt this way. I hated Fr. Kavanaugh for doing it, and more than ever, I hated the fact that he was a part of our lives. One night, I excused myself as soon as I thought Fr. Kavanaugh would let me leave the table, telling him a lie about just remembering that I had left my jacket in the backyard. He looked at me suspiciously, but then he always looked at me suspiciously. Luckily, he was too preoccupied finding fault with my mother to think of some reason to keep me at the table.

It was dark in the backyard but too late in the year for the lightning bugs that frequented the last remains of the peach orchard deep in our backyard. Knowing this made me curious about the small dot of orange light that appeared out of nowhere. A shape formed in the darkness as twigs snapped beneath approaching footsteps. The orange dot became the tip of a cigarette. Butchie McDevitt laughed.

"What do you say, Peckerhead!"

I was too dumbfounded to duck when Butchie flicked what was left of his cigarette at me. It bounced off my shoulder and tumbled to the ground in a shower of tiny sparks.

"Miss me?"

The truth was I really had missed him. His father had long ago grown tired of me sneaking over to the gas station to ask if he had heard anything. "How could I?" he once answered, "the little shit can't write good enough to send a letter, and he's too dumb to make a fucking phone call."

"Does your father know you're back?" I managed to ask.

"Yeah. He don't give a shit."

"Did you see his new tow truck?"

"Yeah, I saw it. Big-ass Ford."

I glanced nervously back toward the kitchen door. "You better leave. Fr. Kavanaugh will be coming out any minute."

Butchie lit another cigarette. "That fat shit? I ain't afraid of him."

He probably wasn't, but I was, especially when he was in the kind of mood Fr. Kavanaugh was in tonight. I pleaded with Butchie to leave.

He stretched and looked around. "Give me your bike."

"What?"

"You still got that cool bike you got that time? Give it to me, and then I'll leave."

I told him that Fr. Kavanaugh had sold my bike at the parish auction, and that was the truth. He had gone nuts and taken it away from me when I asked my mother if I could transfer to public school, a request I foolishly assumed would remain between the two of us. He also hit me in the ear so hard that the inside of my head rang for eight days, misery that paled in comparison to seeing Edward Earhart riding to school every day on the neatest thing I had ever owned. As hard as I tried, I had no luck hating Edward Earhart. He was fat and funny and had no way of knowing that the birthday present his mother and father had bought him at the auction had been my reward for not telling anyone about Fr. Kavanaugh chipping my teeth.

"Call the cops."

"What?"

"He stole your bike, didn't he? Call the cops on his fat ass."

It proved to be amazingly difficult to explain to Butchie that even if the Harrisville police dropped everything they were doing, like chasing speeders or keeping their eyes peeled for people on the Ten Most Wanted List long enough to investigate some kid's claim that a Catholic priest had stolen his bicycle, the things that particular priest would do to that kid after the police left were too scary to think about. Desperate to get Butchie to leave before Fr. Kavanaugh stomped out the kitchen door and found the two of us together, I offered to give him every cent I had on me if he would leave.

"Don't you want to hear about where I've been?"

I was surprised by how disappointed he sounded. I fished a quarter and a dime out of my pocket and handed it to him. "I do, I really do, but right now I've got to get back in the house."

Butchie told me so many stories about his disappearance that I didn't know what to believe. "My mother and her sorry boyfriend kidnapped my ass in the middle of the night while my old man was playing poker up at the Moose Lodge," one version began. After tying him up, they had stuffed him in the trunk of a car that, in his words, smelled like elephant farts, and driven him to either Louisville, Kentucky, or Dallas, Texas. Sometimes it was New Jersey.

He told me that for weeks at a time he was chained to a piano in the apartment of his mother, who looked exactly like Marilyn Monroe. She worked during the day as a bus driver, and at night, she was in charge of a hundred people in a factory that made snow tires. Another version had him being kept in a cage all day with only a coffee can to go to the bathroom in, and in yet another account, he was forced to attend circus school where he was trained to be an acrobat. I learned the hard way not to point out the obvious contradictions in these stories. Doing that embarrassed him and made him mad, so mad that one time he punched me in the shoulder hard enough to make my arm go numb for almost an hour. Butchie had not grown much taller while he was gone, but he was definitely more muscular, and because he now had the beginnings of a mustache, he looked more like a small man than a boy.

It occurred to me eventually that Butchie had simply been born stupid, the way some people are born blind or come into this world with only one foot or with really big noses like everybody in the Rinaldi family. He once told me that when he was a baby, he had been dropped on his head when his father, who was holding him, got into a fight at a bowling alley. I doubted that very much, and in any case, he would have had to be dropped on his head more than once to end up with a brain as defective as the one Butchie had been given to make his way through life.

His big dream was to become a steamroller driver. The thought of working the myriad handles and levers that propelled the hippopotamus-like machine back and forth over steaming asphalt mesmerized him the way the idea of being a fireman or an airline pilot thrilled kids with a more conventional point of view. Somewhere, somehow, he had become convinced that being seen operating a steamroller would make him extremely attractive to girls and result in endless *kooze*, an expression he had picked up while he was gone that apparently meant girls and women and the things people who knew a lot more than me did with them.

Mr. McDevitt treated Butchie as though he had never been gone. He threatened him with gruesome tortures like twisting his balls with a pair of pliers, a threat Butchie totally ignored, or with punishments like sending him back to live with his mother, a warning that never failed to get his attention. Unlike Fr. Kavanaugh, Mr. McDevitt never did the things he threatened to do. Other than the time Butchie stole my bike, Mr. McDevitt never hit Butchie, at least I never saw him do it, and for sure he never gave him a black eye or chipped his teeth.

The world Butchie McDevitt lived in fascinated me. It was a world free of worrying about commandments, mortal sins, venial sins, or Mass on Sundays and holy days of obligation. On nights when he and his father didn't sleep in the gas station, they drove in the tow truck to a wreck of a stucco house at the bottom of Thirty-Eighth Avenue, a crumbling pile of architectural details that, according to my mother, had long ago been the home of a man who had gotten rich selling paper clips and carbon paper to the federal government. Judging by the number of trucks and cars parked in the hard earth yard out front, the place was now a rabbit warren of rented rooms and apartments. The two of them often ate their meals in the oil-drenched disarray of Mr. McDevitt's cramped office at the gas station, devouring things I never got to eat at home: tiny sausages tugged from tin cans, smelly sardines stacked like tiny silver logs on saltine crackers, and pork and beans prepared with nothing more than a can opener. The wild freedom of it all made the two of them seem like bandits on the run.

CHAPTER SIXTEEN

My life took a significant turn for the worse at the end of the sixth grade when Fr. Kavanaugh appointed me head altar boy. That move, announced to my extreme humiliation in the Sunday Bulletin, made me extremely unpopular with a number of eighth graders who, for reasons totally beyond my understanding, coveted the position. Now, in addition to having to show up daily at either the church or the rectory to perform my endless list of janitorial chores, I was saddled with the responsibility of helping Fr. Fowler teach new altar boys how to serve Mass, a job that was a royal pain in the ass. If that wasn't torture enough, because I lived right next door to the church, Fr. Kavanaugh expected me to drop everything and run over to the church every time someone's mother called at the last minute to say her precious son had a sore throat or the runs and wouldn't be able to serve Mass.

It happened all the time. One Sunday morning, I was stretched out on the living room carpet with *The Washington*

Post comic section spread out in front of me, my church shoes kicked aside and what was left of a box of powdered doughnuts at my elbow. As always, I was anxious to find *Li'l Abner*, pausing only long enough when I got to *The Phantom* and *Alley Oop* to see what they were up to. This particular Sunday, *Alley Oop* was cornered in a cave by a bunch of weird-looking guys from outer space. I made a mental note to come back and read every bubble of words after I found what I was looking for. I passed *Blondie* and *Prince Valiant*. *Dick Tracy* was at the top of the next page, talking into his radio wristwatch, and *Mary Worth* was right underneath. Nothing ever happened in *Mary Worth* except for a bunch of stupid talking. *Judge Parker* was the same way. They reminded me of the dumb radio shows my mother listened to in the afternoons while she was ironing.

Out in the kitchen, the telephone rang. I heard my mother say, "Yes, Father. I'll send him right over."

I turned the page, and there she was, Daisy Mae. I smoothed the paper against the carpet. Daisy Mae, Li'l Abner's girlfriend or wife or whatever she was, with her bare feet and really long legs, was chasing Li'l Abner across a log bridge. She had the biggest boobs in the comics. Not as big as the ones on one of Mr. McDevitt's calendars but bigger than on any real lady I had ever seen. She was wearing the skimpy, polka-dot blouse she always wore. Sometimes the people who drew cartoons added lines next to a dog's tail to show that it was wagging or next to a prehistoric bird's wings to show that they we flapping, but I guess they weren't allowed to put lines next to Daisy

Mae's boobs to show the way they bounced up and down when she ran after Li'l Abner. Powdered sugar fell like snow into her bright-yellow hair when I stuffed most of a doughnut into my mouth.

My mother's footsteps crossed the kitchen floor into the hall. "Russell, Fr. Kavanaugh needs you over at the church to serve ten-thirty Mass. Vincent Rinaldi is sick this morning."

Brushing aside the powdered snow, I followed Daisy Mae and her bouncing boobs as she chased Li'l Abner over a hill, almost catching him as they ran past a rickety old cabin with smoke coming out of a crooked chimney.

"Russell Flynn, did you hear me? Fr. Kavanaugh wants you over at the church immediately."

I dropped my head into the comic section and crumpled the pages with my fists. "I just served nine o'clock Mass! Tell him to get somebody else!"

"You know very well he can't do that. There isn't time, and you're right next door." She nudged me with her shoe. "Mass starts in ten minutes. You know better than to get him mad."

I rolled onto my back and looked up at my mother, angry and arguing like the teenager I would soon be.

She took a deep breath, her hands nervously kneading her apron. "Russell, please. You know how he gets when he's upset."

The living room windows rattled as pealing bells from the steeple high above our house announced that Mass was about to begin. It was as though Fr. Kavanaugh was issuing his last warning.

Melvin Delsey, one of the newest altar boys, was in the sacristy when I got over to the church, struggling with the top snap of his oversized cassock.

"You're not Vinnie Rinaldi," he informed me.

"No shit, Sherlock," I whispered in his ear as I helped him with the snap and started pulling my own cassock on. "Vinnie's sick," I explained when I realized how bewildered he was.

Melvin Delsey was a little guy even for the fifth grade. His voice was squeaky, and his cheeks were as puffy as a chipmunk's. His sister, Patricia, who had always been the smartest girl in my class, had bloomed into the best-looking girl at St. Lawrence's, a phenomenon that amazed me, because the only other girls in the school worth looking at, Sandra Thompson and Mary Ann McWilliams, were pretty dumb. Melvin was having trouble slipping his surplus over his head, mainly because his mother had starched it as stiff as cardboard. When Melvin's chipmunk face finally popped through the neck hole, I told him to light the candles while I did the cruets. He told me he didn't know how.

"You're kidding me."

He wasn't kidding, and there wasn't time to show him. I filled the cruets with water and wine and hurried them into the sanctuary while Melvin tagged along in a daze. I had hoped to get the altar candles lit before Fr. Kavanaugh came out of the vestment room, but I didn't make it. He was waiting, the watch on his hairy wrist aimed menacingly at my face when I scrambled back into the sacristy. "Let's move," he growled. "I'll deal with the two of you after Mass."

Fr. Kavanaugh threatened me so regularly that his words barely registered, an immunity Melvin Delsey did not enjoy. He whimpered audibly as Fr. Kavanaugh shoved the two of us out into the sanctuary and the congregation clamored to its feet. High in the choir loft, Mrs. Enright pumped the massive organ to life, a postage stamp-size image of her face visible in the mirror over the tiered keyboard.

Melvin took a stab at the first Latin response, his voice high pitched and uncertain, his pronunciation unrecognizable. Fr. Kavanaugh cleared his throat ominously, an unmistakable warning that Melvin had better shape up, which he didn't. As Mass wore on, his squeaky responses became worse, and by the consecration, the part of Fr. Kavanaugh's neck visible between his white hair and the collar of his alb had turned tomato red. Totally oblivious to the fact that he made new altar boys so nervous they could hardly see straight, much less recite Latin in his presence, Fr. Kavanaugh's anger after Mass would be aimed as much at me for not teaching Latin correctly as it would be at Melvin for mangling every response more difficult than "Amen."

When Fr. Fowler appeared to assist with communion, I signaled to Melvin by tapping my Adam's apple that he was supposed to take one of the patens and follow Fr. Fowler down to the altar rail. Melvin looked back at me, confused. When I tried mouthing the words *go get the paten*, he mouthed back *what*? I was sure he knew what the paten was, because Fr. Kavanaugh had made me spend two hours after school one day, demonstrating to the latest crop of altar boys how to hold the paten, which looked like a gold Ping-Pong paddle, under each person's chin so they could catch the host if it slipped off somebody's tongue. To me, it was a total waste of time; no altar boy I knew had ever caught a host or even a crumb of a host. A kid in my class named David Dexter claimed that his brother Daniel, who was now a senior in high school, had set the record by catching four hosts and two host crumbs while he was at St. Lawrence's. Because David Dexter had also told us that his mother, who was as fat as a tugboat, had been a skater in the Ice Capades, I knew the story was a bunch of crap.

Fr. Fowler, whose patience and kindness Fr. Kavanaugh believed to be signs of weakness, slipped over to where the baffled Melvin was kneeling and whispered something in his ear. Whatever he said made Melvin smile and follow him like a happy puppy to the crowded altar rail.

There are little screwups at Mass, and there are big screwups at Mass, and then there are incidents that turn a person into an altar boy legend. Fr. Fowler had given communion to no more than three people when Melvin, walking backwards the way an altar boy has to when he is placing the paten under each person's chin, got his feet tangled in the hem of his cassock. He staggered, uttered a small cry, and fell smack on his ass. I expected Fr. Kavanaugh to go absolutely nuts, to publicly and extremely loudly, in front of an awestruck congregation, banish Melvin forever from the ranks of the altar boys the way God had banished Adam and Eve from the Garden of Eden. The only thing that stopped him, and possibly prevented the youngest Delsey child from becoming a babbling idiot for the remainder of his life, was the presence of The French Lady.

CHAPTER SEVENTEEN

With the scent of The French Lady's perfume growing stronger with every step he took, Fr. Kavanaugh ignored Melvin's prone body and hurried along the altar rail, mumbling "Corpus Domini nostri" while pressing hosts onto waiting tongues: pink tongues and gray tongues, cracked tongues, and tongues that quivered like fat little fish. One old woman with hairs on her nose had trouble opening her mouth. Her eyes fluttered with the effort, but the best she could do was to make the smallest slit between her lips. Fr. Fowler or Fr. Ellenberger would have done their best to give her communion by pressing the host between her teeth like they were pushing a coin into a slot. Fr. Kavanaugh didn't have the time. He moved on. The old woman's eyes opened. She didn't know what to do. He didn't even seem to notice. The French Lady's scent grew stronger until finally there she was. She closed her eyes and tilted her head back until the enormous brim of her hat was out of the way. With the exception of a few of the women on Mr. McDevitt's naked-lady calendars, she was the only person with purple eyelids I had ever seen. Her tongue was as red as her lipstick, her teeth were as white as pictures in toothpaste commercials, and of special interest to the lucky altar boys like me who got the chance to see her up close, she had one of those movie star dots on her left cheek. Whether it was a real mole or only painted on with black makeup was the subject of intense debate on the St. Lawrence's playground.

Fr. Kavanaugh had trouble removing a host from the ciborium. His big fingers shook. Never before in my life had I heard him sound nervous, but that's definitely the way he sounded when he pronounced the Latin words and started to place the host on The French Lady's long tongue. That is when it happened. Out of nowhere, I got the chance to become enshrined in St. Lawrence's parish altar boy lore, an opportunity to do what so many altar boys dream about and talk about but which so few ever get the chance to actually do. I got the chance to catch a falling host. And I nailed it. The host tumbled end over end and landed squarely in the middle of the paten.

When no host touched her tongue, The French Lady's eyes fluttered open. Fr. Kavanaugh's face turned red as he struggled to remove the host from the paten with his shaking fingers. He glared at me like I was supposed to do something, but I knew the rules, and the rules said that only priests were allowed to touch a host. Finally, he managed to push the host to the edge of the paten with his fat thumb, grab hold of it, and stick it on The French Lady's tongue. He forgot to say "Corpus Domini nostri" again, but maybe he didn't have to, because he had already said it once. I wasn't sure about that rule.

The French Lady went to confession every Saturday evening, her long, black hair concealed by a silk kerchief and everything except her bright-red lipstick masked by sunglasses. She slipped quietly into the church about fifteen minutes before confession was scheduled to end, sliding into the same pew she occupied every Sunday, a spot so close to where I was changing the altar cloth that I could smell the perfume that always reminded me of roses and honeysuckle. She blessed herself, dropped her face into her hands, and remained that way for a long time, longer than anyone else I had ever seen getting ready for confession. My imagination imploded in a futile attempt to imagine the nature of the sins that would bring a perfumed French woman to her knees, sins that might well be unpronounceable in English. By the time she blessed herself again and stood up, the church was almost empty. She then did something that no sane member of the parish would do without a gun held to their head: she entered Fr. Kavanaugh's confessional.

And there she remained for what seemed like an eternity.

By my watch, her record was twenty-eight minutes, easily beating the record formerly held by Mrs. Dolan, who was about a hundred years old and probably took so much time because she wanted to make sure she had covered everything before she died. The big difference between

The French Lady and Mrs. Dolan, besides what they looked like, was that Mrs. Dolan spent just as much time saying her penance as she did inside the confessional. The French Lady was gone in a flash. If she said one Hail Mary before she left, she said it fast.

All I had to do after she was gone was wait for Fr. Kavanaugh to leave. Fr. Fowler and Fr. Ellenberger were long gone. I had finished checking the candles, filling the holy water fonts, and making sure that no one had left anything in the pews, a job that had been more fun than usual because I had found a wrapper from a Hershey Bar someone must have eaten in church, and I was looking forward to showing it to Fr. Kavanaugh so I could watch his head explode.

For some reason, he stayed inside his confessional for a long time after The French Lady left, meaning that I had to hang around, waiting to lock the big front doors and turn off the lights. My five-hundred-word essay about the Incas was due Monday, and I still had work to do, not that Fr. Kavanaugh gave a damn about my problems. Even after finishing the part about the queen of Spain giving Pizarro the green light to screw the Incas out of everything they owned, I was only up to 398 words, and I wouldn't have been that far along if I hadn't risked my life by sneaking my geography book over to the church and doing research while I was supposed to be mopping the boiler room floor in the basement.

That had been just yesterday, a day I had almost become the first kid in the history of the world to die while writing a geography paper. I had been so absorbed reading about what a crud ball Pizarro had been to the Incas that I didn't hear Fr. Kavanaugh's heavy steps on the steep wooden stairs until he was almost at the bottom. "What the hell is taking you so long down here?" he bellowed.

The boiler room door was half open when I heard Fr. Ellenberger call to him from the top of the stairs. "Excuse me, Father, but there has been a rather disturbing phone call."

"Something you or Fr. Fowler can handle, I trust," he yelled back impatiently.

I shoved my geography book onto the top of the boiler and searched desperately for the broom.

"Actually, Father, it was Mrs. Dolan's daughter. Her mother is in the hospital." There was a pause during which Fr. Ellenberger cleared his throat. "It seems that the dear lady would like to confess her sins one last time. She has specifically requested your presence."

I found the broom and started sweeping as fast as I could.

"God help us and save us!" Fr. Kavanaugh muttered while pushing the door the rest of the way open. Either the boiler room floor hadn't been that dirty to start with or he was too distracted by Fr. Ellenberger's interruption to notice that I had not done squat. "Get outside right now!" he yelled into the room. "I want my car washed and waxed before dark! Let's go, move it!"

"Father?" came the meek inquiry from the top of the stairs.

Fr. Kavanaugh ignored his ever-intimidated assistant, pushing me through the basement door and up the steep outside stairs. "You know where everything is. Use the new can of Simonize, and don't forget to Windex all the windows!"

When he turned to leave, I gave him the finger behind his back, something I had seen Butchie McDevitt do to his father a million times. I had found that doing it to Fr. Kavanaugh gave me inexplicable joy.

All I could think about while I slaved away on Fr. Kavanaugh's big New Yorker was that if I didn't get my geography book back, I would run the risk of someone like Patricia Delsey getting a better grade than me on the Inca essay.

Fr. Kavanaugh didn't show up for dinner that night, something I could tell bothered my mother. At first she wouldn't let me take any pork chops or fried potatoes. "He'll be here any minute," she told me, covering the food with a clean dishtowel to keep it warm. I watched the clock hands' slow progress, starving. Two or three times she got up from the table and looked out the back door, wondering out loud where he could be. Shaking her head, she fixed a plate for him and put it in the oven. She didn't even notice when I took a pork chop and some potatoes and began to eat, hatching a plan in my head to sneak over to the church under the cover of darkness and retrieve my geography book as soon as I was done.

It was a plan that didn't work, abandoned in favor of self-preservation. The instant I caught a whiff of roses and honeysuckle in the dark, I ducked behind one of the fat holly bushes separating the rear of the church from the parking lot and froze. The low growl of Fr. Kavanaugh's voice made the hair on the back of my head stick straight out. Through the tangle of pointed leaves I could see that he was speaking into a small, light-colored car parked right next to his Chrysler. From time to time, soft words came from inside the small car, and for the first time in my life, I heard Fr. Kavanaugh laugh. He bent down, rested one big arm on the roof of the strange car, and for a few seconds, his head disappeared from view. When it reappeared, the small car's headlights came on, and as Fr. Kavanaugh watched, it backed away from the church. I stayed hidden behind the holly bush long after Fr. Kavanaugh disappeared through the back door of the church and the last of the unmistakable perfume drifted into the night.

When I finally got back home, I stayed up late rewriting from memory the part of the essay I had already finished and adding some baloney about how if only Pizarro had left the Incas alone they might have grown into a great nation and maybe even invented rockets before the Germans did. Sr. Mary Luke especially liked that part, making a note in the margin that none of us will ever know what great plans God had for the Incas. She gave me an A. She also gave Patricia Delsey an A, but that was OK Unlike her, I had written my last three paragraphs without the help of a geography book.

CHAPTER EIGHTEEN

Because I was staring out the classroom window wondering what Butchie was doing, I completely missed the beginning of the confrontation that led to Patricia Delsey being thrown out of St. Lawrence's for being a heretic. McDevitt's gas station was blocked from my view by the large sycamore tree in our backyard, but my guess was that Butchie had skipped school like he usually did and was sitting on his butt somewhere out of his father's sight, smoking a cigarette. I had told him about The French Lady and the way she came to Mass dressed like someone from the movies with more makeup on her face than all of the other women in church put together, and when I did, he had told me that women draw fake moles on their faces when they want men to know they are not wearing underpants. He told me I could ask his father if I didn't believe him, and it must have been while I was trying to decide if that would be a good idea that Sr. Mary Luke and Patricia Delsey got into it.

The first words that registered when I realized something unusual was happening were "You are testing my patience, Patricia. Please be seated."

I followed the direction of Sr. Mary Luke's glare and saw that Patricia Delsey was completely unfazed. She did not sit down.

Her defiant stance was all the more impressive because she was so tall, taller by far than any of the other girls in the seventh grade and probably as tall as any of the boys except for Thomas "Beanpole" Meltzer, who was taller than most grownups in the parish. There were other things that made Patricia seem older than she was: she was by far the smartest girl in the class and would have been the smartest person, boy or girl, if she had been as good in math as I was, an imperfection that, I was certain, made her mad. She also said things like *on the other hand* and *that's beside the point*, expressions that no one else our age ever used.

"I'm sorry, Sister," she continued calmly, "but I've been thinking about this a great deal, and it doesn't stand to reason that any God as good as we have been taught He is would discriminate against perfectly good people just because they have never been baptized as Catholics."

"Patricia, there are many things that mere mortals are not meant to understand, especially at your young age. We must simply place our trust in the Lord. Now please, take your seat."

Tension in the classroom increased noticeably when Patricia continued to stand. "According to the *Encyclopedia Britannica*, in Ceylon alone there are five million Buddhists and one and a half million Hindus. It makes no sense that all those people would be kept out of heaven just because they don't have the same beliefs that we do. Most of them have probably never even heard of Catholicism."

"That will be quite enough, Patricia!"

If there was a single Buddhist or Hindu in Harrisville, Maryland, at that time, I had never seen them, not that I would have known what to look for. My only encounter with Buddhism had been the previous Christmas when I was at Woolworth's looking for a present for my mother. An ashtray shaped like a potbellied man wearing a red robe had caught my eye. He was sitting in front of a gold-colored dish where you were supposed to put cigarette ashes. While trying to decide if it was worth forty-nine cents, the lady behind the counter explained that it was a Buddha ashtray and pointed out that they also carried ashtrays shaped like a beaver drinking out of a small pond and another shaped like a hollowed-out stump. The beaver was my favorite, but since my mother didn't smoke, I bought her some powder that smelled like green apples, which, that, as far as I could tell, she had never used.

Ignoring Sr. Mary Luke's withering stare, Patricia pressed on, declaring that it was also hard to believe that God would make newborn babies spend eternity in limbo just because they died before they had a chance to be baptized, a failure that was in no way their fault. Shaking her finger to emphasize the point, she argued that any open-minded person had to know in their heart that Methodists and Baptists were every bit as good as Catholics as long as they led their lives the way everybody was supposed to.

John Quinlan, who, it was widely believed, had gotten as far as the seventh grade at St. Lawrence's only because his father, who owned Quinlan's Funeral Home, put twenty dollars in the collection every Sunday, was furiously writing down every word of what Patricia Delsey was saying, apparently believing that there would be a test on it later. When Sr. Mary Luke spotted him scribbling away, she shot down the aisle and snatched the notebook away from him.

"One other point, Sister. I did some research on Muslims...."

"Patricia Ann Delsey, if you don't sit down this very instant, I am going to report you to the rectory!"

The classroom gasped. Patricia rolled her eyes but sat down. No one in their right mind wanted to be reported to the rectory and have their parents summoned to a meeting with Fr. Kavanaugh, an event a hundred times more disastrous than being marched downstairs to see Sr. John Bosco, the Sister Superior who, even though she had white hairs growing on her nose and looked like a witch, was actually pretty nice. The last person to be reported to the rectory was Mario D'Amico when a black-and-white picture of a pile of naked men and women fell out of his religion book. Michael Walsh claimed that he got a good look at the picture on the floor before Lorraine Enright saw it and screamed, and though his description of what the naked people were doing ignited our imaginations, his most stunning revelations have, with the passage of time, proven to be anatomically impossible.

A strong indication that my mind had been seriously dam-
aged by overexposure to religion came that night in the
form of a dream, the first of many weird dreams that no one
who was lucky enough to pass his childhood in the bliss of
public school would ever experience.

In the dream, I was Zacchaeus, the short guy in the
gospel who climbed up a tree to get a better look at Jesus,
only it was the gates of heaven I was trying to get a good
look at, not Jesus. He wasn't in the dream.

There was a huge crowd of people in front of the gates,
lined up like they were waiting for a store to open. The
gates of heaven were very fancy, like the gates at the main
entrance to the zoo in Washington, only much bigger and
made out of gold so bright that the only reason I could look
at them was because I was wearing sunglasses. The part of
heaven I could see from up in the tree looked like a beautiful
park with trimmed, green grass and red and yellow flowers lining a long, glittering path that curved into a forest of
gently swaying trees. Mr. Higgins, Mr. McCloskey, and Mr.
Duda, the ushers from noon Mass, guarded the gates. They
were wearing their blue usher ribbons, only they weren't
ushers. They were angels. I could see their wings. They
were yelling for everybody to stand back from the gates,
but nobody was paying attention to them.

One man in the crowd was riding on an elephant, and
a bunch of others had monkeys on their shoulders. Some
people had bright cloth things wound around their heads,

and others had shaved heads. From up in the tree, I could see that some of the people were wearing sandals, some were barefoot, and others had on fancy gold shoes with long curved toes. Way in the back, jumping up and down, trying to see what was going on, there were about a hundred short people who looked like the natives in Tarzan movies, and even farther back, I spotted thousands of Incas who looked exactly like the Incas in our geography book. They were chanting something in Incan that I couldn't understand.

Mr. Duda pulled a bullhorn from under his angel gown with the arm that hadn't been shot off in the war. "None of you were baptized! You cannot come in! I repeat, you were not baptized! Go back to limbo and stay there!"

One of the Tarzan natives looked up into the tree where I was wiping my sunglasses. "What is baptized?"

"Baptism is a sacrament that cleanses us from original sin, makes us Christians, children of God, and heirs of heaven," I hollered back, reciting word for word the catechism definition that had been drilled into my head in the second or third grade.

Two other people came over and stood next to him looking up at me: an Inca and an Eskimo. They had no idea what I was talking about, but before they could say anything, there was a big commotion up near the gates. The Fallon sisters had pushed their way through the crowd and showed Mr. Duda what appeared to be tickets. He opened the gates just enough for them to squeeze their skinny, old bodies through. Rows and rows of neatly dressed people abandoned the folding chairs where they had been patiently waiting and surged toward the gates. "Protestant baptisms are not valid! Read the rules!" Mr. Duda blared through the bullhorn. There was a huge fuss when he refused to let Abraham Lincoln in.

I put my sunglasses back on. Far beyond the golden gates where the long path disappeared into the forest, my father was waving at me. He looked exactly like he looked in the picture Fr. Kavanaugh had made me tear to pieces. He waved until I waved back, and then he was gone.

No one ever knew for sure if Patricia Delsey was expelled or if she was taken out of St. Lawrence's and enrolled in Harrisville Junior High by her father who was still mad about Fr. Kavanaugh throwing little Melvin Delsey off the altar boys. All Sr. Mary Luke would say about the whole thing was that we all should get down on our knees every night and ask God to shield Patricia and her brother from the perils of public school. I saw no need for such prayers. As far as I was concerned, Patricia Delsey and little Melvin had hit the jackpot.

CHAPTER NINETEEN

———⊗⊗⊗———

Thou Shalt Not Place Thy Foot On The Gas Station Property
Unless Thou Desireth To Be Beaten To A Pulp By Thy Pastor.

Those ominous words had not echoed like thunder from high atop a desert mountain, but they frequently rattled the silverware and caused the salt and pepper shakers to do a little dance when Fr. Kavanaugh underlined them by pounding on the kitchen table like a madman. While it was impossible not to wince, imagining myself being crushed like a melon in the vise-like grip of his huge hands, I could not help thinking how dismal my life would be without an occasional dose of life on the other side of the hedge. There was no way I was going to stay away from the gas station. I would be more careful than ever, but I was going to continue to take my chances.

My original plan was to do it on Saturdays when my mother was working at the St. Vincent de Paul store *and* Fr. Kavanaugh's car was missing from its parking space behind the church. Unfortunately, that plan had a big hole in it, because while I could count on my mother being away from ten in the morning until three in the afternoon, I never knew for sure how long Fr. Kavanaugh would be gone. The next plan I came up with worked better. I would do it when my mother was working at the St. Vincent de Paul store *and* there was a pastors' meeting downtown at the chancery, occasions at which, Fr. Kavanaugh complained to my mother, a bunch of lunatics debated such matters as the most effective way to pray for peace with the Russians when anyone with half a brain knew that a much better idea would be to bomb the living hell out of them. Fr. Kavanaugh hated these meetings with a passion, but I loved them. They meant he would be gone for hours.

These flights to freedom remained a nerve-racking experience until at some point during the spring of my seventh grade, it dawned on me that sneaking over to the gas station was no longer the challenge it had always been. For one thing, Fr. Kavanaugh's car began to disappear regularly for long stretches of time, a surprising occurrence I never connected with the change that took place in my mother. More than ever before, she seemed lost inside her lonely mind. It was like she no longer cared about anything, least of all where I had been or what I had been doing.

Not that I could let my guard down completely. While there was virtually no chance that Fr. Kavanaugh would show up to do business with Mr. McDevitt, a man he referred to heatedly as a heathen, there was always the possibility he would spot me while driving past the gas station in his big Chrysler. It might have been a long shot, but because I knew better than anyone on earth what it was like to be the victim of Fr. Kavanaugh's wrath, I stayed out of sight, often hiding with Butchie in his father's tow truck, listening to observations about life that were far different from anything I was likely to hear on St. Lawrence's playground.

Butchie loved his father's truck, a muscular green and white workhorse with five orange lights bolted to the roof and the words McDevitt's Garage painted in yellow on both doors. He sat in it for hours, pretending he was speeding through the streets of Harrisville while telling me about all the things he was going to do someday. Apparently, being a steamroller driver was no longer his plan. Any dickhead, he informed me, knew that tow truck drivers got ten times more kooze than guys who drove steamrollers.

On these occasions, I did more listening than talking, wondering often what Butchie was really going to do when he got older. I never once saw him write, and there were very few words he could read; I knew that from the time I caught him trying to mouth the words of an advertisement for x-ray glasses on the back cover of a comic book. Accompanying the words he found so mysterious was a picture of some moron gawking through horn-rimmed glass at the silhouette of a woman whose huge boobs were visible inside the outline of her dress. Butchie kept pointing at words and asking me what they said, words like *see clearly under layers of clothes* and *amaze your friends at parties*. He asked me how much the x-ray glasses cost, and I told him one dollar plus twenty-five cents for shipping, all words I could have read by the end of the third grade.

"A dollar and twenty-five cents! You have to be shitting me" was his angry reaction, a reaction underlined by a punch on the shoulder that numbed my arm to the elbow. "They can stick those fucking x-ray glasses up their ass," he sneered, shoving the comic book under the driver's seat where he kept a stack of them. "I seen so many naked women when I sneak around at night that I can't even remember which houses have big tits living in them and which ones have little tits." He twisted the steering wheel back and forth while delivering a remarkably accurate imitation of a powerful engine. "If you weren't such a chickenshit, you could come with me."

Before I could say anything, the driver's-side door flew open. "Get your ass out of the truck. I've got a run to make!" Mr. McDevitt snatched the collar of Butchie's black T-shirt and dragged him out of the tow truck. "Watch the gas pumps while I'm gone, and unless you want to grow up without a dick, put every goddamned cent you get in the register this time!"

Mr. McDevitt threatened Butchie like that all the time, but his anger was different than Fr. Kavanaugh's anger. It was like he meant it but he didn't. Fr. Kavanaugh meant it.

"Your mother know you're over here?" he yelled after me as I slipped out the other door.

"Yes, sir."

He knew I was lying, I could tell by the way he looked at me, but he didn't say anything. He just fired up the engine and took off.

Butchie pushed back his long hair with greasy hands, making no noticeable difference in his appearance. "I'm going to kick his ass someday," he informed me as the tow truck squealed out onto Prospect Street. He was always saying things like that about his father, but he never seemed very mad. It was like the two of them were playing a game.

"Come on, Peckerhead, let's get some Cokes out of the machine. I know how to open it with a screwdriver."

We were on our second bottles when the gas pump bell rang, a sound audible inside our house all day long. Butchie made no attempt to rise from the battered swivel chair behind his father's desk. "Screw them," he said taking another swig of his Coke. "They can get their fucking gas somewhere else."

I got up from the floor next to the Coke machine, brushed off the seat of my pants, and walked over to the big window at the front of the office. "What a neat car," I remarked.

"What kind?" Butchie asked without opening his eyes. He loved cars.

"I don't know," I answered honestly. "Some kind of light-yellow convertible with white walls and a tan top."

Butchie jumped up, spilling Coke all over himself, and hustled over to the window.

"That's her! Goddamn! It's her again!"

I followed him out to the gas pumps where Mrs. DeSimone waited. She didn't smile when Butchie asked if he could check her oil, but she did smile when she saw me. "I see you at church, is that right?" When she said *that*, it sounded like *zat*.

"Yes, ma'am." I had never before heard The French Lady speak. Her voice gave me goose bumps. The scent of roses and honeysuckle filled the air.

She was wearing the same bright-red scarf and sunglasses I had seen her wearing at confession along with tan leather gloves that matched the cover of the steering wheel. "Tell that rude boy to fill me with three dollars." She spoke to me like Butchie wasn't even there. "I only come to this place again because I am almost empty." It sounded like she said *sree* dollars, but I knew what she meant.

Her car was a Studebaker, a word on the chrome trim above the rear license plate that Butchie was trying his best to sound out. "Is that the hottest kooze you ever saw in your life?" Butchie whispered much too loudly as he flipped open the gas cap cover and jammed home the nozzle. "My old man said he'd like to check her oil every day of the week and twice on Sundays."

Mrs. DeSimone's sunglasses filled the rearview mirror, looking back at us. "You, church boy," she called, holding out three dollar bills. I took them and handed them to Butchie. The second the gas flap closed, she took off, waiting at the end of the driveway long enough for a dump truck to rumble past before making a right turn onto Thirty-Eighth Avenue.

Amazingly, Butchie didn't say anything about Mrs. DeSimone calling me church boy. He stood still as a statue, staring after the pale-yellow convertible until it disappeared behind a thicket of trees lining the road. "She's foreign," Butchie finally said, pointing out a fact that any idiot who heard her say three words could figure out. "My old man told me that the last time she came in here. He poked a ton of foreign women when he was in the war, him and his friend Roddy who was in the war with him. I heard them talking about it one night when they were drinking beer." He started to slip The French Lady's gasoline money into his pants pocket but seemed to think better of it.

"She lives back behind the church on that street way down by the creek. I saw her when I accidentally looked through her bedroom window."

I thought about that for a minute. "How do you accidentally look in somebody's bedroom window?" I asked after I gave up trying to figure it out for myself.

"Because, Peckerhead, I snuck into the wrong backyard when I was looking for the house where a girl I seen at the drugstore lives. It was dark as hell."

When we got back inside the cramped office, Butchie went to the cash register and took the three dollars out of his pocket. They must have smelled like The French Lady's perfume, because he sniffed at the bills before putting them back in his pocket. "I didn't see anything good. She was already in bed, reading a magazine with a big, white cat sitting next to her," he told me, flopping down into his father's chair and swinging his feet up onto the desk, "but I'm going back. You can bet your sweet ass on that."

I slid down beside the Coke machine again, trying my best to picture what The French Lady looked like in bed, wondering if she cleaned the purple stuff off her eyelids and wiped the movie star mole off her cheek at night.

"When are you going back?" I asked before I knew I was speaking.

"You ain't got the guts," Butchie sneered, searching through the drawers of his father's desk. "Son of a bitch must have taken his cigarettes with him." Butchie stood up, took the three dollars out of his pocket again, and studied them. He put two in the register and stuck one back in his pocket. "I'm going to the drugstore to get some cigarettes. Watch the place until I get back."

I told him I had to get home.

He thought about that for a minute before leaving. "If you want to come with me when I try to catch that foreign babe in her birthday suit, your ass better still be here when I get back."

I slid back down onto the floor and tried to think up a good lie to tell Mr. McDevitt if he got back before Butchie.

CHAPTER TWENTY

Probably because she had done it as long as I could remember, my mother continued to prepare dinner for Fr. Kavanaugh every night, the very same meals on the very same day of the week that his sainted mother had prepared them back in Wilkes-Barre. More often than not, he failed to show up, and when this happened, my mother didn't seem to know what to do. She picked at her food with one eye on the kitchen door. "I can't imagine what could be keeping him," she brooded. "He must be making a sick call."

I had no idea where he was, but I knew for a fact that he wasn't making a sick call. He didn't allow Fr. Fowler or Fr. Ellenberger to do much, but as far as he was concerned, chores like infant baptisms and sick calls, occasions when there would be little use for his gift of intimidation, were annoyances to which they were entirely welcome.

Even when he wasn't with us, dinner at our house was far from normal if normal meant having a father at one end of the table, a mother at the other end, and a brother or a sister sitting across from me, talking about what everybody had done that day. The relative serenity of Fr. Kavanaugh's absence spawned fantasies. My father, identical in appearance to the man in the forbidden photograph, smiled and asked me if I had hit any home runs that day, and my mother, every bit as pretty as I knew she had once been, wanted to know if I had gotten back my history test yet. There were no cutting comments about the pot roast not having as many carrots or onions as the pot roast back in Pennsylvania or about the meat loaf being overcooked, which in fact it never was, even though all my mother had to work with was an ancient oven with feet that had been installed when the old house was new. Criticism of her cooking made my mother recoil as though she had been slapped. It hurt her and embarrassed her, a fact that became clearer to me as I got older. She looked down at her plate and moved food in circles with her fork. She never once looked him in the eye, like I always hoped she would, and asked him if that were the case, why didn't he feed his fat face over at the rectory with the other priests. I could imagine a lot of things, but try as I would, any picture of my mother telling Fr. Kavanaugh where to go was in some category beyond fiction.

On the blissful nights of his absence, I reached for more of whatever was on the table without fear of having my arm broken, and when I was finished eating, I hurried over to the sink with my dirty dishes and ran up the stairs to do my homework. My strategy for these evenings was to be out of sight if the kitchen door swung open and he came strutting in late as he had once or twice, dropping into his chair and seeming to dare my mother to say one word about it.

It was on one of these nights when, for the first time in my life, I heard my mother argue with him. I had left my bedroom to use the bathroom and was passing the top of the stairs when I heard Fr. Kavanaugh's voice, deep and angry, informing my mother that she had no understanding of the time demands made on the pastor of a busy parish.

"No doubt the needs of one parishioner in particular," my mother shot back.

A long silence was followed by the ominous rumble of Fr. Kavanaugh clearing his throat. I couldn't make out what he said, but I heard my mother very clearly. "You know very well who I'm talking about!" It was the first time in my life I ever heard her raise her voice.

I pictured Fr. Kavanaugh's eyes narrowing in disbelief.

"Did you tell her the same thing you told me?" my mother yelled. A chair scraped the floor. It sounded to me like a hand slapped the table very hard. "Does she cook your meals? Does she wash and iron your clothes? Does she comfort you? That is your word for it, isn't it? *Comfort!*"

Another chair scraped the floor. A second later, the back door slammed so hard that I felt the floor shake all the way upstairs.

I barely had time to make it back to my bedroom before my mother started up the stairs. Later, in the dark, through the aging walls of the house her father had built, I heard her crying.

My mother was still in bed when I left for school the next morning, and she was still in her bathrobe and slippers when I came home that afternoon. We had leftovers for dinner, which was fine with me, especially since my mother said nothing when I made a meat loaf sandwich at the table, a breach of Fr. Kavanaugh's dinner rules that would have incited him to violence. A few days passed before I found her dressed when I came home from school, a circumstance that didn't surprise me halfway as much as the fact that she was at her ironing board pressing a pair of Fr. Kavanaugh's huge, black pants.

That night, when I came downstairs from doing my homework, she was sitting at the table, staring into a cup of coffee. From time to time she stirred it slowly, seeming to concentrate hard on the tiny swirls she created with the spoon. At some point she realized that I had come into the kitchen and informed me wearily that there was tuna salad in the refrigerator and macaroni and cheese on the stove. She pushed herself to her feet and walked slowly to the kitchen window. For a very long time she stared at the darkened granite walls of St. Lawrence's and then said she had a terrible headache and was going up to bed.

Sometimes, during this period, she ate dinner with me, but usually she just sat at the table like a zombie, endlessly stirring her coffee while she waited for me to finish so she could do the dishes. Our nights together had changed drastically. I think, for her, they had become empty and confusing. For me, they were too good to be true. For the first time since I had grown old enough to form memories, Fr. Kavanaugh was not at our dinner table, one eye on his crossword puzzle and the other on me, ready to pounce like an angry lion if I accidently put an elbow on the table or so much as looked hard at the food my mother set on the table before he pronounced grace in the same solemn tone that I imagined God would sound like speaking out of a cloud. Unfortunately, I misinterpreted Fr. Kavanaugh's absence from our dinner table as a sign that my days as the parish slave had come to an end, and one day after school, instead of heading for the rectory, I told Vinnie Rinaldi he could have my job cleaning Fr. Kavanaugh's office if he wanted it.

"Really? I can really have that job? Fr. Kavanaugh said so?" he asked incredulously.

"He said you were the only one I could give it to," I informed him solemnly.

The next day at recess, kneeling at a chalk circle drawn on the blacktop, about to play a game of marbles, I was as happy as I had ever been. Blue skies had washed away the clouds, and the sun was shining on my life. I believe I was whistling. The only warnings that disaster was about to strike were the sudden expressions of terror on the faces of the classmates I was playing with. Before I had time to turn and see what they were gaping at, Fr. Kavanaugh grabbed me by the back of my shirt and yanked me to my feet. He never said a word, slapping me first with the palm of his hand and then with the back of his hand so hard that I thought my neck had snapped.

When I came home from school, my mother looked up from mending one of my school shirts. If she noticed my red, swollen face, she didn't say anything about it. She bit off a thread, shook out the shirt, and dropped it into the ironing basket next to her chair. "Did you see him today?" she asked.

I shook my head as I took the jar of peanut butter from the pantry. It was the first time she had said anything about Fr. Kavanaugh since the night I heard her crying in her bedroom.

"I wonder if he is coming to dinner," she said aloud, standing and wiping her hands on her apron.

I sat down at the table with a peanut butter and jelly sandwich, wishing with all my might that he were dead. What had happened that day was the worst thing he had ever done to me. Every kid on that playground, from first graders to eighth graders, had stopped playing tag or skipping rope and whatever else they were doing to watch me cry. I couldn't stop. No matter how hard I tried, I couldn't stop crying. My face hurt and my neck hurt, and I was so angry and embarrassed that I couldn't see straight.

CHAPTER TWENTY-ONE

A platter of pot roast sat on the kitchen table along with a basket of rolls and a big bowl of applesauce, untouched except for what I had eaten. My mother, who rarely ate anymore, sat stirring her coffee with her eyes fixed on the kitchen door. When I finished, she pushed herself to her feet, put the leftovers away, and did the dishes with all the energy of the zombie she had become. "It's raining," she said almost inaudibly after going over to the door and peering out into the night. A few seconds later, she turned and, without looking at me, headed for the hall stairway. The bedroom slippers she now lived in slid across the linoleum like she was too tired to lift her feet.

I took out my math book and turned to the five problems we were supposed to do for homework. They were word problems, the kind of thing I was better at than anyone else in our class, especially since Patricia Delsey had been expelled. The first one asked if a bus left Point A traveling at forty miles an hour and a car left Point A forty-five minutes later driving fifty miles an hour in the same direction, how long would it take the car to catch up with the bus? It was the kind of problem I usually did in my head while everyone else in the classroom scratched away with their pencils. The first step was to figure out how far the bus was going to get before the car started. There was nothing to these dumb problems, but my face hurt so much from Fr. Kavanaugh hitting me that I couldn't think straight. I crossed my arms across my math book and put my head down to rest for a few minutes. I watched the bus leave Point A. Forty miles an hour times forty-five minutes; point seven five times forty.

I was high up in the same tree that I had climbed the time I saw Mr. Higgins, Mr. McCloskey, and Mr. Duda guarding the gates of heaven. They saw me and waved. For some reason, there was no one waiting to get into heaven. In front of the gates, where the Incas and everyone else had been milling around the last time I was there, the grass was all matted down and littered with empty cups and sandwich wrappers. Mr. Shifflet was picking them up with a long, pointed stick and putting them in a burlap sack that Mr. McCloskey held open for him. Waves of heat rolled up into the tree, twisting its leaves into brown knots and making me so hot I could barely stand it. When I looked down, trying to discover where the heat was coming from, I saw a big, rectangular hole with steep steps descending into blackness out of which the sound of screaming mixed with blasts of howling wind and swirling smoke. While I watched, the hole began to move, coming so close to the tree that I could see straight down into the darkness. The screaming became louder, and the hot smoke swirled wildly up into the tree, stinging my eyes. Fr. Kavanaugh laughed as he walked over to the hole and stood so close that the toes of his big, black shoes stuck over the edge. Mr. Nolan, who owned Madison Ford, tried to climb out of the hole, but Fr. Kavanaugh stomped on his fingers until he let go and fell back into the smoking pit. Mrs. Doyle, who always came to Mass late because it took so long to get all her kids dressed, made it to the top step and grabbed Fr. Kavanaugh's foot before he kicked her hand away. Maybe Mr. Nolan was living in sin with his bookkeeper like Fr. Kavanaugh said, but Mrs. Doyle couldn't help it if her husband never helped her. The one who belonged in hell was Fr. Kavanaugh for being so mean to everyone. I shinnied down the tree, tearing my pants on the hot bark, but before I could push him down the stairs, he spun around and grabbed me. "You little bastard!" he boomed in his deep, twelve o'clock Mass voice. "Your sinful father is down there with the rest of them. No sense you waiting any longer to meet him!"

I couldn't move my arms. I kicked at him with all my might, but it didn't do any good. He threw me into the smoking hole as effortlessly as he threw his dirty laundry down our cellar stairs.

The side of my head was sweaty and stuck to the pages of my arithmetic book. I tried to remember how fast the bus was traveling when it left Point A, but I couldn't because someone kept interrupting my train of thought. It took a minute to wake all the way up and realize that Butchie McDevitt was in our kitchen, a place he had never been before. He was wearing a black T-shirt and black pants, and he was so wet that his long, black hair was matted to his head.

"Wake up, Peckerhead! Time to go!"

"How did you get in?"

"Through the damned door, how do you think? I seen it was only you, so I came in."

My mother never locked the back door even after Fr. Kavanaugh stopped coming over, probably because she was afraid he would kick it in if he decided to come back and found it locked. Butchie saw me looking at the puddle of water forming around his feet. "It's raining like hell, but that don't make any difference. My old man went to the Moose with his friend Roddy, so I'm going. You got the guts to go with me?"

"Go where?"

"Go check out that foreign lady. Where the hell do you think?"

I looked toward the hallway and the stairs and listened carefully. There was no sign of my mother, but I shushed Butchie anyway. "You mean Mrs. DeSimone?"

"I don't know what the hell her name is. The one with the yellow convertible and the big, white cat."

"Big, white cat?"

"I saw it both times I looked in the window."

"Both times? I thought you only went once."

"I went back since then. She was in her big old bed doing something with her toenails. She had white stuff all over her face." It was obvious that Butchie was not used to speaking quietly. I looked nervously toward the stairway and shushed him again.

"Was she naked?" The thought was beyond my imagination.

"She had on this pink bathrobe, but I think she is going to be naked tonight."

Butchie's reasoning made no sense at all to me, but for reasons only he could understand, it seemed to make perfect sense to him. The math book, still open to the five problems I was supposed to do, stared up at me from the table. Going with Butchie would probably do nothing but get me as wet as he already was, I knew that, but I also knew that if by some miracle he did see The French Lady naked while I was home doing word problems, I would hate math for the rest of my life.

"You're afraid your old lady will catch you sneaking back in, ain't you?"

I stood up and looked at him. There was no chance in the world that my mother would come back downstairs, not tonight, not any night anymore, but even if she was sitting at the kitchen table waiting for me when I got back, all I had to do was make up a lie about having to do some job over at the church for Fr. Kavanaugh. Maybe I wouldn't even do that. Maybe I would tell her I went out because I felt like it. I was sick and tired of all the bullshit.

"Let me get my jacket," I said to Butchie.

CHAPTER TWENTY-TWO

I reached the back porch in time to see Butchie disappear like a rabbit through the hedge at the edge of St. Lawrence's parking lot. Tunnels of light from the row of prison-like fixtures atop the school bore uselessly into the wet night, frustrating my efforts to see whether Fr. Kavanaugh's car was hiding in the maze of deep shadows behind the church. Through the pounding rain, I heard Butchie holler that I better move my ass or he was going without me.

We splashed through the streets behind the parish property, all of which were named for trees. Butchie moved furtively along the rain-swept sidewalks, crouching low and using parked cars for cover as we made our way from Chestnut Street to Elm Street where he ducked behind a telephone pole to catch his breath and whispered excitedly in my ear that I had probably noticed he was moving like a commando, a trick he had learned from looking at the pictures in a *Battle Star* comic book he had stolen from Miller's Drugstore. Between deep breaths, he informed me that he would probably join the commandos if he ever changed his mind about being a steamroller driver. Before I could point out that he had already chucked steamrollers in favor of tow trucks, he took off again, charging through a puddle the size of a small pond. The jacket I had grabbed on the way out of the house was soaked, my shoes were filled with water, and my soggy pants were having trouble bending as fast as my knees. We were about to jump over the overflowing gutter at the edge of Hemlock Street when a car sailed around the corner, launching a dual beam of light along the glistening pavement. "Look at that, Peckerhead!" Butchie exclaimed. "Just what we need!" In the headlight glare he had spotted a beat-up bucket wedged under a parked car.

Before I could ask what he was talking about, he was gone again, swinging the stupid bucket wildly.

When we got to Oak Street, Butchie skidded to a stop behind a big, black sedan. "That's it," he shouted into the rain, "right over there!" Spidery tree shadows cast by the streetlight waved eerily across a one-story brick house on the other side of the street. "That's where she lives!"

"I got to pee," Butchie announced out of nowhere, bouncing to his feet and unzipping his fly to take aim at the front tire of the big car we were using for cover. "I never peed on a Chrysler before."

The word Chrysler took my breath away. My heart would not have danced more wildly if Fr. Kavanaugh had suddenly grabbed me by the back of the neck. I jumped to my feet and pressed my face against the big car's rain-streaked window, but even if I had been able to see anything,

I wouldn't have known what I was looking for. It wasn't like he would have left a prayer book on the dashboard or rosary beads hanging from the mirror.

"What the hell you looking at, Peckerhead?" Butchie wanted to know, zipping up his fly. "She ain't in there." A second later, he was on his way across the street. "Let's go! She might be taking off her clothes this very second!"

A big part of me wanted to turn around and run for home, but an even bigger part had zero interest in listening to Butchie crow about how I missed seeing The French Lady parade around her house as naked as a jaybird. I sprinted across the street into her darkened yard. By the time I caught up with Butchie, he had reached the fence at the side of the house. His black tee shirt and pants were as wet as if he had just climbed out of a lake. "That's her bedroom," he informed me excitedly, pointing to a lighted window at the rear corner of the house. He dropped the bucket over the fence with a soggy thud and hopped over after it, agile as a monkey. While I struggled to climb the slippery fence, he worked hard to steady the upside-down bucket under the yellow rectangle of light.

"I could hardly reach the fucking window last time," he muttered, trying to get the bucket to sit flat. There was something in the way, a rock or a root. Butchie cursed under his breath and kicked hard at whatever it was, but the thing wouldn't budge. He moved the bucket back and forth under the window, got it as steady as it was going to get, reached for the brick windowsill, put one foot on the rocking perch, and pulled himself up. The arrangement wobbled wildly for a few seconds, almost spilling him, but finally stabilized enough for him to motion me to climb up behind him where, wiping raindrops away from my eyes, I peered through the narrow space between the sill and the bottom of the venetian blinds. The view of The French Lady's bedroom was so perfect that I thought I was going to pass out.

The biggest bed I had ever seen was right next to the window, so close to us that I could have counted the pink flowers stitched into the thick, yellow blanket. Stacked against a huge headboard were more pillows than we had in all the bedrooms in our house put together. The white cat Butchie had told me about was on the bed, licking a paw lazily and rubbing it around on its head. While I watched, the cat stopped, stared over at the window for a long time, then went back to cleaning its head. The French Lady was on the other side of the room, wearing a shiny, pink bathrobe while she sat at a table with a big, curved mirror attached to it. I could see her reflection perfectly. Holding onto Butchie's shoulders, I watched her scoop white cream out of a jar and rub it all over her face with the tips of her long fingers, turning her head one way and then the other while she swirled the cream in quick circles until it disappeared into her skin. When she was done, she screwed a gold lid onto the jar and picked up a little mirror. She studied her face for a long time, making funny faces by stretching her mouth wide open and closing it again and then opening her eyes as wide as she could while she rubbed the sides of her nose. When she was done doing all of that, she reached behind her head with both hands and did something to her long, black hair that made it fall straight down her back. I could tell by the way the bucket began rocking that Butchie was beside himself. We rocked so hard that the cat stopped licking its paw and stared hard at the window.

The French Lady stood up and stretched, arching her back and reaching for the ceiling. "Gigi, what in the world are you looking at?" she asked the cat in a voice that, through the closed window with the rain pelting down, sounded hollow and far away.

Butchie and I held our breath like we were underwater until the cat stopped looking at us and went back to licking its paw and rubbing its furry, white head. The French Lady, who had come over to the side of the bed closest to the window, turned her back and stood so close to us that, if the window had been open, either one of us could have reached out and touched her. To my open-mouthed astonishment, the pink robe dropped away from her shoulders. The bucket rocked violently. If I hadn't been there and Butchie had told me about it, I would never have believed him. Her bare butt was right in front of us. It was whiter than the rest of her body, so white that it looked like she was wearing underpants, only she wasn't. I whispered in his ear for Butchie to be quiet even though he hadn't said a word. He was as still as a rain-soaked statue.

The French Lady slipped into bed, easing the cat aside and pulling the yellow blanket with the stitched flowers up around her shoulders. We saw her boobs for about two seconds. They disappeared under the blanket in a flash, but as far as I could tell, foreign-lady boobs didn't look any different than the boobs on Mr. McDevitt's calendars.

"Holy shit." Butchie breathed the words more than spoke them. He was frozen in place, both hands gripping the brick windowsill. I whispered in his ear that we should leave before we got in trouble. He shook his head emphatically and whispered back that I could leave if I wanted to but that his father wouldn't be home from the Moose until after midnight, so he was going to stick around in case anything else happened. I was trying to decide what to do when out of the blue, through all the noise of our pounding hearts and the driving rain, I heard Mrs. DeSimone call out in her foreign lady accent, "You can come in now!"

Fr. Kavanaugh, wearing the light-blue bathrobe I had often seen in my mother's laundry basket, opened the bedroom door so fast that he must have been on the other side with his hand on the knob the whole time. Butchie and I fell off the bucket together, landing in a tangle of arms and legs in the wet grass. While I struggled to get back up, disoriented as a drunk by the sight I had just seen, Butchie leaped to his feet and groped in the dark for the bucket. I was halfway to the fence when Butchie, who had wasted no time regaining his perch outside the window, called after me, struggling hard to keep his voice down. "You have to see this, Peckerhead! You have to fucking to see this!"

Fr. Kavanaugh, as big and bare as Moby Dick, was on top of The French Lady grunting like a hog, his huge, bare ass bouncing up and down between her raised knees. I didn't know whether to pee in my pants or go blind.

There are details of that night outside The French Lady's bedroom window that have refused to fade with time. The first indelible memory is the way that big, white cat just sat there while all that bouncing and grunting was going on, licking its paw and rubbing its head. Just as amazing to me was the way The French Lady chewed gum the whole time as calmly as if she were reading a magazine. Those two images return calm and soundless. The third one does not; it replays itself in stereo with the volume turned all the way up. Butchie McDevitt, somehow keeping his balance on that wildly rocking bucket, bangs on the window with his fist and screams, like a person who had lost his mind, "Ride 'em cowboy!" He screams it over and over.

That did it for me. I took off into the rain, stopping at the fence just long enough to turn and see the venetian blinds fly open in Butchie's face. He froze while Fr. Kavanaugh, about to explode with anger, struggled like a man possessed to force the window open. Their faces could not have been more than a foot apart.

CHAPTER
TWENTY-THREE

Butchie and I ran through the wet night like cats chased by a bulldog. When we reached my backyard, soaked and gasping for breath, Butchie kept right on going, disappearing through the hedge toward the gas station. I leaped onto the back porch, skidded to a stop on the slippery decking, and searched for signs of my mother before pushing the door open and collapsing with my back against the kitchen wall. My heart was out of control. Rainwater streamed from my matted hair and soaked clothes. There was no way in the world Fr. Kavanaugh could have seen me. All the way home, I had repeated those words to myself, splashing through puddles in the dark and escaping death as we cut through a yard on Chestnut Street where a berserk dog shot out of the night and would have mauled us to pieces if its chain had been three feet longer. Fr. Kavanaugh had seen Butchie's stupid, grinning face right outside The French

Lady's bedroom window, there was no doubt in my mind about that, but because I was all the way over by the fence, there was no way he could have known I was there. I pulled off my shoes and emptied them into the small pond that was forming on the floor around me. He didn't see me; it would have been impossible. If there had been any doubt in my mind about that, I would still be running.

After using a handful of paper napkins to dry the floor, I stripped naked in the cellar, hid my wet things under the stairs, and snuck up to my bedroom wrapped in a towel I had found in the laundry basket. My mother's bedroom was dark, which was pure luck because my mind wasn't working well enough to make up a story about why I was walking around the house wearing nothing but a bath towel. From the side window of my bedroom, I could see the gas station. There was a light on in Mr. McDevitt's office, but while I watched, it went out. Mr. McDevitt would be out most of the night playing cards at the Moose, but Butchie was safely home. I dropped into bed, my heart pounding so hard I could feel the blood pulsing through my fingers and toes. I heard my mother get up and go into the bathroom, and after a few minutes, I heard her bedroom door close again. Staring up at the pale bedroom ceiling, I wondered if Butchie had known that people grunted like Fr. Kavanaugh when they screwed.

The last thing I remember thinking was that Mr. McDevitt wouldn't let Fr. Kavanaugh do anything to Butchie. The thought slowed my racing heart. Butchie was lucky. If it had been me that Fr. Kavanaugh had seen through The

French Lady's window, there would be no one on earth to protect me. My only choice would have been to run away, fleeing into the rainy night with the seven dollars I had in my Roy Rogers bank and some extra underwear in my school knapsack. Where would I go? Would I ever finish school? These were the scary things I worried about until I fell asleep.

I woke up twice. The first time, it was still completely dark outside my bedroom windows. I listened, not sure but thinking that I had heard something. I got up and looked toward the gas station. No lights were burning. Somewhere in the darkness I heard the sound again. I went to the rear window, the one overlooking our backyard. Blacker than the night, something that looked like a big bear hurried across our property toward the church. I dropped back into bed, smart enough to know that there were no bears in Harrisville but not smart enough, or simply too tired, to understand what I had just seen.

The second time I awoke, my bedroom was echoing with the blare of sirens and shaking with the vibrations of heavy engines. Flares of red light spilled through the side window and arced across the ceiling. Rescue equipment and police cars had besieged the gas station, their emergency radios squawking static-drenched words into the fading night. I got dressed as fast as I could. At the top of the stairs, I ran into my mother.

"You stay right here in this house, Russell Flynn! Whatever those crazy McDevitts have done now is none of your affair!"

I squeezed past her in too much of a hurry to argue. Outside, the rain had stopped. Near the gasoline pumps, two policemen were talking to Mr. McDevitt. I walked right up to them, looking for Butchie.

"I was out all night playing poker," Mr. McDevitt was telling the policemen. One of them wrote what he said in a notepad. "I saw the office door was busted in, and then I found him. Right there where he is now, on the floor behind the desk. At first I didn't see him." He spoke more quietly than I had ever heard him speak.

"Anyone see you playing poker?"

Mr. McDevitt looked hard at the policeman who asked him the question.

"Got to ask you."

Mr. McDevitt took a deep breath. "Guy named Roddy Spellman. We had a few beers at his place after we left the Moose."

Mr. McDevitt kept looking toward the gas station office while he answered questions about Roddy Spellman. He told them about being in the war with Roddy. The policemen both nodded like maybe they had been in the war too. That's when one of them noticed me.

"What are you doing here?"

"I live next door. The sirens woke me up."

"Well, get back home."

I looked up at Mr. McDevitt. "Where's Butchie?"

He stared at me blankly. To my amazement, he put out his hand and rubbed my hair. He had never actually been mean to me, but he had never before done anything like that.

I had never even seen him do anything like that to Butchie.

"Do like the man said. Get the hell out of here before that old lady of yours comes over here and has a shit fit."

"Was that your boy's name, Butchie?" one of the policemen asked Mr. McDevitt as the three of them walked toward the gas station that was already filled with other policemen and men in bright-yellow fireman coats.

The tow truck was parked against the concrete curb Mr. McDevitt made Butchie paint white every year, a job Butchie hated almost as much as cleaning the restrooms. With waves of nausea sweeping my body, I sat down on the truck's running board and closed my eyes, trying to understand what had happened. I had never known anyone who died. All I could think about was how alive Butchie had been, not just alive but beside himself with joy, banging on The French Lady's window and laughing like an idiot the whole time we ran home through the rain. It was like seeing Fr. Kavanaugh and The French Lady naked was the greatest thing that had ever happened to him. My father had died, and both of my grandparents had died, but I never knew them when they were alive, and somehow that made this very different. I had known Butchie and done things with him. I had seen him go away and listened to his crazy stories when he came back. Now he had gone away again and would never be coming back. It was impossible to understand.

Two of the men in the yellow fireman coats squeezed their way out of the gas station door and rolled a stretcher toward the waiting ambulance. The body on it was covered with a white blanket just like in the movies. There was a bump in the blanket where Butchie's head would be and another one where his feet were. When I remembered the bearlike figure I had seen hurrying through our yard in the dark, I put my head between my knees and threw up. Butchie didn't believe in heaven and hell, I knew that. He said it was all a bunch of bullshit. I didn't know what to believe anymore. It was OK with me if there wasn't any heaven if it was just some place where everybody hung around and prayed all day, but hell was different. There had to be a hell. What sense did anything make if there was no place for people like Fr. Kavanaugh to burn until they split open like a hot dog on a grill?

As the two men in the yellow coats started sliding the stretcher into the ambulance, a hand fell out from under the blanket, and something small and black dropped onto the ground. It rolled around in a perfect circle and stopped next to a weed growing through a crack in the pavement.

"Fifteen years old. Goddamned shame," one of the men said, slamming the ambulance door shut. "You see the way his neck was broken? Looks like he was attacked by a damn gorilla."

The ambulance left the gas station quietly, trailing its pulsing, red lights out into Prospect Street. I stood up and walked toward the thing that had fallen out of Butchie's hand, somehow aware that my mother was staring out of our kitchen window, blessing herself and begging her parents to forgive her for what she had done to their beloved tennis court and rose garden. I reached down and picked up a small, black button with strands of thread attached to it like the tail of a tiny, black comet.

"I thought I told you to get out of here!" The policeman who had been asking Mr. McDevitt all the questions was hurrying back toward his car. "I'm not going to tell you again!"

There was no point in giving him the button. There was no point in telling him I knew for certain whose shirt it had come from. All he would do was ask me a bunch of questions while the other policeman with the notebook wrote down what I said, and after I told them everything, I'd probably get sent to reform school for peeking in The French Lady's window. They wouldn't believe the part about Fr. Kavanaugh any more than they would have believed me if I had told them that when I was six years old, he had hit me so hard he chipped two of my teeth. I dropped the button into my pocket.

❧

On my way back home, I saw where Fr. Kavanaugh had slipped and fallen on the way up the rain-slicked path between the gas station and our backyard. Even though it was still pretty dark, I could see the mess he had made in the mud as he struggled to get back up. I could imagine him cursing to himself as he became aware of the slick, red clay on his shoes and pants and all over his hands. Beyond the hedge on the other side of our yard, the church was dark. Except for the pulsing, red sweep of the emergency lights against its massive, granite walls, the lone hint of life at St.

Lawrence's appeared at the top of the soaring steeple where a gold cross reflected the first rays of the sun.

Our house was just as dark. If my mother had come downstairs to see what was going on, she had now gone back to bed. So many crazy thoughts were bouncing around in my head that I didn't know what to do. I couldn't just go back to bed and pretend like nothing had happened. Seconds after I sat down on the back porch steps to think things out, a light came on in the church basement, a bright-yellow rectangle punched into the dying night.

CHAPTER TWENTY-FOUR

Rain-drenched forsythia bushes at the base of the church slapped at me with wet leaves as I crept close to the lighted window and peered into Mr. Shifflet's basement workshop. Fr. Kavanaugh, his wide back to me, was busy at the cluttered workbench, a scattering of unfolded newspapers catching the red mud he hurriedly scraped from a pair of his large shoes. When he finished, he folded the newspapers carefully and dropped them into the beat-up metal trashcan next to the workbench. I didn't notice the pile of black clothes at his feet until he picked them up and stuffed them into a paper grocery bag. He pushed the bag to one side of the workbench, spread more newspapers, and placed the shoes on top of them. For what seemed like an eternity, he did nothing. With both of his enormous hands on the edge of the workbench and his head down, he just stood there. I couldn't see his face, but I knew his eyes were closed. Maybe he was wishing that the whole thing had never happened, and maybe he was praying for

God to help him. Whatever he was doing, when he finally finished, he turned and looked around the room, searching for something. After rummaging through the shelves where Mr. Shifflet kept everything from spare votive candles to Christmas decorations, he scanned the room again and said, "Fuck." He clearly said *fuck*. I couldn't hear him from outside the window but I could see his lips move, and that was exactly what he said. Out of the blue, it came to me that he was looking for the shoe polish! He needed to polish his shoes so no one could figure out what he had done, but because he never shined his own shoes, he had no idea where the shoe polish was. He made me do it, the way he made me do everything else. His eyes fixed on the boiler room door. He was getting warm, but he still hadn't found it.

The shoes were all the way across the room, so it was hard to tell how well Fr. Kavanaugh had managed to clean them. Even if he had gotten every bit of mud off them, there would be plenty more on the pants and shirt he had stuffed into the grocery bag. I watched him disappear into the boiler room. The shoeshine kit was on top of the wood crate that held the plaster camels and shepherds belonging to the manger scene, but Fr. Kavanaugh didn't know that. He was going to be busy looking for a while. I dove through the wet bushes and sprinted toward the basement door at the rear of the church. All I had to do was snatch that bag from the workroom and show it to the police. As I ran, I felt for the black button in my pocket. I'd show that to them too! I'd bet all the money in the world that the same kind of button was missing from the black shirt Fr. Kavanaugh had stuffed into the bag. My hopes soared, and then, just as I reached the back steps, they died. Even with clues like that, the police wouldn't believe me. For all I knew, half the Harrisville Police Department had made their first communion at St. Lawrence's. They wouldn't believe Fr. Kavanaugh had killed Butchie any more than they would believe that he went around saying *fuck* when he was looking for shoe polish. There had to be something else I could do. Maybe I could send the bag to the archbishop with an anonymous letter telling him everything. Maybe I could send it to *The Washington Post*. No! I had it! Mr. McDevitt! I'd show the muddy priest's clothes to Mr. McDevitt! He wasn't a Catholic. He didn't give a shit about some stupid rule that said nobody was allowed to lay hands on a priest. When he found out that Fr. Kavanaugh had killed Butchie, he would kick the living shit out of him. He might even bash in his fucking head in with one of his greasy wrenches.

I almost broke my neck racing down the steep concrete stairs in the shadowy morning light, barely managing to grab the pipe handrail with both hands and spin to a stop just before I hit the bottom. Through the small rectangles of glass in the basement door I could see the boiler room door. It was halfway open, but there was no sign of Fr. Kavanaugh. I twisted the knob. The door wasn't locked, but the old hinges groaned the way they always did when I pushed it open. I held my breath and waited. No Fr. Kava-naugh, no shadows moving on the floor near the entrance to the boiler room. Five seconds was all I needed. I could almost reach the bag of clothes from where I was standing, and the shoes were right next to it on the workbench. What was I waiting for? My father would have done it; I was sure of that. Butchie would have done it in a heartbeat. Just as I took a deep breath, Fr. Kavanaugh marched out of the boiler room, carrying the shoeshine kit. All he had to do was glance in my direction, and I would be as dead as Butchie, just as dead as I would already be if Fr. Kavanaugh had any idea that I had seen his big, bare ass bouncing like a beach ball between The French Lady's knees. He dropped the kit on the workbench and began rooting through drawers, looking for something. I was close enough to see that he had shaved and that his thick, white hair was combed. The pants he was now wearing were neatly pressed as was the black, long-sleeved shirt with the Roman collar showing at his neck like a small, white square. I was so close that I could see two long scratches on the side of his face and a swollen bruise under his eye. Almost as if he knew someone was taking note of these things, he took a white handkerchief from his pants pocket, unfolded it carefully, and patted at the scratches. He studied the handkerchief then turned and went into the small bathroom next to the boiler room.

I shoved the basement door open and grabbed the bag. I grabbed the shoes and stuffed them in with the muddy clothes. Fr. Kavanaugh's ass was grass. Outside, the morning had become a little brighter. Holding the bag in one hand and grabbing for the handrail with the other, I was about to jump over a wet swirl of leaves around the drain at the bottom of the stairs when Fr. Kavanaugh's voice exploded like thunder.

"You little bastard!"

Pee squirted down my leg as I stumbled up the stairs with his big fingers clutching at the back of my shirt.

"Give me that bag, you little son of a bitch!"

Halfway to the top, I stumbled, scraping my shin against the concrete stairs. For a second, his hand was around my ankle.

"I'll break your fucking neck!"

I kicked free and made it to the top step. He was so close to me that I could hear his heavy breathing and feel his desperate fingers scrape my back. I knew if he caught me, he would break my neck the way I had heard the ambulance guys say he had broken Butchie's. I spun around and shoved him as hard as I could. He grabbed at the bag, ripping it from my hands as he staggered backwards. His eyes widened, his mouth flew open, and for one last time, I saw the scratches on his face and the swelling under his eye. His arms flailed desperately as he toppled backwards, managing a sound that wasn't a word and wasn't a scream, a strange sound that stopped altogether when he hit the bottom of the stairs like a bag of cement.

He was perfectly still, the palm of one big hand facing the early morning sky, the other lost in the tangle of wet leaves. Nothing moved. His head was turned in a way that no one could turn their head on purpose no matter how hard they tried.

If anyone ever wondered what he was doing with a grocery bag full of dirty shoes and muddy clothes, I never heard about it. Before I started home, I took the black button from my pocket, threw it down the stairs, and watched it bounce crazily into the shadows surrounding his still body. I remember thinking that I should feel something, but what I felt was nothing. I remember thinking I should run, but I didn't. What I did was walk home in the gathering light and fix a bowl of Cheerios.

PART 2

VINNIE

Chapter One

In those days, before air conditioning became commonplace, the church was already stifling as noon Mass began. Women fanned damp faces with copies of the Sunday bulletin and shushed cranky children, acutely aware that Fr. Kavanaugh was not a patient man. Men tugged at neckties and furtively checked watches. On both sides of the altar, fans large enough to propel small airplanes pushed heavy air at their discomfort. Time moved in slow motion, punctuated by bursts of Latin and the starched scurrying of me and the other altar boy, Vinnie Rinaldi, who, as usual, was so nervous in the presence of Fr. Kavanaugh that he was on the verge of throwing up. Fr. Kavanaugh, his bear-like back turned on all of us, growled along, arms extending, head nodding, the biggest fingers I had ever seen pinching colored ribbons that marked the leathered book, flipping bunched pages: the Introit, the sing-song repetition of the Kyrie, the priest's powerful entreaties, "Kyrie eleison, kyrie eleison," our memorized responses, "Kyrie eleison,

179

christe eleison," Vinnie's contributions coming in hesitant spurts, the congregation behind us sweltering, coughing, shuffling. Finally, mercifully, the gospel then, as though a time-out had been called, the thunderous collapse of hundreds of Catholics into butt-worn pews. As though it were part of the liturgy, Vinnie and I genuflected at the foot of the altar and hurried to pull the chains on the droning fans before Fr. Kavanaugh reached the pulpit.

Fr. Kavanaugh hesitated before starting the readings, carefully removing his eyeglasses and wiping them with a handkerchief produced from the hidden folds of his vestments. After checking the lenses at arm's length, his eyes swept the sea of upturned faces. He was confident that most of his parishioners stood no chance of salvation. He knew the troublemaking children they sent to his school, he knew which women never came to Sodality meetings, and he knew the men who drank too much at the Knights of Columbus Hall on Saturday nights. Night after night, sitting at our kitchen table, he declared in words punctuated by his pounding fist that he knew things about them from their disgusting confessions that a decent person could never even imagine.

His voice always surprised. Coming upon a reference to "sins of the flesh," he raised his eyes, their penetrating beam targeting specific members of the congregation. Heads spun toward the spotlighted sinners. Those in his glare were desperate to blend back into the safety of the flock but had no idea how to do it. As he always did, he delivered the damning words of the reading a second time, underlining them this time with bullhorn volume. A startled infant screamed at the top of its lungs. Fr. Kavanaugh leveled a blistering beam of disapproval at the mortified mother who immediately rose and stumbled her way to the end of the pew, genuflected as best she could without dropping the wailing child, and hurried toward the back of the church. When the sound of her fleeing footsteps evaporated behind the closing vestibule doors, Fr. Kavanaugh cleared his throat and resumed his damning tirade with renewed venom.

After turning off the fans, Vinnie and I had taken our seats on the backless altar boy stools at the right hand side of the sanctuary, the two of us separated by the ornately carved and cushioned chair the priests used at High Mass. Our stools had no cushions to soften the butt-numbing effect of the hardwood. Vinnie, whose nervous stomach kicked into gear when he was within fifty feet of Fr. Kavanaugh, had gone to the bathroom three times while we were waiting in the sacristy for Mass to begin, and it was obvious that he had to go again. His eyes were tightly shut, his legs wiggling, as he mumbled desperately to himself.

"Stop that infernal squirming over there," Fr. Kavanaugh bellowed across the sanctuary. Every eye in church turned toward us. I sat up straighter and tried my best to imitate a statue. Vinnie looked like he was going to puke.

Fr. Kavanaugh glared at us long enough to scare a faint whimper out of Vinnie and then turned his attention back to the wilting congregation. "Listen to what Saint Matthew tells us in today's gospel," he commanded. Glancing down at the missal, he read, "At that time, Jesus said to his dis-

181

ciples, 'Beware of false prophets who come to you in sheep's clothing but inwardly are ravenous wolves. By their fruits you will know them.'" Then, to my horror, he focused his narrowed eyes on me. "Tell me, Mr. Flynn, what does Saint Matthew mean by those words?"

While I hoped and prayed that I wasn't expected to actually answer, everyone in the church stared at me, waiting. Not a single person cleared their throat, not one baby cried. Mr. Duda, the one-armed usher, came halfway down the main aisle and gestured with his only hand for me to speak up.

My mind raced. *Saint Matthew. Sheep. Wolves.* We must have talked about this in school, but I had long ago stopped paying attention in religion class. The words sounded like they had something to do with phonies, people who acted like good Catholics but really weren't. That had to be it. Fr. Kavanaugh had his hands on his hips, glaring at me. He looked as big as King Kong.

"You're getting him really mad. Say something," Vinnie whispered frantically across the cushioned chair that separated us.

"Say something! Say something!" everyone in church chanted. Up in the choir loft, Mrs. Enright put music to their words, and hundreds of profusely sweating people sang out, "Say something, Russell Flynn! Say something!" Louder and louder, they chanted the words in time with the organ.

Suddenly, as always, I was no longer a thirteen-year-old altar boy dressed in a red cassock and a starched, white surplus. I was me, wearing a pinstriped Brooks Brothers suit and a maroon power tie. Vinnie Rinaldi saw me change before his eyes and threw up all over his Sunday shoes.

"Say something, Russell Flynn! Say something!" The music and words reached a crescendo.

I jumped up, knocking over my stool. "All right, goddamn it, I'll say something!" I screamed as loud as I could. "What that gospel means is that Father Thomas Xavier Kavanaugh is the biggest goddamned phony who ever wore a Roman collar!"

Babies screamed. Women wailed. Fr. Kavanaugh's face blazed red, he floated out of the pulpit, spreading his arms like wings and ballooning in size until he looked like a giant Jesus in the Macy's parade. He drifted toward me as his powerful voice turned to thunder. "How dare you speak to a man of God in that manner. You! You, Russell Flynn are a disgrace to St. Lawrence's parish! Despite the efforts of your good mother, despite my repeated warnings about the sins of the flesh, despite the good nuns who instructed you since the first day of kindergarten, you have managed to become the vilest sinner in the history of St. Lawrence's Catholic School!"

I fled the altar, the way I always did, jumping over the communion rail and sprinting down the center aisle. Mrs. Enright's organ shook the church to the tune of a new chant: "Sinner! Sinner!" Sr. Superior forced her way toward the aisle screaming at the top of her lungs. "Catch him! Catch him! Bring him to my office!" Mr. Duda reached for me with the only arm he had.

———✸———

A blank ceiling, the sound of running water, my heart racing, pulsing like a drum inside my ears, I pushed onto my elbows and looked toward the sound of the water. It occurred to me for the hundredth time that I should get my money back from that lousy psychiatrist. What a worthless little twerp he had proved to be. Steamy mist drifted through the partially open bathroom door. Some of my clothes, my tie and suit jacket and a badly wrinkled white shirt with lipstick stains I could see all the way from the bed, were draped over the leather chair on the far side of the room. Shoes, socks, pants, and underwear were scattered on the floor between the chair and the bed. I looked again toward the bathroom. The sound of the shower had stopped. I sat all the way up and saw myself in the mirror on the far wall, an unappealing montage of graying hair in wild disarray and the face that looked less and less like the one that had once been me. I cursed at what I saw and turned away.

A black cocktail dress hung on the corner of the mirror. Other things, black also and neatly folded, waited on the dresser. I didn't remember her taking the time to do any folding last night, but that didn't surprise me. I tended to have tunnel vision whenever a good-looking woman was stepping out of her clothes.

The bathroom door opened all the way, and out of the mist she came. Marsha. Her name came to me as soon as I saw her. Unfortunately, other things came back to me at the same time, most notably the fact that she was the wife of my biggest client, a general contractor from Maine known as much for his volcanic temper as for his vast real estate holdings. A familiar question scattered all remnants of sleep and the dream that too often accompanied it. What the hell had I been thinking? Of all the women at that party, of all the women I knew, what in the hell had I been thinking?

She had brought a towel with her from the bathroom, but it wasn't covering a damn thing. She was drying her hair with it. The shower had left her skin pink and steaming. Her breasts, big but not enormous, just about right, with nipples the color of plums, jiggled as she rubbed her hair, tilting her head one way and then another as she did. She shook out the towel, fixing her eyes on me.

"Come on, Lover Boy, get your ass out of that bed. Do you have any idea what time it is?"

She turned as she spoke and went over to the dresser. Her body was firm and fine. Maybe I wasn't so stupid after all. She took her underpants from the neat pile on the dresser, shook them out, and stepped into them, wiggling her perfect, pink butt as she pulled them up. When she turned around, she was hooking her bra with the straps in front of her, the way they all do. She twisted it around her body and slipped her breasts into the cups with a snap of finality.

"Let's go. Put your eyes back in your head and get dressed. You have a flight to catch, remember?"

I lay back down and patted the bed beside me. She picked up the damp towel and threw it, hitting me square in the face. "You must be kidding."

What the hell. It was always worth a try.

185

CHAPTER TWO

I had witnessed people driving like her, but until she roared out of the hotel garage and onto the busy streets of Boston, I had never known how terrifying it was to be in the same car with them. She drove with a get-out-of-my-way mentality, both hands clamped to the steering wheel, quick glances over her shoulder, quicker lane changes. She smiled when she saw my foot working the invisible brake pedal on my side of the car. I did my best to smile back. Weaving through a sea of brake lights, we somehow made it out of the North End and through the tunnel alive. As we neared Logan Airport, traffic became a horn-blowing mess, a detail that did not faze her. If anything, she became more competitive, swearing quietly at any driver who dared get in her way. "Come on slow balls," she muttered, "move your ass!" *Slow balls.* I had never heard anyone use that expression before last night.

Marsha. Marsha. I repeated her name to myself, preparing for the big goodbye, knowing that the worst mistake a man could make was mixing up their names. I once whispered the name Cathy, or maybe it was Barbara, into the ear of a Donna. I don't recommend it. Other than that one incident, which could not have happened at a worse moment, my track record for keeping them straight was right up there. I had a better-than-average knack for remembering names. Not that I could remember them all; that would have taken a memory freak.

She zeroed in on a slow-moving airport cab, swooping right up behind it, once more forming the words *slow balls* with her lips. She rode its back bumper, flicking her eyes up to the mirror every second or so. "Idiots like this guy drive me crazy," she snarled. I didn't know what she wanted from the guy; there was a solid wall of traffic in front of him. I didn't get far in my attempt to point that out before being stopped short by a pair of narrowed green eyes. She was a knockout, a fact that was just as obvious in the morning rush hour as it had been last night at the Christmas party, every bit as beautiful but in a different way. Her hair this morning was free and loose; her makeup had a lighter touch. Last night, she looked like a movie star: sparkling earrings, hair held high with a tiara fit for a queen. Athletic, that was it. My guess was tennis. Not golf. Definitely not golf. The game would be much too slow for her, not to mention that she might kill somebody driving a golf cart.

The traffic in front of us came to one of those inexplicable screeching stops, brake lights flashing, tires squealing, vehicles swerving on to both shoulders. She swore in words that sounded like an Italian curse and then asked me what time my flight was. I glanced at the clock in the middle of the dashboard and told her we had plenty of time, exactly the same thing I would have told her if we had been running late. Her fingers drummed impatiently on the steering wheel.

Daisy Mae. That's who she reminded me of! Daisy Mae, the incredibly sexy heartthrob of *Li'l Abner*, one of the comic strips I read religiously when I was a kid. Daisy Mae, the first major fantasy of my life, wholesome, big boobed, and sexy as they come. I narrowed my eyes, trying to picture Marsha in that skimpy, polka-dotted top and the tight, tattered shorts that Daisy Mae always ran through the Sunday comics in. In a perfect world, the two of us would still be back at the Omni instead of being stuck in traffic on Harborside Drive.

That was exactly the kind of thing I had no intention of ever telling Dr. Kite. There was no reason for him to think of me as some kind of a nut. A guy having a little problem with bad dreams, I could go that far with him, but I wasn't a wacko with real issues. On the way to my first session with him, I reminded myself not to let it slip that I still couldn't think about any of those old comic strips—not The Phantom or *Alley Oop* or *Li'l Abner*— without a bunch of other shit about those Sunday mornings flooding into my head. There wasn't any point in getting into that comic strip business with Dr. Kite. For one thing, it wouldn't have done a damn bit of good. How old was he? I was fifty-one. That would make that little twerp about what, forty, early forties? Even if I did tell him about the comic strips, it wouldn't mean a damn thing to him. By the time he was a kid, they didn't read the comics anymore. They didn't do anything but watch cartoons on television.

"Is your mother's funeral tomorrow?" Marsha asked, glancing over her shoulder to see if there was any chance of picking up a car length or two.

"The funeral was a month ago." I didn't know if she noticed that it had taken me a minute to understand her question.

She took her eyes from the stalled traffic. "A month ago? I thought that was why you were going back."

Maybe I had told her that last night. I couldn't remember. What I did remember was that it had been another one of those nights when I realized I wasn't as young as I used to be. Not by a long shot. I had disguised my lack of staying power pretty smoothly, I thought, by giving her a half-assed excuse about needing to get some sleep because I had to make a flight in the morning. If I said anything about a funeral, I hadn't meant to.

"I have to go back home to take care of a few things." When that didn't sound like enough of a reason for leaving town right before Christmas, I sketched a picture of the big old house my grandfather had built. "It's old and it's big and it's filled from the cellar to the attic with two generations' worth of junk. I've got to go back and get it ready to put on the market."

"No brothers and sisters?"

"Just me."

She nodded, no doubt giving me points for being such a dutiful son. There was no reason to spoil the effect by confessing that I had skipped my mother's funeral without the least twinge of remorse.

Just as inexplicably as they had slowed to the pace of a herd of grazing cows, the cars in front of us began moving again. With squealing tires, Marsha made a lane change that triggered car horn pandemonium. "In any case, I'm sorry about your mother," she told me calmly. "I remember how sad it was when my own mother died." It was beyond my understanding how a person could make a driving move like that and speak at the same time.

"She was old." That was the only thing I could think to say about my mother, the only thing that wouldn't have sounded mean and bitter. I had tried half-heartedly to sound like a grieving son the day the woman from the hospice called me at the office and informed me that my mother had passed away "peacefully" during the night. If that was true, it was a miracle. My mother's mind never experienced anything close to peace after the morning she heard shouting in the church parking lot and peered through the kitchen window to see what was going on. Beyond the hedge, Mr. Shifflet, the parish janitor, was screaming hysterically.

"His neck's broke like a damn chicken! Just like a damn chicken!"

I'm not sure what her reaction would have been if it had been my body that Mr. Shifflet had tripped over at the bottom of the stairs behind the church that morning, but when she realized that he was screaming about Fr. Kavanaugh, her troubled mind disintegrated, leaving her in a state of insanity that extinguished what little interest in life she still had. The once-silent prayers she said while ironing or doing the dishes became clearly audible, revealing that for all the years of my youth she had not been praying to God, or to the Blessed Mother, or to some trusted patron saint but to her dead mother and father, begging them for forgiveness for the sins she had committed, sins, she acknowledged repeatedly, that were not worthy of forgiveness. She shuffled around the house, dusting, or sweeping, or changing pillowcases, declaring her wickedness. Every evening, still in her housecoat and slippers and unaware that her hair had been in rollers for days, she prepared the pot roast and meat loaf dinners that Fr. Kavanaugh had demanded of her. She sat and waited for sounds of footsteps on the back porch that only she could hear, and when she heard them, she rose from the table, opened the kitchen door, and smiled. I watched her do these things until I was old enough to move out, just as I watched her wash and iron the clothes that bastard had left at our house until there was nothing left of them but threads.

⸙

"This will be fine, behind the van," I told her. "The United entrance is just beyond that sign."

"I can get you closer than this."

And she did, accelerating into the striped crosswalk gap directly in front of the busy terminal doors with a move few stunt drivers would have attempted.

I grabbed my suitcase and carry-on bag from the trunk, rehearsing in my mind exactly what I was going to say. Fear of being killed with her at the wheel was reason enough to break off this little relationship before it went any further, but the fact that she was the wife of my most valuable client was a much bigger reason. Last night had been nice, there was no doubt about that, a prime woman on the loose and me with no more of a game plan for the evening than to shake hands with clients and wish them a Merry Christmas. Out of nowhere, I had felt a hand on my arm, and there she was, all by herself and looking like a million dollars. She waved away what must have been a quizzical expression on my face. "Oh, him," she had said, picking a glass of champagne from a passing tray. "Can you believe it? There was a message waiting at the desk when we checked in. One of his construction projects burned to the ground."

She looked around the room and took my arm. "He never even unpacked." She said it like she still couldn't believe it. "I told him he was going back without me. I'll be damned if I was going to rush back to the sticks. What is there to do in Portland this time of year?" She smiled and squeezed my arm. "You've been up there. You know what I'm talking about." She downed the champagne and announced that she was ready for a real drink. As we crossed the floor, she brushed against me. Not enough for anyone else to notice but enough. She knew what she was doing, and I knew what she was doing. Sometimes it just falls into a guy's lap.

I hesitated before lowering the trunk lid, wondering if I could get away with seeing her one more time, two at the most. A woman like her could always think up an excuse for coming down to Boston. The debate between the big head and the little head lasted only a few seconds. Having an affair with a woman whose husband represented more billable hours to the firm than any other two clients combined would be insane, no matter what she looked like coming out of the shower. Like the endless line of taxis arriving at the terminal this morning, another good-looking woman would be along shortly. Maybe not quite as fine, maybe without her unique spunky personality, but what the hell, they were only cab rides. I could catch one on any corner and get out whenever I wanted. The trunk lid rocked the car when I slammed it shut. There was nothing left to do but get it over with. She would understand. All I had to do was say it the right way. I had done it many times before. I just hoped she wouldn't make a scene in front of all these people.

She was waiting for me with the window rolled down. "Give me a goodbye kiss," she said.

I leaned over and saw miniature images of my face in her sunglasses. We kissed. A car horn blared behind us. I took a deep breath and began my speech. She interrupted.

"Last night was fun, but it's over. Mum's the word." She half-whispered the words, pressing a finger to her lips "Got to get home to Papa." She flashed a final smile. "I'll leave your car at the Omni."

She glanced quickly past me before whipping into a nonexistent gap between two taxis. Before I totally understood what had happened, a Toyota with suitcases strapped to its roof filled the space between me and the curb. Where her beautiful face had just been, a fat woman holding the remains of a doughnut looked up at me quizzically.

CHAPTER THREE

"Do you consider your conduct with women reckless?"

We had been nearing the end of another carefully timed therapy session. I could tell by the way Dr. Kite's eyes had started glancing at the strategically placed digital clock on the small table to my right.

I never liked him; that was probably the reason we weren't getting anywhere. He was a twerp, I can't think of any better way to describe him, sitting in his black leather swivel chair, his legs crossed in that tight way I don't like to see men cross their legs, one knee sitting on top of the other knee, balls mushing together, tasseled loafer wagging, Montblanc pen poised to record my answer.

It was the third time I had seen him, and this was the first question he had ever asked me. "Do you consider your conduct with women reckless?"

"Well, I don't know..."

Dr. Kite held up his hand. One of the rules he had laid out in the first session was that I was not allowed to say "I don't know" when he asked a question. Since this was his first question, I wasn't in practice yet.

He waited, pursing his lips around the pen, wagging that foot, mushing his balls.

"I never thought of it that way." That was the best thing I could think of saying, and besides, it was the truth. Fun, yes. Reckless, no.

"Mr. Flynn, you have an affair with the wife of a professional football player, and you don't consider that reckless? You spend the night with the fiancé of one of your law partners, and you don't consider that reckless?" That was three questions now in one minute, or was it just the same question asked three different ways? His eyes darted again toward the clock. We never went a minute longer than forty-five minutes. He slowly closed the notebook that somehow remained balanced on his skinny top knee and carefully placed the expensive pen in the breast pocket of his suit, a black pinstriped suit just like the one I sometimes wore in the dreams. I had never described that suit in detail. He didn't have to know everything. All he had to know was enough for him to tell me why I couldn't get laid anymore without having that stupid dream.

That's why I started telling him about the various women. At first, I told him about just one of them, I can't remember which one, thinking that would be enough for him to get the idea. I didn't get into detail, using polite terms like "sleeping with her" instead of "screwing" or whatever. I wasn't paying all that money to entertain him. I just wanted to get to the point where he would look up from his notes, nod his head knowingly, and say, "OK Mr. Flynn, here's what you have to do. Take three of the small white pills and one of the large orange pills that I'm going to prescribe two hours before you anticipate having sexual intercourse" or perhaps for him to say, "Oh yes, Mr. Flynn, you are suffering from Screwdream Syndrome, a condition very common in men your age. All you have to do is avoid copulation with women who have freckles." Or whatever. As I understand it, that's what psychiatrists do. They listen, they ask questions, they point something out that the patient has never realized, or they prescribe a little of this medication or a little of that medication and, bang, problem gone. Or at least things get a lot better than they were. I could live with just having the dreams every once in a while the way I used to.

Actually it wasn't dreams plural; it was just one dream, one basic dream with different people popping in and out of it. Sometimes The French Lady was in it, waiting to go to confession over at the side of the church, the left side as I looked out from the altar. That would be the epistle side. Sometimes my mother was waiting outside the confessional on the opposite side of the church, the gospel side. Sometimes they were both in the same dream, staring across the expanse of pews at each other. My mother hated The French Lady, but I can't remember if The French Lady even knew who my mother was. In any case, none of that made any sense, because confessions were always on Saturday afternoons, and the dreams were always about Sunday Mass, noon Mass specifically, the crowded one that Fr. Kavanaugh never let any of the other priests say. Sometimes even Butchie McDevitt was in the dream, hanging around the baptismal font all the way in the back of the church, smoking a cigarette. That part made even less sense. For one thing, in the whole time I was a Catholic, I never saw anybody smoke a cigarette in church. For another thing, if they had ever tried it at Saint Lawrence's, Fr. Kavanaugh would have stopped right in the middle of Mass and personally dragged the person smoking the cigarette out of the church, and thrown him or her down the front steps into Prospect Street. The other reason that particular detail didn't make any sense was because, as best I could remember, Butchie never set foot inside of Saint Lawrence's. Visiting a church, any church, would have been at the bottom of his to-do list.

I had come up with a strategy. I'd tell Dr. Kite as much about the dream as I thought he had to know, and because it was obvious that there was a relationship between the dream and having sex with them, I'd specifically mention one, maybe two, of the women. As far as I could see, there was no reason to tell him anything about The French Lady or about Butchie, and I sure as hell wasn't going to get into any of the business about my mother and Fr. Kavanaugh. My tendency to end up in bed with any good-looking woman who showed the least bit of interest in screwing would give him plenty to work with. If it wasn't, he sure as hell wasn't as good as he was supposed to be.

A woman I had hooked up with a couple of months ago, Carolyn, the receptionist at my dentist's office, was the one who had told me about Dr. Kite. I liked Carolyn; she wasn't one of the ones you had to pretend you were falling in love with. With her, it was the good old wham-bam, do it, and scram. She usually clicked on the television set or flipped open a magazine while I was still fishing around for my underwear. Great attitude. Neat as a pin little apartment right off of Commonwealth Avenue; I can't remember the address, but I wouldn't have any problem finding it again. The way she came to tell me about Dr. Kite was a little weird. I was getting dressed, she was sitting at this old-fashioned dressing table she had, smoking a cigarette and doing something with her hair, and she asked me, as casually as you can possibly imagine, if I wanted to go to Mass with her the next day. It must have been a Saturday night.

I didn't know if I hadn't heard her right or if she was joking or what. In fact, that's exactly what I said to her.

She said it again. How about coming over about eleven-thirty and we can go to noon Mass together. Noon Mass. Noon Mass, of all the Masses she could have suggested.

I think I was sitting on the edge of her bed, putting on my socks. "Are you kidding?" I asked her.

"No," she said, looking at me in the mirror without turning around. "I like to go to Mass. I go every Sunday."

This was a woman who had just been balling me like we were competing in a screwing contest. I pointed that little fact out to her.

"So?" she said.

"So?" I was too dumbfounded to articulate how contradictory her attitude was.

She stopped fooling with her hair and picked up the cigarette that had been idling in an ashtray. "Do you think because I like a little sex now and then I'm not good enough to go to Mass? Is that your problem?"

Of course, I told her no, that wasn't it at all. It wasn't her, it was me. I hated churches. Priests were a bunch of phonies. I guess I went off on the subject. I said something about sex giving me nightmares about my old pastor. It slipped out.

"Honey, you need a shrink," she said, exhaling.

"A what? A psychiatrist?" I tried to laugh. "Don't be ridiculous."

But here I was, face to face with one, gripping both arms of his overstuffed patients' chair to keep from sinking any farther into the ridiculously thick cushions. This man expertly eyeing me and the clock at the same time, wagging his tasseled loafer noticeably faster as the end of the session approached, was the same psychiatrist who had helped one of Carolyn's girlfriends deal with her fear of small dogs. Didn't stop her from being afraid of them, Carolyn had made that very clear, but had gotten her girlfriend to the point, in less than a year, where she could walk past a Chihuahua or a Pekingese on the sidewalk without wetting her pants.

"That will do it for today, Mr. Flynn. I'll see you again," he swiveled in his chair and flipped open the appointment book on his desk, using a ribbon bookmarker like the ones in a Sunday missal, "Thursday."

I struggled up out of the chair and headed for the door on the far side of the room, the door that opened directly into the elevator lobby, not the one that led back to the reception area. Apparently, the well-planned psychiatrist's office was arranged to eliminate the possibility of patients coming face to face with each other. In that way, men who wanted to get laid without being haunted by visions of their old pastor would not have to make eye contact with women who peed in their pants when small dogs yapped at their heels.

CHAPTER FOUR

The waiting area for my flight was a zoo. Outstretched legs blocked the narrow aisles. Kids sat on the floor and on their parents' laps. Over near the glass wall of the terminal, people stood staring out at the parked airplanes. I spotted a seat not far from where I was standing. It was next to where a jockey-size man was sitting, and there was nothing on it but a suitcase. As I stepped over big feet and small children to get to it, the jockey-size man watched me with a worried look. When I got close to him, I saw that he was wearing the same kind of shoes that Dr. Kite wore. Twerp shoes. I never had anything against tasseled loafers or the people who wore them until I started going to see that little fruit. In fact, I had a pair of them myself. Perfectly good Florsheims that I chucked down the trash chute in my apartment building shortly after my sessions began.

"Are you saving this seat for someone?"

The short guy didn't even look at me, even when I asked the question again, so I lifted the suitcase onto the floor and flopped down. He still didn't look at me. Maybe it wasn't his suitcase. Maybe he was deaf. Maybe he was from Peru. If somebody came back to the seat, I'd get up. In the meantime, I unzipped my carry-on bag and scrounged around for my ticket to see where I was sitting. Row 29, Seat B. I memorized that snippet of information and stuffed the ticket back into the bag. The little man with the Dr. Kite shoes burped without excusing himself. While hoping that I wouldn't be sitting next to him on the plane, it dawned on me that something didn't seem right about what I had just read. I took the ticket back out and read it again. Row 29, Seat B. Unless we were flying on an airplane with a hell of a big first-class section, my seat was in coach. I cursed, maybe to myself, maybe not, and struggled back to my feet.

The woman at the United counter tapped a message on her keyboard, tilted her head, stared at her monitor, shook her head, tapped in another message, and stared at the monitor again. "Sorry, Mr. Flynn, I can't upgrade you. Your flight is full."

I tried not to curse out loud, but I was getting more pissed off by the second. An hour and a half of being crammed into a coach seat, all six foot three and 220 pounds of me, quite possibly stuck next to a burping Peruvian. I wanted to strangle the new girl in my front office. Karen? Karen or Kristin, I couldn't remember which it was. I had told her first class, always book me first class, no matter how short the flight. How the hell hard is that to remember? Big tits. No brains. The skinny ones weren't as much fun to interview, but they were always smarter.

Someone in line behind me cleared a throat, trying to hurry me. I lowered my voice and spoke conspiratorially to the woman at the computer. "Look, I fly a ton of miles on United every year. You and I both know there is always some way to upgrade a ticket."

She took a deep breath. "The flight to Baltimore is completely full. There is nothing I can do except inform you in the event that we have a last-minute cancellation."

I narrowed my eyes and looked at her hard. When nothing happened, I told her my name was Russell Flynn, spelling out my last name for her and informing her pointedly that I would be waiting to hear from her. "Right over there." I cocked my thumb over my shoulder in the general direction of the seat I had left. She flicked a smile and asked the throat clearer behind me if she could help him.

After removing the burping man's suitcase from the seat again, I flopped back down with the intention of evaluating my law firm's method of hiring secretaries. I had gotten as far as admitting to myself that I should stay out of the process all together when I noticed that a little boy in the seat across the way was staring at me. His father was reading the sports page, and his mother had her eyes closed. She was young and very pretty in the face, a little on the plump side but good looking in that let's-go-for-a-hike-today kind of way. The entire family looked wholesome, like those families you see in vitamin pill commercials. I winked at the boy. He looked startled at first, but then he smiled and tried to wink back, contorting his entire face, tilting his head and trying again but getting no closer to a wink than closing both eyes at one time. His mother opened her eyes and looked at him. I checked my lousy ticket again then slipped it into the breast pocket of my jacket.

I never went anywhere with my mother when I was little, not that I can remember anyway. Things were different then, of course. The little boy across from me was four or five years old, not that I spent enough time around kids to know for sure. People didn't fly around with their kids back when I was four or five years old. Maybe people who lived in Hollywood or New York City did but not people who lived in Harrisville, Maryland. Every once in a while, word would get around that someone had taken a train to visit relatives in Connecticut or North Carolina or had ridden a Greyhound bus to Atlantic City, but my mother and I never did anything like that. She took me to the grocery store or to the stores up on Baltimore Avenue when I was too little to stay home by myself, but that was about it. Not that my bizarre childhood was typical of anything.

The young mother smiled at her son and asked him what he was doing. He looked up at her with his wink-contorted face, and she laughed. "You better stop doing that, or you'll look like that all the time when you grow up."

She laughed, and he laughed. During one of the sessions with Dr. Kite, he asked me if my mother ever laughed. Right out of the blue, as though that had anything to do with anything. As much as I already disliked him at that point, I reminded myself that the guy was supposed to be good and gave him the benefit of the doubt. Did my mother ever laugh? I thought about it while his eyes darted from me to the digital clock, like he was keeping track of how long it would take me to come up with the answer. I already knew the answer, because I thought about it once when I was watching a television show about one of those perfect families with two nerdy kids and a father who was always wearing a sweater and a tie. They were sitting at the kitchen table, and one of their sons said something dumb that they thought was funny, and they all started laughing, not laughing at him because they thought he was stupid, just laughing like they were all happy as hell, and finally the boy who had said the dumb thing started laughing too. I never sat at a kitchen table where people did anything like that. If I said something dumb, the least I would get was a dirty look from Fr. Kavanaugh, and more than likely I would get a swift swat upside my head with the back of his enormous hand. If anyone ever tried to make a television show about the things Fr. Kavanaugh said and did at our kitchen table, the Vatican would do whatever it took to keep it off the air. "No," I told Dr. Kite, "my mother never laughed." I couldn't even picture her smiling.

The little boy across from me was still trying hard to wink, looking like a pint-size version of Igor in *Young Frankenstein*. His mother pushed him playfully. "Joey, stop that! You look awful."

He laughed and laughed.

Remember this moment, Joey, I thought to myself. *Freeze it and treasure it and never forget it. You just experienced more love and kindness from your mother in one minute than I did in my entire childhood.*

Chapter Five

I ran my eyes across the lighted notations on the departures board, hoping I had misread the message. United Flight 935 to Baltimore, Gate C-14. *Delayed.* No reason given, no new departure time noted, no *sorry, folks, we screwed up again* message, nothing but indifferent block letters smirking at me. I looked back at the glass entrance doors, at the cars and taxis coming and going beyond them, but she was long gone.

There was no one to be mad at but myself. I didn't give a damn about my flight being delayed; in this case, it was like finding out that a root canal had been postponed. I was in no big hurry to get back to Harrisville. In fact, the more I thought about it, the more I wondered why the hell I was going at all. The thing that made me mad was that I had been so distracted by that woman's prize body this morning, so distracted by the take charge, get-your-butt-out-of-bed way she had about her, that it had completely slipped my mind to call the airline and verify that my flight was on time.

It's something I always do, or have one of the secretaries at my office do. If I had done that one simple thing, I would have discovered that I had plenty of time to work a little bit of the old charm and sweet-talk that lovely creature back into bed. She had been something. Not many of them had that tough-cookie personality, but I liked it when they did. I liked women who didn't let some man dictate the way every damn thing in their life was going to be, and it didn't take a psychiatrist to figure why I felt that way. In her entire life, my mother never once asserted herself. My mind had just begun to drift down that well-worn trail when I was poked sharply in the back. An agitated woman with frizzy hair barked that if I had seen what I needed to see, maybe I could get my ass out of the way so she could check on her own flight. I was too impressed to be annoyed. Never in a thousand years would my mother have asserted herself like that.

The line in the coffee shop was a little long, but since my flight wasn't boarding anytime soon, I decided a hot cup of joe would be worth the wait. I didn't notice the priest at the end of the line until my nose was almost touching the starched, white rim of the Roman collar against the back of his skinny neck. I took a deep breath, fighting an overwhelming impulse to forget about the coffee and leave. Closing my eyes didn't help; all it did was bring to life an unnerving image of Fr. Kavanaugh's massive back and shoulders. I did my best to slam the door on the flood of memories screaming for recognition and held my ground, reminding myself that I had adjusted my attitude on the subject of priests a long time ago by coming to the realization that if they were all like Fr. Kavanaugh, the Catholic religion would have been reduced decades ago to scattered congregations of religious nuts who got a kick out of being screamed at every Sunday about their sinful ways. The ordeal came to a merciful end when one of the women behind the counter handed the priest with the skinny neck his coffee. He nodded thanks, blew across the top of the steaming cup, and disappeared into the waiting area.

I sat down harder than I meant to, spilling hot coffee onto my hand and uttering a surprisingly descriptive curse. A dark lady with a bright-green scarf covering her hair looked up from her Danish and smiled, revealing the limitations of her English vocabulary. The coffee I had managed to save was surprisingly good. I drank deeply and tried hard to redirect my thoughts. These next couple of days were going to be tough. Everything about going back to Harrisville was going to be tough. In order to do what I had to do, I would have to go inside the house. There was no getting around that point. On the positive side, there would be no reason to go inside the church next door, no reason that I could think of to even set foot on St. Lawrence's property. Being back in the house again couldn't possibly be any worse than the dreams that had been driving me crazy if for no other reason than that the bastard in the middle of those weird experiences was no longer ruling the world from a chair in my mother's kitchen.

There was no partition between the area where I was sitting and the wide, mall-like concourse, just a row of rectangular planters growing plastic plants. People streamed past in bunches and in ones and twos, wheeling suitcases, travel cases slung over their shoulders, and shopping bags in their hands from which brightly wrapped packages occasionally peeked. It was always awkward when people I knew reminisced about the wonderful Christmases of their childhoods. To me, the Christmas season meant a party at the Omni, gift wrapped bottles of Johnny Walker Black and Wild Turkey for our clients, and expensive perfume or a piece of jewelry if a relationship happened to overlap the holidays. Hurried footsteps beyond the planters created a steady rhythm against which amplified announcements continually intruded. Now and then, individuals broke out of line to stare up at the flight information boards. An old woman about my mother's age—the age my mother would have been—came into view, stabbing at the floor with a cane, walking much slower than everyone else. People passed her on both sides the way they would pass a slow car on the freeway. There was a man with her, her son maybe, trying hard to walk as slowly as she was walking. Occasionally he bent over and said something to her. As they disappeared from view, she laughed and took his arm.

I felt no guilt about missing my mother's funeral. Without a second's hesitation, I had told the woman who called from the hospice that it would be impossible for me to make it. When she said nothing, I piled details onto the lie: there was a weeklong conference for tax attorneys coming up that I was scheduled to moderate. It was to be in Chicago.

A hundred and twenty people had already made reservations. There was no possible way the conference could be postponed. Not a single word I hurried into the silent phone had been true. After a long pause, the woman had said, "I see." I explained that the funeral arrangements had been made and paid for many years ago and the details were on file at Dillon's Funeral Home in Harrisville. That much had not been a lie. I told the doubtful woman that I had Dillon's phone number somewhere and that I would call them as soon as I got off the phone.

I had done that much. I had found the phone number and made the call that set my mother's funeral arrangements in motion. A somber-sounding man at the funeral home had put me on hold for an eternity while he went to look for the file I told him would be labeled *Rose Marie Flynn*. When he finally came back, he read the details of the arrangements, as much to himself as to me, then started droning through a bunch of questions that must have been typed out on a checklist. What were the favorite flowers of the deceased? She had always had pots of geraniums on the kitchen windowsill, but since I had never seen geraniums at a funeral, I told him to use his own judgment. Was St. Lawrence's still her parish, he inquired? Yes. Should he call the pastor or would I? Please do it, if you don't mind, I told him. Each of my answers was followed by a silence during which, I assumed, he made notes. I told him there was no need for a wake; I doubted if any of her friends were still alive, not that she ever had any. No, regretfully, I would not be there. I reiterated every detail of the nonexistent conference in Chicago that I could remember. He didn't seem impressed. I didn't give a shit.

I yawned and looked at my watch. The way things were going, I wouldn't get into Baltimore until late afternoon. So far I had avoided thinking much about the next couple of days. In fact, the extent of my game plan consisted of driving to the house in a rental car, doing what had to be done, and flying back to Boston tomorrow. No doubt everyone else in this waiting room had much more exciting plans for Christmas Eve and Christmas Day, days that, because of the experiences of my weird youth, meant little more to me than that my office would be closed for a few days. If I was lucky, I'd be back in Boston in time to catch the last of the holiday parties and maybe even find that Santa had left a good-looking woman under the mistletoe, all decked out for the holidays and full of cheer. The wonderful image of women and mistletoe and Tom and Jerrys in front of a warm fire reminded me that Christmas had its good points after all.

The dark-skinned lady with the bright-green scarf around her head stood up and brushed Danish crumbs from the silky material that wrapped her body. She actually made a little bow in my direction before she left. Across the room, the priest who had been in the coffee line was looking at me. When our eyes met, he seemed startled and quickly turned his attention to the book on his lap. A half minute passed before he raised his eyes without raising his head and was startled all over again when he realized my attention was still fixed on him. His eyes dropped to the book again, but

I continued to watch him. He had a big nose, very big, and was wearing wire-rimmed glasses. If he thought he knew me, he had the wrong person. I hadn't spoken to a priest since I moved to New England right after I finished law school, and that was a lifetime ago.

With his head lowered, he looked like he was following the words in the book with his long nose. The thought made me laugh. He had one of the biggest noses I had ever seen. A *Rinaldi* nose. That's what we called them at St. Lawrence's when I was a kid. Everyone in the Rinaldi family had noses like that. In fact, one of the youngest Rinaldi kids had a nose so big for his little face that he looked like a puppet. I wondered if that poor kid still remembered being called Pinocchio on the playground when there were no nuns around to hear. His only hope was that his nose had stayed the same size while the rest of his body grew, because if his nose had grown as fast as everything else, he would look like an anteater by now. I stood up, stretched, and couldn't help laughing. An anteater. What a cruel thought.

I glanced out into the concourse. A man and woman looked up at the flight information board, shook their heads, and continued down the long concourse. A small boy chased them, reaching for his mother's hand.

Chapter Six

My eyes swept the waiting area, which was now more crowded than ever. People were standing in the jammed aisles, some were speaking with seated companions, and others stared blankly toward the boarding doors, no doubt wondering like me when this show was going to get on the road. The priest from the coffee shop had found a seat next to the little boy's father right across the aisle. He was looking at me again. We made eye contact for a second. He seemed embarrassed all over again and looked down at the opened book on his lap. Most people would have called it a prayer book, but I knew exactly what it was. It was his breviary, his "office," the book from which priests were required to read certain prayers every day of the week. Unwanted Catholic trivia like that floated through my brain like flotsam from a sunken ship, a totally unwelcome state of affairs attributable to my unconventional upbringing. *Unconventional.* That was a charitable term for what my childhood had been. Even if I lived as long as Methuselah, there wouldn't be enough time to forget half the religious crap I had been force-fed like a foie gras goose.

"Mr. Flynn?" The woman from the United Airlines counter interrupted a reflection that had gone far enough. "I'm afraid there have been no last-minute cancellations. There is nothing we can do to upgrade your ticket to Baltimore."

"Great." My one-word reply had a nasty edge to it that was intended for a certain full-bodied secretary in my office. Unfortunately, the woman from United didn't know that. Her expression revealed a monumental struggle for self-control before she turned and walked away.

The priest was instantly on his feet, standing in front of me. "Flynn! I thought so! Russell Flynn from Harrisville, Maryland!"

One second, I was thinking about how much pleasure it was going to give me to fire a secretary when I got back to my office, and the next second, I was staring blankly at a big-nosed priest who knew my name. My mind had shifted gears so fast that the only word I could get my mouth to say was "yes." The priest's hand shot out. Before my mind reengaged, I took it.

"You know, I've been sitting right over there trying to decide if it was you. It's been a million years, but I thought it was." He continued shaking my hand and stammering, "What a small world!"

The expression on my face must have made it clear that I didn't have a clue who he was?

"Father Rinaldi," he said, pointing a finger at himself. "Vincent Rinaldi, from St. Lawrence's! You remember me.

We were altar boys together."

My mind raced; worlds collided. I squinted my eyes, concentrating on his face. Vinnie Rinaldi; it couldn't possibly be. He belonged in a different world, not the world I was living in now. His hair was almost entirely gray, but it was still thick and curly, and he still had the same shit-eating grin plastered across his face. Memories that I didn't need came reeling out of the past. Mr. Rinaldi, his father, had worked out a sweet deal with Fr. Kavanaugh, forcing every kid at St. Lawrence's to wear a brand of shoes that were sold only at Rinaldi's Shoe-A-Rama up on Baltimore Avenue. I never figured that out as a kid, but I knew it now, just as surely as I knew that shenanigans of that nature wouldn't even register on the radar screen of Fr. Kavanaugh's sins.

"How many years has it been?" he asked, shaking his head in obvious wonder. "Twenty-five, thirty? Wait a minute, I know." He puzzled the numbers in his head, noting out loud that we had graduated from the eighth grade in 1955 before coming up with the answer. "Thirty-seven years since we've seen each other. Heavens above!" He had overlooked the fact that my career at St. Lawrence's Catholic School had ended abruptly during the summer after the seventh grade, but he had gotten the years right.

We stared at each other. Vinnie repeating several more times what a small world it was while I struggled to understand how the worst altar boy in the history of the Catholic Church had ever managed to become a priest.

"No doubt you're going back home for a Christmas visit.

God bless us." He shook his head, flashing the idiotic grin for which he had been famous when we were kids. "What row are you sitting in?" he asked, picking up his briefcase and rooting through it, looking for his ticket. Before he found what he was looking for, the same woman who had sentenced me to sitting in the coach section all the way from Boston to Baltimore came on the speaker system and announced that our flight would soon begin boarding.

Vinnie jumped up, leaned close to my ear, and confided, as though he were admitting to a serious character fault, that he needed to use a real bathroom before he boarded because the sound of flushing airplane toilets frightened him. As he hurried through the hoard of stirring passengers, he yelled over his shoulder that we would catch up with each other on the plane. "May your butt get stuck in the toilet seat," I found myself whispering in his direction, realizing with a smile that the words sounded like a sarcastic wish from a fortune cookie. Enduring a flight sitting in coach was going to be bad enough without reminiscing about the good old days at St. Lawrence's.

All around me people were getting to their feet, stretching, and zipping up carry-on bags. A list of rows that could board had been announced, but I hadn't been paying attention. The young father sitting across from me folded his newspaper as the mother patted the boy on his knee. "Come on, Joey, let's go get on the airplane," she said, getting to her feet. Joey was still working on his winking technique, but he wasn't getting anywhere fast. Winking doesn't come easily to little kids.

"Joey, stop doing that! It makes you look like a little monster." She shook her head in the direction of her husband, but I could tell she wasn't mad. She had no idea that it was all my fault.

Joey's family made their way over to the boarding line that was lengthening out onto the concourse. A dozen or so people ignored the bottleneck and made a beeline for the gate, apparently forgetting that they were no longer in their native New York. I leaned back in my seat. There was no rush. I had flown enough to know that all of us were going to take off at the same time. For a minute, I wondered how dumb it would be to just leave and have my office book another flight back to Maryland—a flight with a first-class ticket. It was a temptation, but it was also a dumb idea. It was time to get it over with. I had put this trip off twice already. In any case, all thoughts about leaving the airport came to an abrupt halt when I saw a spectacular redhead stand up and raise both long arms high above her head on the far side of the waiting area. Hips, shoulders, and everything else swayed in a yoga-like rhythm as she stretched away the long wait she had endured with the rest of us. Stretching done, kinks gone, she started rooting through a purse the size of a shopping bag, no doubt looking for her boarding pass. I joined the stream flowing toward the boarding area. *What the hell,* I thought. I had just as much chance of sitting next to that gorgeous thing as I did of ending up next to Vinnie or a burping Peruvian.

CHAPTER SEVEN

The first-class passengers looked as smug as fed cats with their drinks and headsets and United Airlines blankets spread across their laps, as though the wide leather seats were sleighs about to take them on a coddled dash along the East Coast. Only one of them, a trim woman in a business suit, had the humanity to make eye contact with me, a lowly coach passenger, as I squeezed through their exalted world toward the modern-day steerage section. I smiled, she smiled, and that was that. The flicker of interest that flamed briefly in her bespectacled eyes had been snuffed out by the airline industry caste system. In the last row of the first-class section, a man so overfed that he ballooned beyond his seat stared menacingly at anyone who dared to brush against him, which, since his cascading body blocked all but about twelve inches of the already narrow aisle, included virtually everyone in our slowly moving caravan. I turned sideways in an attempt to squeeze past him, but it did little good, earning me a glare that seemed to ask if there weren't a backdoor that people like me were supposed to use to board the aircraft.

Seat by seat, the logjam in front of me lightened. I looked down at my boarding pass again: Seat 29B. A man and a woman squeezed into two seats in Row 24, but just as I started moving again, the woman decided she would rather sit in the aisle seat. Smiles of apology, seats switched, no one in front of me now, and there she was again. The redhead, stretching on the toes of high-heeled boots almost up to her knees as she attempted to stuff the red leather jacket she had been wearing into the overhead compartment. Black panty-hose showing between her boots and short skirt, she reached as high as she could, trying to make room for the jacket. Could it be? I counted the rows, and bingo, things were suddenly looking up in the coach section. As I waited for her to finish, she cursed with soft but surprising language.

"Here, let me do that."

She flashed a smile that conveyed not the least bit of concern that I might have heard the sailor-like curses that had escaped her very red lips. She thanked me as she wiggled across two seats to the one against the window. I checked the tag above the aisle. The window seat was A. I was in the middle, in Seat B. The jackpot! The holder of my ticket, and only the holder of my ticket, was entitled to sit next to this gorgeous woman all the way from Boston to Baltimore. The overstuffed grouch in first class had no idea what he was missing.

OK, you've played this game before, Russell, I reminded myself like an experienced golfer teeing up a ball, like a seasoned tennis player lining up a serve. *No need to rush, not in this case. You've got almost two hours to reel her in. We both reached for the same seat belt, and our hands touched. There were laughs and smiles.*

"I brought that jacket with me because I saw on *The Today Show* that it's going to be cold in Baltimore. In the high thirties, the weatherman said." She made a shivering gesture, accompanied by a big smile. A gold earring, one of those really big hoops, shook free from under her hair. She was wearing a little too much makeup for my taste, but what the hell. It was too early to stick out my hand and introduce myself. I wasn't trying to sell her a vacuum cleaner. Everything was going just fine.

I clicked my seat belt closed. There were still a few stragglers making their way down the aisle, followed by a flight attendant who was closing overhead compartment doors, one plastic slam after another. The seat between the aisle and me was still empty. Up front, an enormous woman squeezed through the first-class partition, huffing and puffing and jostling passengers on both sides of the aisle. She plowed into the coach section like a tugboat, producing, I was sure, the same alarmed prayer in the mind of everyone sitting next to an empty seat: *Please God, not me.* People sighed audibly as she passed, like roadside trees swaying in her wake. A cruel mind would have wondered if she had been allowed on the airplane with just one ticket. I weighed over two hundred pounds, and even though I worked out three times a week and ran on weekends, I barely fit between the armrests of my seat. Stopping to check her boarding pass, she sagged like a deflating weather balloon into the seats on both sides of the aisle. If she weighed an ounce she weighed three hundred pounds. She breathed deeply, looked farther down the aisle, and chugged on. Someone in the back of the plane groaned.

The redhead grabbed my arm, laughing. "You should have seen the look on your face when you saw that woman coming down the aisle." She laughed like someone who enjoyed having a good time. That was a good sign. The fingers that lay lightly on my sleeve were long with dark-red nails that made them even longer. There were expensive-looking rings on two of those fingers, and on the hand in her lap, there were two more rings. One was a very large diamond. The one nestled against it was clearly a wedding band, a stop sign I had run many times. She slipped her hand away and adjusted her seatbelt then smiled and shook her head, obviously still thinking about the fat lady. She looked at me, and the smile became a laugh that jiggled her voluptuous body. The devil on my left shoulder had been winning for most of my life, and his chances of seeing me go astray one more time were looking good. Just as I was about to introduce myself, she looked past me. Her smile disappeared for a second then returned, more playfully than before. She put her lips close to my ear. "I'm afraid you're going to have to be a good boy on this flight," she whispered, "not that I would expect anything else." She nodded toward the aisle.

I turned just as Vinnie, dopey smile, Roman collar and all, dropped into the aisle seat next to me and squeezed my arm with the enthusiasm of a long-lost friend. "Do you know what this is, Russell?" he asked, bending forward to see who was in the window seat. His eyes widened noticeably, he nodded uncertainly, but he was not flustered enough by the face, the figure, or the attire of our fellow seatmate to forget that he had just launched a rhetorical question. "My presence in the seat next to you," he continued with accelerating enthusiasm, "is yet another proof that God listens to our prayers, big and small." Each word was accompanied by an enthusiastic pat on my arm. "As I walked down the tunnel to this airplane, I prayed with all my heart that God, through His almighty powers, would see to it that my seat was the one right next to you." The shit-eating grin for which he was famous in grade school overwhelmed his face. "Can anyone doubt His existence?"

As he leaned forward to push his briefcase under the seat, he glanced quickly again toward the window, his eyes widened once more, this time dramatically, as he gave the briefcase a quick shove and sat bolt upright in his seat. The redhead had crossed her long legs, no doubt exposing more thigh than permitted under FAA regulations on domestic flights. As the last of the passengers pushed past on the way to the back of the plane, one of them said, "Good morning, Father." This acknowledgement of his state in life seemed to fully restore Vinnie and refocus his thoughts on the manner in which God had seen to it that he ended up in the seat next to me.

"For all I know, you were praying for the same thing, Russell," he sighed. Vinnie buckled his seatbelt and patted my knee again. "Small world," he muttered to himself. "What a small, small world."

CHAPTER EIGHT

Father Vincent Rinaldi blessed himself as the big plane revved its engines into a vibrating frenzy and lunged forward on the takeoff roll. The redhead closed her eyes and wrapped her long fingers around the ends of the armrests. Beyond the window, brown grass and runway lights gained speed as they disappeared behind us. I loved this part. It was like a giant carnival ride. The big jet strained to become airborne, striving with all its might to lift off the ground with that enormous woman sitting somewhere back in the tail section. The Wright brothers might have stuck to building bicycles if they had known that airplanes would someday be asked to leave the ground with loads like her on board.

A final effort, a few bumps, a teasing hop, then the rumble of the runway ceased, and we were flying. Patches of bare earth and winter grass blended into a seamless brown-green carpet as we soared into the air. An adjacent runway, striped in yellow and scuffed by landing wheel rubber, came into view, shrunk quickly to the size of a driveway, and then to a strip of ribbon, before disappearing as the pilot banked and locked onto the course that would carry us down the East Coast.

It was a safe bet that behind his closed eyes, Vinnie was praying. For all I knew, the redhead was praying too; take-offs and landings do that to both saints and sinners. Below her short skirt, black pantyhose drew delicate patterns on her long, thin legs. Her knees were a little boney, but it was a pretty good guess that she had never been kicked out of bed because of them. My eyes swept her fine body before focusing once more on the magic taking place beyond the window. She would be there for the rest of the flight, but the allusion of leaving this world without having to die first would be gone in less than a minute.

Human beings on the earth below had shrunk to invisibility; cars and trucks looked like crawling beetles; high-voltage transmission lines shortcutting across the landscape assumed the delicate appearance of threads. The everyday details of the world—the tightly packed houses, a sprawling shopping mall anchored in a sea of asphalt—lost their importance. As the wing outside the window sliced through the first traces of cloud, ponds and lakes glowed gold in the midmorning sun, and the earth organized itself into quiet rectangles of greens and browns. From up here, it was almost possible to forget that life down there was such a never-ending hassle. Clouds sweeping past the big jet's silver wing thickened, and in seconds, all traces of the earth vanished. The sound of the plane's powerful engines suddenly changed pitch. The redhead stiffened almost imperceptibly, but her eyes remained closed. Vinnie glanced at me and forced a smile. "Small world," he said for the umpteenth time before aiming his big nose at the seat in front of him and shutting his eyes again.

My eyes returned to the window, distracted for only a second by the museum-size diamond nestled next to the redhead's wedding ring. She was not only married but pampered, another hurdle I'd cleared a time or two. The world, its hazy edges beginning to curve out of sight, appeared to be anything but small, an observation that always reassured me. I needed this planet to be as big and wide and time-consuming to navigate as possible. I needed all the insulation that time and distance could provide between the life I had escaped to and the nightmare of my childhood.

The big jet was no longer straining. We had reached the top of a long, imaginary hill so high that the earth below had dissolved into an abstract composition of muted colors. The engines caught their breath, vibrations ceased, and coded chimes signaled the flight attendants. Some of the people I could see from where I was sitting had reopened their eyes. A lady on the aisle one row up who had never closed hers took a deep breath and removed a paperback book from the seat pocket in front of her. Vinnie and the redhead had not yet resurfaced. Vinnie was still praying, his lips moving the way my mother's used to.

The redhead opened her eyes and stretched, one tanned arm almost brushing my face, gold bracelets colliding, her perfume swirling invisibly. "Excuse *me*," her words cutting short a yawn, "I must have dozed off." She shook herself the rest of the way awake and extended her hand. "My name is Veronica Curtis." She said it in an oh-by-the-way manner, a playing card tossed casually onto the table. My response was every bit as casual. I had eased into this game a thousand times before.

"Father Rinaldi," Vinnie chimed in, leaning forward and reaching his hand across my seat. He had come back to life, assured by the relaxed mood that had returned to the cabin that we had survived the takeoff. From the rows around us came movement, chatter, and bursts of relieved laughter, the usual confirmation that more people than would ever admit it were overwhelmed by the unnatural act of rocketing into the sky.

Veronica Curtis, the redhead who now had a name, hesitated for a second, then shook Vinnie's hand with the tips of her long fingers.

"This man between us and I go way back, don't we Russell?" Vinnie had donned the shit-eating grin that he obviously couldn't help.

"Are you two together?" Veronica wondered aloud, sounding as confused as she looked.

"Good god, no!" My words escaped without the least sensitivity to Vinnie's feelings.

He took no notice. "Just an incredible coincidence. Russell and I haven't seen each other since we were altar boys together in grade school."

"Altar boys?" she asked, freeing her fingers from Vinnie's hand.

I winced.

"That's right. Ad Deum qui laetificat juventutem meam. Those were the days, weren't they, Russell?"

"I'm sorry, I don't speak Spanish. I can't even understand the people who come to take care of our lawn." Veronica sounded perfectly serious.

Laughter snorted from Vinnie's long nose. "Goodness no, that wasn't Spanish, it was Latin, the first response an altar boy ever memorized back in our day. Isn't that right, Russell?"

"I miss the Latin Mass, Russell, I really do," he continued eagerly, "not that I have any quarrel with Holy Mother the Church, mind you." He added the last words quickly, apparently fearing that one of our fellow passengers might misunderstand and report him for spreading heresy. "Reciting the Confiteor, saying the Suscipiat, responding with a loud and clear et cum spiritu tuo to every Dominus vobiscum. Ah, Russell, those were the days."

Vinnie's Latin had come a long way, but then again, it would have been impossible for it to get any worse than it had been when we were in grade school together. He leaned forward, addressing Veronica. "I bet this man still remembers every Latin response in the Mass. Russell was a real whizbang as an altar boy. In fact"—he seemed about

229

to drown in nostalgia—"wait a minute, yes, I remember it for certain, you even helped Father Fowler teach Latin to the new altar boys, didn't you, Russell?" A crescent smile underlined his banana-like nose. Vinnie was beside himself with the memory.

"He probably doesn't want to brag" was Vinnie's way of explaining my silence to Veronica. "Undoubtedly he's too embarrassed to admit it, but of all the kids at our school, Russell here was our pastor Fr. Kavanaugh's very favorite."

Veronica gave me a strange look, and I shook my head, a gesture that did not escape Vinnie. "Oh yes you were, Russell! It was obvious that Fr. Kavanaugh held you in very high esteem. A fact that, I must confess, caused me to envy you. An exemplary priest, simply an exemplary priest." Vinnie's voice trailed off as he wrapped up a glowing review of Fr. Kavanaugh's life on earth. "The manner in which that extraordinary man of God was taken from our midst was a tragedy felt by every member of the parish. Russell will second me on that point."

"What happened to him?" Veronica asked before Vinnie had a chance to notice that I had seconded nothing.

Vinnie removed his glasses and scratched his nose before answering in a hushed tone that implied that he was about to reveal confidential information. "The Harrisville Police Department concluded that he died in a freak accident. I have seen the report. It states that he was most likely lost in prayer when he stumbled and fell down the poorly lit stairs leading to the church basement."

"How awful."

Vinnie held his glasses at arm's length and examined them dramatically before sliding them up the long slope of his nose. "I for one do not believe that is what happened." Vinnie looked at me, raising and lowering his eyebrows in a knowing manner that made my heart jump. "No sir, I do not believe for one minute that is what happened."

In all the years that had passed, I had never heard anyone question the official version of Fr. Kavanaugh's death, and even though I had always considered Vinnie to be more or less an idiot, I feared that he was about to drop a giant bomb.

"I consider myself a bit of an expert in the methods of Sherlock Holmes. *The Speckled Band*, *The Five Orange Pips*, *The Musgrave Ritual*, ah, *The Musgrave Ritual* — name any of Sir Arthur Conan Doyle's stories about his master detective, and I can recount for you in detail the crime, the clues, and the outcome of each. Indeed, if God had not called me to the priesthood, there is no doubt in my mind that I would have become chief of detectives on some major police force."

I relaxed. This was the Vinnie I knew at St. Lawrence's. He knew no more about what happened to Fr. Kavanaugh than the man in the moon.

"That wonderful priest was murdered!" Vinnie announced dramatically.

The bottom fell out of my stomach. Veronica gasped.

"In using the Great Detective's methods to arrive at that conclusion, I asked myself, can it be merely a coincidence that our dear pastor's death occurred on the same night that a hoodlum was murdered less than a hundred yards from the spot where Fr. Kavanaugh's body was found?"

"A hoodlum? Were there many hoodlums in your neighborhood?" Veronica interrupted.

"Only one," Vinnie answered, "but he was a bad one. His father ran the gasoline station next door to Russell's house. As unsavory a father and son duo as ever walked this earth. One day when I was walking past the gas station on my way to the library, the younger one called me a name I will not repeat and knocked me to the ground. It is no exaggeration to say that I feared for my life."

Vinnie, apparently reliving the horror of that long-ago day, did not notice my struggle to keep from laughing out loud.

"But I digress," he continued. "I can't quite remember the name of the hoodlum who was found dead in the gasoline station on the other side of your house, Russell, but surely you do." He quickly looked past me and added, "I know it sounds uncharitable to refer to fellow human beings as unsavory, Mrs. Curtis, but in this case, I am simply stating a fact. I'm certain that Russell and his mother found it extremely difficult living next door to such miscreants."

"Did you figure out who murdered the priest?" she asked.

The Roman-collared Sherlock Holmes shook his head. "I'm afraid the perpetrator of that foul deed will carry his guilt to the grave."

In fact, the perpetrator of that foul deed never experienced guilt. Guilt, no. Fear of discovery, yes. It was months before I managed to sleep all the way through the night, and when I did fall asleep, I was terrified by nightmares in which the entire Harrisville Police Department stormed my bedroom, kicked down the door, and slapped me in irons before I knew what was happening. I never went to church again, and my mother was too stunned by Fr. Kavanaugh's death to even notice. Fr. Fowler came over to the house several times trying to convince me that returning to my duties as an altar boy would do me a world of good and, just as importantly, would fill Fr. Kavanaugh with joy as he looked down from heaven.

As he looked down from heaven! Assuming there was such a place, Fr. Kavanaugh had as much chance of being in heaven as Machine Gun Kelly.

CHAPTER NINE

The sight of the approaching refreshment cart interrupted a train of thought that never failed to put me in the mood for a stiff drink. I was about to ask Veronica if she would join me when Vinnie dove into a new subject.

"By the way, Russell, what takes you back to Maryland?"

When I told him, he almost sprained his arm blessing himself. "Your mother passed away? Oh dear God. May her soul rest in peace."

Veronica patted my arm. "That is so sad," she said.

With perfect timing, a flight attendant wearing a Santa Claus hat stopped at our aisle. Without a second's hesitation, Veronica said she would have a Canadian Club and water. I asked for a Johnny Walker Black. The attendant, not bad looking if you didn't mind a few miles on the odometer, passed out Christmas tree napkins and little bags of nuts and asked Vinnie what he was having. She called him Reverend. He corrected her and then said piously that he would just have ginger ale, hitting the word *just* noticeably harder than the other words in his answer.

Hoping that Vinnie would busy himself praying for my mother, I turned my attention to more important things.

"The holidays are here again," the redhead replied when I asked her why she was flying to Baltimore. "Time to do the Christmas thing with my daughter." She rolled her eyes into her head, an obvious invitation to ask if she was looking forward to the task, a question she had already answered. "Hardly," she replied when I did ask. "Her husband drives me up a wall." She sighed. "To tell you the truth, my daughter does too. It's our annual attempt to be civil: hug each other, drink eggnogs, and smile at presents we don't need. I'd much rather stay home with my cats."

The detail I was most interested in had been had left out of her answer. "Is your husband joining you?"

"Lord no. Dominic isn't Laura's father, and he wouldn't come with me even if he was."

Another box checked off. "Do you need a ride to your daughter's house? I'm picking up a rental car at the airport."

"How sweet," she sighed, squeezing my arm. "Unfortunately, she and her obnoxious husband are meeting me when we land."

I was trying to decide what my next move should be when Vinnie, sniffing sin in the making, bolted into action. "Russell," he declared, grabbing my right arm, "you and I really must spend time together when we are home."

While I struggled to find the right words to make it clear that I had no desire to rekindle a relationship we never had in the first place, Vinnie filled the air with words designed to jam my communications with Veronica. Had he mentioned that he taught theology at Boston College or that he was honorary chairman of the school's annual clothing drive? Did I care to guess how many sweaters, pairs of pants, usable socks, and whatnots they had collected this past fall? "Say, Russell," he interjected without waiting for my guesses, "you would certainly get a lot of satisfaction out of volunteering to help with the drive next year. The work we do is elixir for the soul. Remind me to get your phone number."

I attempted to turn my attention back to Veronica.

"I've got a great idea, Russell!" Vinnie continued, his eyes lighting up, "I'll be helping with the children's Christmas Eve Mass at St. Lawrence's tonight! Why don't you come? We can get together for a cup of eggnog at the rectory afterwards. What do you say?"

The muscles in my face refused to obey when I attempted a smile. Returning to the house I spent my miserable childhood in was going to be more than enough to deal with; chancing an encounter with Fr. Kavanaugh's ungodly spirit inside the church he once ruled like Attila the Hun was the last thing I had any desire to do. As I was about to make this crystal clear, the young boy I had seen in the airport came skipping down the aisle. He smiled and waved at Vinnie, who seemed mildly startled, then spotted me, and stopped, pulling loose from his mother's hand. He had apparently been working on his winking technique and wanted me to see how he was progressing. The first few attempts involved much too much mouth twisting and nose wrinkling, but his last effort showed promise.

"Joey, what are you doing?" his mother laughed, retrieving his hand and apologizing to the two of us.

"I'll pray for the child," Vinnie solemnly told the mother who reacted with a puzzled look as she dragged Joey away.

"That poor child obviously has a serious nervous disorder," Vinnie whispered to me as the flight attendant arrived with the refreshment cart. She reached across Vinnie with our drinks, then handed him his, calling him Reverend again. Veronica raised her glass to me and smiled. "Cheers." Her teeth were much more perfect than the ones Mother Nature normally hands out.

Vinnie went right to work on his ginger ale, pausing between gulps to reinforce his Christmas Eve invitation. "Yes. Yes. I'll see you at Mass, and then we'll have an eggnog together. Maybe two." He downed another slug of ginger ale and set the plastic cup on the seat-back tray in front of him. "Tell me, Russell, where do you attend Mass in Boston?"

I took a sip of the scotch, wiped my mouth with the Christmas napkin, and took another sip, a good long one. Vinnie must have thought I had not heard him because he rephrased the question. "I mean, what parish do you belong to, Russell? Perhaps I know your pastor." Because he was opening a bag of nuts with his teeth, his words were slightly muffled.

"I'm not in any parish."

He pushed a palm full of macadamias into his mouth. "What was that?"

A perceptive person would have understood what my answer meant, but Vinnie, for someone as educated as he must have been, didn't seem to be all that perceptive. He cocked an eyebrow as though he were waiting for me to clarify my answer, possibly expecting me to explain that I wasn't a member of any particular parish because I preferred to attend Mass at the Cathedral or at some historic church in Back Bay. I looked at him silently, but no light came on behind his eyes. He munched away as he waited for me to speak.

I drained the rest of the scotch and fired both barrels. "Vinnie, I couldn't tell you the last time I saw the inside of a church."

It took a few seconds. The nut chewing slowed and then stopped. Vinnie swallowed hard and stared at me until he caught himself and looked away. For the longest time he seemed to be studying the seat in front of him, shoveling nuts into his mouth one after another until he realized the bag was empty. He started to turn his head in my direction, stopped, reached for the black briefcase at his feet, put it back without opening it, then closed his eyes. The flight attendant said, "Excuse me, Reverend" once more as she reached past him to take the money I handed her for the two drinks.

CHAPTER TEN

I wasn't telling the truth about not remembering the last time I had seen the inside of a church. It had been almost exactly a year ago, when I let myself be talked into attending Mass by a woman who saw no conflict between her fondness for sex and the pleasure it gave her to go to church every Sunday clutching the well-worn prayer book she had received from her parents the day she made her confirmation.

Crunching through salt spread on the snow-cleared sidewalk in front of the church, I was as shaky as a man boarding a flight for the first time since surviving a plane crash. With its time-stained granite walls and pointed arches, the place looked ominously like St. Lawrence's. I stopped at the foot of the worn steps and looked up at the small, gold cross held high by a slate-shingled steeple.

"Why don't we skip this and go get some breakfast," I asked as warmly dressed families hurried past us.

Carolyn, daytime dental hygienist, nighttime lover, and

amazingly comfortable Sunday Catholic, took my hand. "Come on, Russell, no one in there is going to bite you."

I reached for the holy water font as we entered, a move that came back without thinking. Like The French Lady, Carolyn marched to the front of the church, high heels clicking, head held high. With a nod, she indicated that the two of us were going to squeeze into the first pew whether the people already seated there liked it or not. I flipped down the kneeler, knelt, and crossed myself without thinking. Rather than say a prayer, I did some math. It had been almost forty years since I had done this. I looked around wondering how much had changed. There were paperback missals in the racks on the backs of the pews. Apparently no one except Carolyn brought their own prayer books to Mass anymore. A simple, cube-like altar faced the congregation. The old, elaborately carved altar atop a tier of marble steps had been relegated to the role of backdrop. Fr. Kavanaugh would have had a stroke.

Carolyn paged through her prayer book until she located the readings for the second Sunday of Advent, marked the place with a thin, green ribbon, and closed her eyes as peacefully as an angel. From somewhere behind us, a choir filled the church with the longing sound of "O Come, O Come Emmanuel." Strange feelings stirred uneasily. I wanted to leave. I had never had the chance to make up my own mind about any of this. By the time I was in the fourth grade, Fr. Kavanaugh had added to my workload the job of setting up the manger scene every Christmastime. Like everything in my youth, it was an unwanted responsibility that involved lugging crates of large figurines up the steep steps from the boiler room, unpacking them under the ever-present threat of bodily harm if the herald angel's golden horn got bent or if I placed the shepherd with the lamb draped over his shoulders too close to the Wise Men. The only thing I remember Fr. Kavanaugh allowing Mr. Shifflet to do was hammer together the wooden stable itself and run an extension cord to the Star of Bethlehem that hung from the straw roof.

Fittingly, the place Carolyn had dragged me to was named The Church of the Nativity, and just as at St. Lawrence's, the manger scene was on the gospel side of the altar, right in front of where we were seated. The statuettes were not in the same league with the set my Grandfather Cornell had donated to St. Lawrence's long before I was born. They were stiff as robots, unlike the painted plaster set my grandfather had ordered from Italy, figurines molded with such delicate precision that it was possible to see the Blessed Mother's fingernails. Beata Madre, the cardboard carton she lived in most of the year was labeled. If there was a way to forget details like that, I had never learned it.

A bell rang, the congregation clamored to its feet, and a small procession started down the center aisle from the back of the church. Three people, two women and a man led the way, followed by two altar boys and a priest wearing the purple vestments of Advent, another of the countless nuggets of liturgical knowledge that decades of rebellion had failed to erase. One of the altar boys was actually a girl with red pigtails, another tidbit of change that would have left Fr. Kavanaugh speechless.

When he arrived at the altar, the priest turned and waited while the final echoes of the beautiful hymn melted to silence. He wished everyone a "good morning," and everyone wished him a "good morning" back. If not equals, the members of this parish were at least on speaking terms with their priest. Like a dancer learning new steps, I found myself a good second or two behind everyone else when it came time to stand, kneel, or sit, but by far, the biggest adjustment was experiencing the Mass in English. It was such a startling experience that I found myself converting the responses into Latin as though I were a contestant on a Vatican game show. In the name of the Father—*In nomine Patris.* Lord have mercy—*Kyrie eleison.* The Lord be with you—*Dominus vobiscum.* I stumbled through part of the Confiteor and screwed up most of the tongue-tying Suscipiat, but for the most part, I put some pretty good numbers up on the liturgical scoreboard.

In the middle of the gospel, a woman carrying a baby and followed closely by a small girl dragging a well-worn teddy bear by its paw, made her way down the center aisle. Their timing was equivalent to arriving at a football game at the end of the second quarter. I cringed, having witnessed many times at St. Lawrence's the price to be paid for such a transgression. Fr. Kavanaugh's thundering voice would have publicly damned the mother and frightened the child to death. The priest saying this Mass, a fortyish man with the square jaw and bent nose of a prizefighter, looked up from the missal from which he had been reading and smiled as though their late arrival had been fully expected.

To my amazement, when it was time, Carolyn got up to go to communion. "Aren't you going?" she whispered to me. I shook my head and watched dumbfounded as she made it all the way down the aisle without being struck by lightning or turned into a pillar of salt.

"No, I didn't go to confession, not that it's any of your business," she replied when I asked her about it in the car after Mass. "Why, what's your problem?"

"Well, unless they've made a radical change to the rules, screwing somebody you are not married to is a mortal sin."

"Give me a break."

The things this woman and I had been doing together just the night before would have been in the running for the "Sins of the Year" award back in the old days.

"For Christ's sake, get over it" was her reply when I made that point. She flipped down the sun visor and peered into the small mirror behind it, opening her mouth wide and cocking her head from side to side to check her lipstick. "You have to be an imbecile to believe all the crap they taught us." She dabbed the corner of her mouth with a fingertip. "God and I have an understanding. We reached it a long time ago."

I started to say something but found I was speechless. That was one of the most interesting things I had ever heard anyone say about God.

"Anyone can have an understanding with God," she informed me, flipping the sun visor back up.

The speakers in the cabin ceiling came to life. "Howdy, folks. Captain Taylor here from the flight deck. You-all sitting on the left side of the aircraft might want to take a peek at a snow-covered New York City, which is about to pass under our wing. The ice skaters in Rockefeller Center and the holiday shoppers running around like a bunch of rabbits are much too small to see from way up here, but they're down there." I thought he was going to break into a country Christmas song, but he caught himself and returned to the mundane. "The current temperature on those busy streets is twenty-nine degrees Fahrenheit, and the temperature in Baltimore, where we are headed for an on-time landing—let me see—is a slightly more comfortable thirty-five degrees. I'd tell you what the temperature is in my hometown of Waycross, Georgia, but it might make you feel bad." With a good-natured chuckle, he wished us all a happy holiday season and signed off.

Vinnie, distracted from the funk of realizing that a fellow altar boy had become an unrepentant sinner, shook his head. "Happy holidays, seasons greetings," he lamented, looking up at the speaker above his seat. "Are we no longer allowed to utter the word Christmas or acknowledge the birthday of Our Lord Jesus Christ?" He sighed. "What has this world come to?"

The enormously fat lady from the back of the plane waddled to a stop next to our row. "Where did the pilot say New York City was?" she asked, out of breath, leaning toward the window and enveloping Vinnie in her folds like a bug smothered by a pillow. "My ex-aunt lives in New York City."

Vinnie's reply was muffled. Maybe, like me, he was wondering what an ex-aunt is.

"I would die if I ever got that fat," Veronica whispered, placing her hand over mine. "Where on earth do women like that buy bathing suits?"

Not even the frightening thought of a woman that big romping in the surf could keep me from resuming the hunt. "When will you be back in Boston?"

"As soon as I can," she replied. "The sooner I get away from my daughter and her obnoxious husband the better."

"Maybe we can get together for dinner," I said as quietly as I could and still be heard above the jet's droning engines. Veronica's leg pressed against mine.

Loosening my seat belt and doing my best to twist away from Vinnie, I motioned for Veronica to write her phone number on the Christmas napkin that had come with my scotch. Her handwriting was overly decorative in a curlicue kind of way, but I could read it just fine. I folded the napkin and stuck it in my jacket pocket, silently mouthing the words *I'll call you.*

Veronica slipped a hand over mine, her many rings launching tiny flares of reflected light. "Wednesday afternoons are best," she whispered. "Dominic spends every Wednesday afternoon at his karate studio."

She had my attention. "Your husband runs a karate studio?"

"Only on the side. He and his brothers, Vito and Tony, own a trash collection business, the third largest in New England."

Dr. Kite's question resonated like distant thunder. *Do you consider your conduct with women reckless?* I never had before, but I had never before pictured myself sliding down the chute of a trash compactor. Oblivious to my sudden silence, Veronica rooted through her large leather purse, her tanned arm out of sight to the elbow, until she located the object of the search: a small, rectangular bottle with a long, black cylindrical cap. When she shook it, the potion it contained shone amber gold in the sunlight streaming through the aircraft window.

"There you are," Veronica said to the bottle. She dropped it into a small, fabric bag, pushed the big purse out of the way with her foot, and unsnapped her seatbelt. "Excuse me, please. I have to go to the little girls' room." She patted my hand and gave it a little squeeze.

We both looked at Vinnie, the one who had to get up first. His eyes were closed, and he appeared to be praying again, in all likelihood, for my soul. "Excuse me please," Veronica said again, louder, reaching past me and shaking Vinnie's arm until, startled and confused, he blinked and stared at her.

"I have to go to..." she stopped abruptly, uncertain if it was proper to say *little girls' room* to a member of the clergy. Instead of chancing it, she nodded toward the back of the airplane.

Vinnie sprang out of his seat, apparently thinking that Veronica was experiencing an emergency. Before I could get up and follow Vinnie into the aisle, Veronica squeezed across my lap, a maneuver that made me thankful for tight airline seating. Only a blind man or a saint would have failed to observe that her black skirt was tight enough to reveal the triangular outline of her underwear. My eyes must have lingered on this enticing detail long enough for Vinnie to catch me, because he shook his head sadly, his weary demeanor acknowledging that little else could be expected from a Fallen-Away Catholic, the blackest of black sheep. He slipped back into his seat and refastened his seat belt. After taking a deep breath, he closed his eyes and blessed himself, no doubt beseeching the powers of heaven to grant him the wisdom to save a sinner like me from the road to hell.

"That is a married woman!" he began when he resurfaced, completely unaware that the vision of having a dumpster as my final resting place had rendered the need for spiritual counseling temporarily unnecessary. His voice dropped to a confidential whisper. "How many times have you pursued married women in this manner?"

I looked at him and attempted to lighten the situation with a little humor. "I have no idea, Vinnie. It's a hobby. You know, like collecting stamps."

"A hobby! Russell, how far have you fallen? Have you forgotten the sixth commandment? Have you forgotten how Sunday after Sunday, Fr. Kavanaugh warned us about the sins of the flesh?" He folded his hands and looked toward heaven, his view interrupted by the curved plastic ceiling of the aircraft. "When was the last time you went to confession? Tell me the truth."

The first few air pockets created miniature waves in my drink, but that was about it. Vinnie stopped preaching and glanced around the cabin nervously. Seeing no signs of an impending air disaster, he turned his attention back to the business of saving my soul. "Russell, of all the people in our class at St. Lawrence's," he began earnestly, "you are the last one I would have thought would turn his back on Holy Mother the Church. For goodness sakes, you were the head altar boy."

I downed most of what was left of my drink, and in an attempt to get him to focus on someone else's soul, I asked if there was anyone in our class for whom he had predicted eternal damnation.

"There was indeed," he answered without hesitating. "I can't remember her name, but even as a seventh grader, she was eager to spread heresy. I pray for her soul every day, but I fear there is little hope."

I polished off the scotch. "Heresy?"

He nodded. "Heresy, indeed. There is no other word for it. Don't you remember her rising to her feet in the middle of religion class and proclaiming, as bold as can be, that the Catholic Church was not the one true religion, that it was not the Mystical Body of Christ on earth? I can still picture the cocksure manner with which she defied Sr. Mary Luke's commands to sit back down. Her name escapes me. She was tall."

"Patricia Delsey."

"Patricia Delsey! That's her! If I recall correctly, Fr. Kavanaugh expelled her from St. Lawrence's that very afternoon." Vinnie shook his head at the memory. "No doubt she rues the day she threw away her chance to obtain the quality of education that only Catholic schools can provide."

CHAPTER ELEVEN

Vinnie's description of what Patricia Delsey did that memorable afternoon in religion class was a bit overstated. Patricia had dug in her heels—as she had a tendency to do—and argued in her typically adult manner that it only stood to reason that people like Buddhists and Hindus and the nice Protestants who lived in her neighborhood would be rewarded in the hereafter for a life well lived the same as Catholics. The problem was that she was only in the seventh grade when she made her stand and that she did it in 1954 when Catholic grade school students were expected to limit their dialogue with priests and nuns to "Yes, Father" and "Yes, Sister." While she was not burned at the stake, her desk was empty the next morning, and by recess, wild rumors were flying. Half the kids on the playground were certain she was in chains in the basement of the rectory, and the others were just as positive she had been carried off to the Sisters of Notre Dame de Namur motherhouse in

Baltimore where she remained strapped to an iron bed, undergoing electric shock therapy.

Neither rumor was true. Patricia finished the seventh grade at Harrisville Junior High School where, because Fr. Kavanaugh was no longer around to stop me from going to public school, I began the eighth grade the following September. My mother never said a word about my leaving St. Lawrence's, and because Fr. Kavanaugh's sudden death had turned her into a zombie, she might not have noticed if I had given up school all together.

While I was trying to remember where Patricia Delsey had gone to law school after she graduated from some expensive college whose name I couldn't remember either, the plane hit a patch of air so choppy it rattled the plastic doors of the overhead bins.

"What's happening?" Vinnie gasped, clutching my arm.

"Just a little turbulence. Relax."

"I should have taken the train."

"We're fine, Vinnie. This is nothing. I had to go to Lima on business a few years ago. Try flying across the Andes sometime."

"No thank you."

On the flight to Peru, we had encountered flying conditions so severe that a series of bone-jarring jolts threw passengers from their seats, breaking one man's arm and sending two flight attendants to the hospital with head injuries. Telling Vinnie about these things was a mistake. Just as he folded his hands and began to pray audibly, the plane bounced wildly from side to side, causing the fold-down trays to flap madly and sending plastic cups and napkins flying. Chimes sounded, and Fasten Seat Belt signs flared to life. Vinnie's fingers dug into my arm, and as though his giant nose were a human air raid siren, he began to wail.

"Oh God, save us! We're going to crash!"

Some of the people I could see from where I was sitting spun their heads to stare at him, their eyes and mouths open in alarm, until a reassuring Southern drawl turned their attention to the cabin speakers.

"Captain Taylor from the flight deck, folks. We've flown into a pretty darn good patch of choppy air, but there's not a thing to worry yourself about. This old airplane is designed to handle conditions a heck of a lot rougher than what I see popping up on the radar up here in the cockpit. Just pull your seatbelts tight, and stay in your seats until things settle down. Cabin crew, you-all take your seats."

Vinnie's head swiveled as he followed the hasty retreat of the flight attendants to the rear of the plane. "The pilot sounds worried," he whimpered.

"He's not worried, Vinnie. We'll be fine. It's only turbulence."

On cue, the plane seemed to drop off a cliff, filling the cabin with roller coaster ride screams that gave way to gasps when the belly of the plane collided with what felt like an unyielding concrete road.

Vinnie grabbed my arm, petrified. "We're going to die. You must confess your sins and save your soul while there is still time."

I turned my head toward the rear of the plane, wondering what had become of Veronica. "Vinnie, relax. We are not going to die."

"How can you be so sure? Lean close to me. I'll help you. How long has it been since your last confession?"

I had not been to confession since the night I shoved Fr. Kavanaugh down the stairs behind St. Lawrence's church, an act driven by fear and hate that no doubt canceled out every prayer I had ever said and made a mockery of every catechism question I had ever memorized. Not that I was about to tell Vinnie that. Not that I was about to tell him anything. I didn't even know the word for killing one's pastor. Years ago, I tried to look it up and was surprised to learn that while there was a word in the dictionary for killing anyone and anything a person could imagine, there was no term for killing one's pastor, no doubt because the fathers of the church never anticipated that anyone would ever do such a thing.

The plane began bucking like a bronco. Wild vibrations shook the floor while somewhere below our feet, it sounded like a giant bowling ball had broken loose and was careening wildly through the cargo department.

"Come on, come on!" Vinnie implored. "We could be smashed to smithereens any second. A year since your last confession, two years? Think!"

Out of curiosity, I counted the years that had passed since the summer after my seventh grade. "Thirty-eight years," I told him.

Up front in the first-class section, a woman wailed as the plane yawed like a ship on a turbulent sea.

"That's a good start, Russell," Vinnie whispered in a shaky voice. "In all those years, how many times have you sinned against the sixth commandment?"

It was obvious that he assumed the only sin I was guilty of was having sex with women, married and unmarried. Compared to the whopper that had blackened my soul for most of my life, those transgressions were like trimmings around a Thanksgiving turkey. I had absolutely no idea how many times I had sinned against the sixth commandment, and even if I took the time to come up with an estimate, I wasn't going to talk about it in confession or anywhere else.

While Vinnie waited in vain for me to save myself from the fires of hell, cabin lights flickered, passengers prayed aloud, and the fat lady from the rear of the plane reappeared at Vinnie's side. She attempted to fall to her knees but became wedged between Vinnie's seat and the seat across the aisle. She blessed herself and began to confess her sins at a volume that drowned out the chaotic din filling the cabin.

"Bless me, Father, for I have sinned," she bellowed, using the exact words we had been taught at St. Lawrence's. "It has been twelve hours since my last confession. No, wait." She unfolded her hands and counted on her chunky fingers. "Eleven hours."

"My dear woman," Vinnie admonished so softly that I could barely hear him, "please lower your voice."

"I ate seventeen glazed doughnuts this morning at the airport. No, wait, fourteen glazed and three jelly-filled. I am once again guilty of gluttony," she sobbed. The remarkable extent to which the cabin had quieted made it clear that many passengers had put aside their fear of dying and tuned in to the unusual confession taking place in their midst.

"These are all the sins I can remember," the woman continued loudly. "No, wait. I almost forgot about the big one."

"The big one?" Vinnie whispered.

"Yes, Father. Last Friday night, after bingo, I..." She stopped abruptly, noticing my presence for the first time. "I can't tell you the rest until he leaves."

There was no way I could go anywhere with her plugging the aisle like a giant cork. "I'll hold my ears," I told her.

"And close your eyes."

As loudly as she was speaking, holding my ears made no difference. Everyone within twelve rows could hear her.

"I just want to double-check before I go any further," she continued. "If I confess something really bad, you can't tell anyone about it, right?"

"That is absolutely correct. It's called the seal of the confessional," Vinnie replied before once again admonishing her to keep her voice down.

"No matter how gross the sin is? No matter how horrible?"

"A priest cannot disclose to anyone what he hears from penitents, no matter how grave the sin is. For instance, if someone confessed to me that they had committed a murder, I would not be allowed to tell the police or anyone else."

"I didn't murder anyone!" the fat lady screamed.

"I did not say you did, madam. I was simply giving you an extreme example of the absoluteness of the seal of the confessional."

There was a pause during which the only sounds picked up by my covered ears were the drone of the plane's engines and various metallic rattlings. "OK. Where was I?" she resumed in what was apparently the only volume she ever used. "Oh yes. Here we go. Last Friday night, on my way home from bingo, I..."

That was as far as she got before a flight attendant appeared. "Madame, you will have to return to your seat. Captain's orders." She placed her hands on the fat woman's shoulders and attempted to tug her toward the rear of the plane.

"I have one more sin to tell before we crash."

"Excuse me?"

At that moment, the pilot made a welcomed announcement. "That last patch of turbulence was a doozy but except for a few more little old spots on the radar, it looks like the rough weather is behind us."

There was scattered applause in the cabin, confusing the fat woman. "Do you mean we are not going to crash?" she asked the flight attendant, straining to speak over her shoulder.

"No, ma'am. We were never going to crash. Now please take your seat. The seatbelt sign is still on."

With a great deal of difficulty, the woman swiveled her body toward the rear of the plane, nearly knocking Vinnie silly with her enormous breasts. "Then I'm not going to tell you what happened after bingo," she announced with a sigh of relief.

※

"I'm back, Reverend. Excuse me," Veronica purred, bending close to Vinnie's ear, her lipstick redder, her perfume recharged. After an aborted attempt in which he forgot to undo his seatbelt, Vinnie stumbled out into the aisle, and Veronica brushed past his seat and squeezed over me, losing her balance in a burst of giggles as the plane bumped through a small patch of air pockets.

"Aren't those bathrooms funny with all that stainless steel and that strange blue water in the toilet?" she marveled, falling into the seat next to the window and making a half-hearted attempt to push her skirt closer to her tanned knees. "After I came out, they made me stay back there in an empty seat because of all the bumping. Wasn't that scary? I had to wait for that big tub of lard to squeeze back into her seat before I could come back down the aisle."

"I don't know how charitable it is to call someone a tub of lard," Vinnie admonished with Boy Scout earnestness. "She may well have an eating disorder."

"She has a disorder all right. It's called eating like a hippo," Veronica replied before glancing toward the windows on the far side of the aisle. "Look at those puffy clouds!" she exclaimed like a child. "We're on top of them! Isn't that just the neatest thing?"

When Vinnie tuned to look at the clouds, Veronica slipped a folded note into my hand. *Remember when we get back to Boston, only call me on Wednesdays when Dominic is busy at his karate studio. Remember, only Wednesdays.* The last three words were underlined twice.

"Augie forgot," she whispered.

"Who is Augie?" I whispered back.

"He was this cute guy I met on the Cape. One Monday morning, he came over to the house to surprise me, and Dominic opened the door."

"What happened?" I asked quietly while Vinnie contemplated the canyon of clouds moving past the windows and raved about the wonders of God's creation.

Veronica shook her head sadly.

"As some of us were taught by the good nuns and priests," Vinnie declared, poking me in the thigh with his finger, "the rewards for a life spent observing the commandments will be even more wonderful."

I slipped Veronica's note into my pocket. My determination to ball it up and throw it away had far more to do with the fear of ending up in a dumpster than with the observance of commandments.

CHAPTER TWELVE

We were still a good sixty miles from Baltimore when the pitch of the engines changed noticeably, and the plane began its long descent. Vinnie stiffened as we bounced gently through the last traces of turbulence. "Almost there," he declared nervously, then lowered his voice to inform me that he would be hearing confessions during both the children's Mass and midnight Mass tonight at St. Lawrence's. "It would be a perfect time for you to make your peace with God, Russell."

"I'll think about it," I answered without thinking.

"You think about it, and I'll pray about it," Vinnie whispered excitedly and seemed on the verge of jumping into the aisle and breaking into a song and dance about the blessings of a Christmas confession when he was startled into silence by the groan of wing flaps hinging into place as the plane banked steeply and locked into its final approach. He shut his eyes, blessed himself, and had begun praying, more audibly than he realized, for a safe landing when the landing gear dropped into place with a resounding thud, causing him to place an unintended degree of emphasis on the word "Jesus."

Veronica's eyes were closed, and her long fingers woven into mine, the biggest diamond that dumpster revenue could buy flashing a totally unnecessary reminder that bidding her goodbye at the airport would be a great way to ensure myself a happy and healthy New Year.

Beyond her window, wet roadways superimposed a businesslike grid on the snow-covered Maryland country-side as it rose steadily to meet us. The big plane tipped its wings one way and then the other as gently as a gliding bird while I watched a Home Depot with a crowded parking lot take shape beside a divided highway where a Greyhound bus sped passengers toward Christmas. Close behind the speeding bus, a green and yellow moving van, toy-size still but growing larger by the second, flashed the painted silhouette of its sailing ship trademark and disappeared below our wing. For all I knew, that road was the same one I fled north on the day after I graduated from law school with no more of a plan for the future than to look for a job wherever I happened to be when the dilapidated Plymouth I had driven all through college finally died.

My thoughts returned to the present when the nervous silence of our descent was broken by the voice of a child.

"I hope we don't crash into Santa Claus."

"We won't," a gentle voice assured the girl as laughter warmed the cabin and caused me to wonder once again what my childhood would have been like if my father had lived. I had thought about it a million times, confident that everything about my life would have been different. Maybe I would have ended up living in Boston anyway, but it would have been because I moved there, not because I fled there. More than once, after a few drinks, I found myself fantasizing about a life in which I visited my parents at Thanksgiving and Christmas and flew them up to Massachusetts in the summer to spend time with me on Cape Cod.

I glanced out the window again to watch the real world rising to meet me, a world in which the defining moment of my wonderful childhood had taken place on a dark set of stairs behind a church. There were patches of snow on the final road we crossed, bare December trees, a fence topped with barbed wire, a string of blue runway lights, and then the wide runway itself. I had never tried to convince myself that pushing Fr. Kavanaugh down those stairs was an accident. The closest I ever came to exonerating myself was admitting that after what he had already done to Butchie that night, it was either him or me. I can't remember thinking that way at the time, but what I do remember dawning on me as I hurried home in the dark was that there was no longer anyone to stop me from quitting the altar boys and going to public school. The sense of freedom attached to that realization may well have been the reason I fell asleep that night the second my head hit the pillow.

The plane returned to earth with a screech of rubber and rocketed down the runway until the roar of reversed engines spilled passengers into the aisle where they began

to yank shopping bags filled with brightly wrapped presents from the overhead bins. For them, it was Christmas
Eve. For me, it was just a gray Thursday, a day with a task
to be done that would cut my ties to Harrisville forever.

The captain's cheerful voice brought the intercom to
life. "Didn't I tell you we were going to make it just fine.
You-all have a merry Christmas and a happy New Year and
everything else. Thanks for flying United." He sounded
like a guy I would have enjoyed having a few drinks with.

Giant candy canes and teams of reindeer strung with miniature lights did their best to transform the baggage claim
area into a winter wonderland for the shoulder-to-shoulder
throng anxiously awaiting the appearance of familiar pieces
of luggage on the relentlessly marching carousel.

The fat lady from the back of the plane spotted hers first,
a child-size pink suitcase that looked much too small to hold
anything that would fit her. I had just begun to feel sorry
for her and the lonely world anyone her size must live in
when she was embraced by a slightly overweight version of
John Wayne and two small girls who danced merrily around
her in a circle wider than most Christmas trees. She hugged
John Wayne back with a ferocity that lifted his boots from
the floor then did her best to stoop low enough for the girls
to pin a corsage to her coat.

"Bumpy!" a very young boy cried out to me from his
father's shoulder.

"It was very bumpy on that airplane," I answered. "Were you afraid?"

The boy thought about it and nodded. His father looked at me and smiled. "But he's not afraid anymore because Santa Claus is coming tonight. Right, Joey?" Joey tried one last time to wink at me as he and his father disappeared into the crowd of travelers making their way to the busy glass doors in the distance and then into the wonder of the night ahead. I watched them go, thinking what a great thing it must be to believe in Santa Claus or in anything else, for that matter, that gives joy to life. It was a thought I promised myself to ponder some night in front of a fire when I had a tumbler of scotch in my hand.

Veronica slipped up beside me, squeezed my arm, and whispered that she would love to give me a little Christmas kiss but was afraid her daughter would show up just as she did and have a fit. She stood on the toes of her boots, scanning the mob of hugging and squealing greeters. "She's late for everything. Probably couldn't decide what to wear. Give us a little peck."

Vinnie, alert as always to mischief in the making, wiggled in between us, struggling to snap the long handle of his two-wheeled American Tourister into place. "Don't forget, Russell Flynn, we have a date tonight after the children's Mass at St. Lawrence's." He waved vigorously in the direction of a woman who was unmistakably a Rinaldi. "A good confession and then an eggnog or two," he confided with a goofy wink. "Until then," he added, patting my shoulder, "may the spirit of Christmas descend upon you like a gentle snowfall."

May the spirit of Christmas descend upon you like a gentle snowfall? Where did those words come from? Had Vinnie read them on the inside of a Christmas card, or was he capable of a thought so simple and nice?

"Oh, there you are! There you are!" Veronica squealed." It was not her daughter she had caught sight of but two large trunks matching the red leather bag hanging by long straps from her shoulder. As I wrestled her luggage to the floor, someone squealed, "Mother!" A dozen mothers turned at once, but only one of them had ever raised a daughter who looked like this one. She was at least as tall as Veronica, which put her at six feet or six one. Her hair wasn't red like her mother's; it was straight and very long and so blond that it was almost white. A beauty mark on one cheek, blue eyelids, ruby lips, and a jewelry box worth of rings fought for attention with a full-length mink coat worn over blue jeans and high-heeled leather boots. She waved madly in Veronica's direction while a toy-size dog that looked like it had been bleached to match her hair went crazy trying to escape from beneath her coat.

Veronica turned toward me and mouthed the words *Wednesdays, only Wednesdays.* I smiled, but I was lying. No dumpsters for me.

CHAPTER THIRTEEN

Viewed through the windshield of a rental car, the stage on which the events of my youth took place appeared much too harmless to have witnessed the nightmares that took place on it.

There had been one change to the set, a major one: McDevitt's gasoline station was gone, replaced by a state-of-the-art enterprise dubbed Kim's Gas & Go. The church was still solidly there. Nothing about it had changed. Its granite gray walls and rocket-like steeple still dominated Prospect Street, an overstated show of force on a street of aging homes and ancient sycamore trees. My family's house, the grandest one on Prospect Street when my grandfather built it, stood wearily between St. Lawrence's and what had been the gasoline station where Butchie McDevitt spent most of the days of his short life. From where I sat, waiting for the traffic light at the corner of Thirty-Eighth Avenue to turn green, all but the roof of our screened porch was obscured by the unruly hedge my mother had planted in a futile attempt to isolate what had been left of her genteel world from the unwelcome arrival of Butchie and his father. The upper floors of our two-and-a-half story Victorian peered down on the neighborhood from behind the hedge, unaware that its carpentry scrollwork and shutter-trimmed windows were desperately in need of paint.

The driver of the car behind me leaned on his horn, interrupting the flood of memories threatening to overwhelm me. I made a right turn onto Prospect Street, then a quick left, and pulled to a stop under a metal-clad canopy spanning four islands of gas pumps. To say the slick, rectangular building spanning the site was a radical departure from Mr. McDevitt's greasy three-bay garage was a major understatement. At Kim's Gas & Go—If You Need It We Have It bragged the bright neon script above an uninterrupted span of plate glass.

After the gas pump rejected my credit card for the third time, a short, dark man wearing a baseball cap with reindeer antlers appeared out of nowhere.

"The card's good," I protested much too strongly, attempting to mask a sudden panic that my bookkeeper, overwhelmed by issuing year-end tax statements and bonus checks to the staff, had forgotten to pay my Visa bill.

"That's what they all say." The man tried his best to act like he was serious until a high-pitched burst of laughter ruined his game. "Your credit card good. My pump bad," he confessed, kicking the base of the pump hard enough to put another dent in it. From the pocket of his Kim's Gas & Go jacket he produced a short-handled tool and reset the pump with a practiced twist. "You come inside and pay when finish. We have good coffee too. Hot. Very good. One dollar." Hurrying toward the store, he continued to push the coffee. "One dollar. Just one dollar."

I set the freezing pump handle, stuffed my hands deep into my pockets, and watched while dancing numbers raced to keep up with the pulsing flow of gasoline. Behind the plate glass windows of the store, plastic Christmas wreaths and looping garlands of tinsel vied for attention with holly-bedecked signs advertising specials on eighteen-packs of Coke, eggnog, Tylenol, and frozen pizza. With stripes of red and white tile capping the silvery reflections caught by a continuous wall of glass, the structure would have been the most radical piece of architecture in the county when Butchie and his father were alive.

Midway between the gas pumps and the slick convenience store, a cluster of small manholes unknowingly marked the location where, in my other lifetime, I watched the rescue squad slide Butchie into an idling ambulance, his entire body covered by a fire department blanket except for the hand that fell free and left the message that named his killer. On my way into the store, I stopped as close as I could remember to the spot on the oil-stained concrete where the damning black button had spun to a stop. I recalled once more waiting until they slammed the door on Butchie and drove off, the light atop the ambulance spinning unforgettable red arcs into the night. Countless times over the years, I had closed my eyes, turned that button over in my fingers, and felt again the black thread woven through the four tiny holes

Inside the store, a very heavy woman wearing a Washington Redskins jacket leaned elbows first on the cash register counter, laboriously reading numbers from what appeared to be a well-used paper napkin. The man I had met at the gas pump was now behind the cash register, patiently punching lottery machine keys. "You give me that number already," he informed the woman in the Redskins jacket.

"You sure, Mr. Kim?"

When Mr. Kim nodded, the reindeer antlers on his cap came alive. "I be right with you," he said in my direction. "Coffee in back, near sandwich counter. Fresh. One dollar."

The woman between us dragged her finger down to the next number on the napkin and resumed her uncertain recitation. I stuck my wallet back in my pocket and headed for the coffee.

There was not a square inch of empty space on Mr. Kim's shelves. Bread, jars of vegetables, cans of chili and beef stew, Cheetos, Fritos, cupcakes, socks, mittens, plastic knives and forks, giant packages of toilet paper, six-packs of every soft drink known to man; you name it, and Mr. Kim sold it. Inflatable reindeer and snowmen swung from the ceiling grid. Vinyl-strap lawn chairs and Styrofoam coolers crammed the tops of the refrigerated cases. Boxes of candy canes and rolls of wrapping paper were stashed everywhere, apparently in anticipation of a last-minute Christmas rush, which, according to my watch, Mr. Kim was banking on taking place in the next few hours.

I took a sip of Mr. Kim's coffee, stirred in a little hazelnut flavoring, and took a warming swig. I had paid a hell of a lot more than a dollar for coffee that wasn't as good as Mr. Kim's. Up at the front of the store, a small traffic jam had formed behind the woman buying lottery tickets. The late-afternoon sky beyond the glass wall had grown dark and heavy, and the streetlights in Prospect Street had already come on. When I took my place at the end of the line, the customer in front of me, a gallon container of milk hanging at his side and a loaf of bread and a sack of cat food clutched to his chest, turned and gave me the word. "Snow. Snow as sure as you're born." He nodded conspiratorially, and I nodded back. Suddenly remembering that I could use something to read on the flight back to Boston, I set off in search of a detective novel, fully confident that there was a rack of paperbacks somewhere in Mr. Kim's maze of merchandise.

While searching for the paperbacks, I uncovered, between a pile of reindeer sweatshirts and stacked cartons of windshield wiper fluid, an amazing assortment of condoms. Out of habit, I checked over my shoulder to make sure no one was watching before taking a closer look. The multitiered display of slick, rectangular packages staring me in the face would have been the target of church crusades and police raids when I was growing up here in Harrisville. At some point in the march of time, what we called rubbers had become condoms and ceased being sold out of machines bolted to men's rooms walls in bars and gasoline stations. No longer was it necessary for guys on the hunt to keep a supply of quarters in the glove compartments of their cars. Arrayed before me were a dozen brands packaged in every color of the rainbow and covered with marketing promises using expressions once confined to books delivered in plain, brown wrappers. Butchie would never have believed how open the pursuit of what he called kooze had become. Gone was Big Tex with his twenty-gallon hat and knowing wink. Now, somewhere in the modern-day corporate world, staffs of graphic artists and merchandising experts earned handsome livings designing condom packaging with the same degree of sophistication that sold shampoo and makeup.

"Doing some shopping?"

I spun around like I had been caught doing exactly what I was doing and came face to face with a very attractive woman about my age who was smiling at my embarrassment. A charcoal turtleneck showed above the collar of her long, black winter coat, its shoulders dusted with the snow that had apparently begun to fall outside. Wisps of silver accented her short, dark hair. She wore no earrings, no eye makeup. If she was wearing lipstick, she wasn't wearing much, and as far as I could tell, the only color on her cheeks had been applied by the frigid Christmas Eve air. If I had ever seen a better-looking woman her age, I couldn't remember where. Sophia Loren maybe.

"I thought it was you when I saw you from the side," she said, appraising me with a squint of concentration. "I can definitely see it in your face. You're Russell Flynn, aren't you?"

I spread my hands in a gesture meant to signal that I had no idea who she was or how she knew my name. Not until that instant did I realize that I had absentmindedly picked up a package of condoms. *Durex. Extra Sensitive.* As casually as my state of mind permitted, I hid it behind my back.

"Father Rinaldi, who, by the way, seemed shocked to discover I had become a nun, told me you were back."

I edged backwards, hoping to return the condoms to the general vicinity of the display rack without her noticing. "Vinnie? You know Vinnie?"

"I went to grade school with him. As a matter of fact, I went to grade school with you."

I still had no clue who she was. As far as I could remember, no girl at St. Lawrence's had shown the least indication that she was going to end up looking like this woman.

"No kidding." To disguise my furtive action, I attempted to sound as casual as possible. My first stab at replacing the pack of condoms went low, my hand striking what felt like the bottom of the display unit. I sensed the entire case sliding backwards.

"Give me that thing," she ordered, holding out her hand as though she had caught me in class with a Hershey Bar. She took the pack of condoms and stuck it next to the other purple packages. "You don't have to say a thing," she instructed when I opened my mouth to explain, not that I had any idea what I was going to say.

"Give up?" she asked, oblivious to the fact that I had never been more embarrassed in my life.

Once again I made the helpless gesture, this time with two empty hands.

"We both left St. Lawrence's after the seventh grade."

I was still too unnerved by the condom debacle to think straight.

"We graduated from Harrisville High School together. If I remember correctly, you went to the University of Maryland."

I recovered enough to nod my head. "I did go to Maryland."

"Need another clue?" she asked. "My father was a professor of history at Maryland. I don't know if you ever had him when you were there."

My mind kicked back to life. Only one person in our grade school class had a parent who was a professor of anything. "Patricia Delsey?"

Patricia smiled and took my arm, leading me away from the condom display. She fixed herself a cup of coffee, and I made another for myself. "Father Rinaldi told me some interesting things about you."

"All bad?"

"All bad." She blew away the steam swirling above her coffee.

CHAPTER FOURTEEN

꩜

She was truly a beautiful woman, mature and classy and with an unmistakable aura of self-confidence that had always made a women attractive to me. I hadn't dated a woman my own age for a long time, but I was open-minded. Greased by a lifetime of habit, and having been too distracted to catch the fact that she was a nun, the old wheels started turning. I wondered if she was married. Deciding it wouldn't be smooth to move too quickly, I eased toward the subject with small talk. "I guess Vinnie told you we were stuck on an airplane together for what seemed like a week."

"He didn't put it quite that way. He's convinced that it was God's plan for the two of you to run into each other after all these years." She smiled across the top of her coffee. "He thinks God sat you side by side on that flight so you would have someone to bare your troubled soul to."

"What an idiot."

"Maybe. Maybe not." She sounded half serious, half teasing. I was beginning to really like her.

Mr. Kim came hurrying down the aisle, the antlers on his Christmas cap bouncing crazily with every step. "Good afternoon, Sister," he said to Patricia as he passed.

It took a second or two for the meaning of his greeting to sink in, but when it did, my face apparently twisted into the shape of a question mark.

"Three of Mr. Kim's grandchildren are at St. Lawrence's," Patricia announced happily. She took a long sip of her coffee and savored it before lobbing the next bomb about herself. "I'm the principal."

This one-two punch almost floored me. When I was a student at St. Lawrence's, Sr. Superior, our principal, had wispy chin whiskers and—cruel rumor had it—once played left tackle for the Green Bay Packers. The woman I was drinking coffee with was cut from a very different mold.

"Which reminds me, I came over here to get some tape to repair a broken halo. We're getting ready for the children's Christmas Eve Mass." She had obviously been in Mr. Kim's store before, because she went directly to an end display stocked with every brand of tape and glue known to man.

"What did you do after you left high school?" I asked as she picked up a roll of tape, studied it, flipped it over and read the small print. "I went to Barnard, then to law school at the University of Pennsylvania." She put down the tape and selected an economy-size container of Elmer's Glue.

"An unusual path to the convent."

"You have no idea." She balanced the glue in her hand as though she were weighing it. "This should do the job." I didn't know what the rules of her order were, but I had decided she must be wearing a little makeup. Either that or she had lips the color of a pink rose.

We got in line at the cash register behind a man wearing a red Coca-Cola jacket who was trying to get Mr. Kim to sign for a stack of soft drinks he had wheeled into the store. While Mr. Kim studied the invoice, apparently in more detail than the deliveryman thought was necessary, Patricia tolerated my attempt to connect the dots between the doubting seventh grade girl she once was and the nun she had become. I learned that after law school she had gone to work for a succession of firms on Wall Street—"three, no four in all," she corrected—ending up as the head of the last company's office in Tokyo.

"Impressive."

"I guess. In Tokyo, they found me an apartment big enough to accommodate three or four families. And they insisted I have a driver." She shook her head as if it had all been a dream.

I sensed an opening and asked out of habit, "A husband?"

She turned and stared at me for a minute as though weighing her answer. "There was a husband, Russell, a husband and two young children." She looked me straight in the eyes as she continued. "They were killed by a drunk driver while I was in Manila on a business trip."

An old man staggered into line in front of Patricia, jostling her so hard that she had trouble holding onto the Elmer's Glue. I started to reach for his shoulder, intending to do no more than point out that there were other people waiting. Patricia stopped me, signaling silently that she didn't mind. Bits of dried leaves and grass plastered the old man's uncut hair and clung to his tattered sweatshirt. He raised a paper bag to his lips and sucked on the protruding neck of a bottle.

"You take that booze out of here before I call the police, old man," Mr. Kim bellowed from behind the counter. "How many times I tell you!"

The man cursed under his breath and took another drink. "You don't know a goddamned thing about running a gas station," the drunk declared loudly. "You wouldn't know a carburetor from a fucking distributor cap."

"I tell you before. Old man, this is not a gas station, it's a mini-mart with gasoline pumps."

"What a bunch of horseshit."

Mr. Kim put down the Coke man's invoice and reached for a telephone. "You remember what the police tell you last time. They not kidding."

The man cursed again, his words extremely vulgar, but turned and headed for the door. When he noticed Patricia, he raised the bottle as though making a toast. "Merry Christmas, pretty lady." She shook her head and smiled patiently when he offered her the bottle.

"What do you have there, Sister?" Mr. Kim chirped, attempting to regain his good humor as the Coca-Cola man wheeled his empty cart out the door.

Patricia showed him the Elmer's Glue and tried to pay for it. Mr. Kim refused to take her money. "I see you at the children's Mass tonight. My grandson Marco is going to be a shepherd." I'd never seen a man look prouder.

Patricia walked with me as I made my way to my car. "I'm on my way over to the church," she explained, pointing in the direction of St. Lawrence's. From behind us came the sound of breaking glass. The man in the filthy clothes had hurled his empty whiskey bottle against the concrete pavement. As we watched, he hollered indistinct words in the direction of Mr. Kim's store then dragged his feet toward the rear of the building and the tangle of trees and underbrush behind it, a small piece of jungle that appeared unchanged since my youth. As I watched him disappear into the growing darkness, a bizarre possibility jolted me. Butchie McDevitt's father had been roughly my mother's age. That would put him in his midseventies now.

Patricia took note of my curiosity. "We've had to call the police more than once when he wandered onto the school grounds. The county has tried to place him in homeless shelters several times, but they haven't had any luck keeping him there."

"This is crazy, but I was wondering if he's the man who owned the gas station that was on this property when I was a kid."

"Really? What was his name?"

"McDevitt."

She thought it over before shaking her head. "If I ever heard his name, I can't remember what it is."

The cold afternoon was growing colder. Patricia turned up the collar of her heavy coat, sunk her hands into its deep pockets, and dug out a pair of extremely red mittens.

"Are you sure you're a nun?" I teased as she pulled them on.

She laughed. "These were an early Christmas present from a little girl in the fourth grade." She smiled, holding them up for me to see. "I love them."

"I can't imagine Sr. Superior wearing red mittens when we were at St. Lawrence's."

"A lot of things have changed, Russell. You should poke your head in the door of the church this evening and take a look."

"And what would I see?"

"Maybe you'd see what going to church is supposed to be like."

I shook my head. "See that big wreck of a house behind you? I've got to go through it from basement to attic and see if there is anything worth keeping before I meet a realtor there tomorrow."

"On Christmas Day?"

"That's the deal. I told her if she wanted the listing she'd have to meet me tomorrow. I'm flying back to Boston at seven o'clock."

She hugged herself with the red mittens as she stared through the wet snow at the darkening silhouette of my childhood world. "I remember being jealous because you had such a short walk to school."

I laughed. "What I remember thinking was that the kids who didn't live where I did had no idea how lucky they were."

She turned and fixed her eyes on me. "Because of Fr. Kavanaugh?"

"How did you ever guess?"

A smile brightened her face.

"Did you know that my father once told him to go to hell?"

"Seriously?"

"Seriously. I'm sure you don't remember, but one day in the seventh grade, I interrupted religion class and informed Sr. Mary Luke that I truly believed there was salvation outside the Catholic Church."

"You have no idea how well I remember that day."

"Really?" She sounded incredulous.

I nodded. "In fact, you can tell Vinnie that it's all your fault that I turned into whatever he thinks I am today."

She studied me thoughtfully, wondering, I'm sure, if I was kidding. I reminded her that she was in the middle of telling me about the time her father told Fr. Kavanaugh where to go.

"Oh yes. Where was I?" She closed her eyes, found her place, and, taking a deep breath, picked up the story. "That night Fr. Kavanaugh called our house. My mother answered the phone but quickly handed it to my father. In a tirade that I could partially hear from across the room, Fr. Kavanaugh bellowed that based on the heretical statements I had made in class that afternoon, it was his conclusion that the entire Delsey family was on the road to eternal damnation."

She brushed snow from my hair with her mittens and smiled. "I don't know how well you remember my father, but he was, almost without exception, reserved and polite. Sounding exactly that way, he calmly informed Fr. Kavanaugh that he would phone him right back, hung up, and asked me to tell him, word for word, what I had said in class that day. After I did, he called Fr. Kavanaugh back and informed him that anyone who disagreed with the common sense statements I had made that afternoon was either poorly educated or an idiot. My father listened, murmuring 'is that right' from time to time, and then, enunciating each word as though he were talking to a person who had difficulty understanding English, said, 'Kavanaugh, why don't you go to hell.' He hung up, informed me I had been expelled from St. Lawrence's and that my younger brother Melvin had been thrown off the altar boys. Picking up the newspaper he had been reading, he said it might be the best thing that had ever happened to either of us."

I smiled at her story and at the image of Fr. Kavanaugh hurling the phone across the room after Patricia's father hung up.

"You've come a long way since being expelled from St. Lawrence's," I observed when she asked me what was so funny.

"In what way?"

"Apparently you are back to believing all of it."

"All of what?"

"You know. God, heaven, hell, purgatory, the Catholic Church. Everything the priests and nuns were so determined to shove down our throats when we were kids."

She studied me for longest time before quietly answering. "What I believe with all my heart, Russell, is that we all have to believe in something."

I leaned back against the car, folding my arms across my chest. This wasn't little old Sr. Sister Mary Luke pitching platitudes and clichés, the questioning of which would be beyond her comprehension. This wasn't Fr. Kavanaugh hammering a cowering congregation over the head with the inevitability of eternal damnation for any man, woman, or child who did not cower before him and the juggernaut of dos and do nots that he commanded. This was an intelligent, educated woman, a woman who had had the courage to stand up in the middle of seventh grade religion class and confidently dismiss the concept that only Catholics had any shot at getting into heaven. The memory of that afternoon had remained with me through all these years, the sunny fragrance of spring beyond the classroom windows, the quietly confident insistence of the tall, young girl who had become the beautiful woman who was speaking to me now with the same quiet confidence.

I could tell by the way she was looking at me that she wanted to say more. "Go ahead and say it," I prompted.

That caught her off guard but just for a second. "Russell, why did you come back here?"

"My mother died last month, and I'm selling the house," I answered, nodding at the snow-shrouded silhouette at the edge of Mr. Kim's pavement. "Like I said, I've got to go through the whole place before it goes on the market." I laughed. "As though there are any memories from a happy childhood over there that need saving."

"I'm sorry about your mother. I'll remember her in my prayers."

I shook my head but managed to say thank you.

She removed her hands from the warmth of the deep coat pockets, pushed back one sleeve, and glanced at her watch. "Father Rinaldi thinks God brought you back here so you could find your soul." She said it matter-of-factly in the same tone with which she would have said "Father Rinaldi thinks you came back to find your old Marty Marion baseball glove."

"Vinnie is nutty as a fruitcake. He always was."

From the steeple of St. Lawrence's, barely visible in the snow-laced sky, the soft notes of "Adeste Fideles" admonished me for saying a thing like that on Christmas Eve.

CHAPTER FIFTEEN

All along Prospect Street, houses awaited Christmas with more illuminated expectation than I remembered. Soft, blue lights completely outlined the house where Mrs. Enright, the parish organist, had lived when I was a boy. Strings of white lights glowed like tiny stars in the shrubbery of the house across the street from the church, and everywhere I looked, window candles warmed the cold night air. The once-grand Victorian I grew up in was the only home on the street whose windows and shrubs took no notice of the special night. It loomed in unlit stillness like a ship anchored in dense fog, its deep porch, the long second-floor windows, and the wide attic dormers as joyless as ever.

To the right of the house, crowding the narrow driveway and the remains of a privet hedge, the massive stone church loomed over all, glowing from within in anticipation of a Christmas Eve liturgy starring an army of costumed school children. St. Lawrence's remained strong and enduring and overpowering, a mountainous survivor mocking the worn pile that had been the grandest residential structure in all of Harrisville when my Grandfather Cornell built it.

With wet snowflakes drifting like tiny parachutes through the branches of a sycamore that had been old when I was young, I stamped my freezing feet against the wet sidewalk and asked myself again why I had ever thought it was necessary to revisit the scene of my screwed-up boyhood when all I had to do was call the realtor and tell her to have Goodwill take whatever they wanted from the house and send everything else to the dump. My hands and ears were colder than my feet. St. Lawrence's, its luminous stained-glass windows afire like a row of holiday fireplaces, looked more inviting than I was willing to admit. He was gone. Long gone. Maybe the experience inside the church would be different now, and maybe it wouldn't. I pushed my hands deeper into my coat pockets, found the house key, and turned it over with my numbing fingers. I hadn't flown all the way down from Boston to stand outside in the cold.

The lights worked, mildly surprising me, but it was so cold inside the house that I could see my breath. The thermostat in the short hallway between the living room and kitchen responded with a faint metallic click when I turned up the setting. Deep in the cellar, the ancient furnace protested this unexpected prodding with a series of unsettling noises. I debated turning the temperature back down before deciding I was cold enough to risk an explosion.

To my amazement, my mother's ironing board still occupied the corner of the kitchen where it stood my entire childhood. The same army of flowerpots lined the wall of windows facing the church, the plants they once sustained now nothing more than tangles of dry stalks bleached white as tiny skeletons. A religious calendar that had lost its grip on the wall next to the refrigerator lay face up on the linoleum floor, insisting the month was still the long-ago March when my mother left the only house she had ever known to be driven, decidedly against her will, to an assisted living home where her pathetic downward spiral dragged on unmercifully. Because his feast day is in March, a picture of Saint Joseph filled the space above the rectangles of days. I knew feast days, I still remembered Latin, and I knew that priests wore white vestments on Christmas Day, knowledge the good nuns at St. Lawrence's had deemed even more important than the ability to diagram sentences.

Without thinking, I pulled a chair away from the kitchen table and sat down. Across the room, the high, gray walls of the church seemed closer than ever, creating the unsettling specter of an ocean liner nudging silently against a pier.

I turned toward the kitchen counter where my mother had spent much of her adult life nervously attempting to fix Fr. Kavanaugh's dinners exactly the way he remembered his own *sainted* mother preparing them. The chair where he reigned night after night patiently awaited his arrival. I fixed my eyes on the back porch door through which he came and went as though our house belonged to him. Had one happy mealtime ever taken place at this table? Did I ever once experience a big Thanksgiving dinner like the ones my grade school classmates took for granted? I pounded the table with my open hand, recalling the incredible bullshit Fr. Kavanaugh fed my simple-minded mother and wished his unholy soul to hell for what he did to Butchie. *Let it go,* I told myself, closing my eyes. *The bastard is dead. No one knows that better than you.*

The front doorbell rang, scattering thoughts I could live without. As I crossed through the living room, I stopped and stared at the carpet where I once spread the Sunday comics in an effort to imitate the way I imagined kids with normal lives lived. Before the pathetic futility of such wishful thinking had time to fully register, the doorbell chimed again, sounding a two-note cadence unchanged by years of idleness. Patricia Delsey smiled when I opened the door.

"I ran into Father Rinaldi while I was delivering the repaired halo next door. He insisted I come over and remind you of your date to join him for eggnog after the children's Mass." Her breath was visible as she spoke, her face flushed with the healthy sting of winter air. "May I come in before I freeze to death?"

I held the door open, surprised but happy to see her again so soon. The red mittens reappeared as she swept snowflakes from the sleeves of her long, black coat and followed me back to the kitchen where the temperature was only slightly warmer than on the front porch.

"I turned up the thermostat, but so far the furnace has produced more noise than heat."

She smiled, her eyes taking in for the first time the interior of the old house whose every detail I knew by heart. "It looks even closer from in here," she stated, turning toward the windows. "St. Lawrence's, I mean. You really did grow up close to it."

"Forty-three feet."

"What?"

"It's exactly forty-three feet from the side of our house to the base of St. Lawrence's Church."

"You actually measured it?" she asked incredulously.

"More than once."

She laughed. "But you didn't consider yourself lucky to live so close to the school, not even when it was raining or as cold as it is today?"

"Lucky? I wouldn't wish the experience on my worst enemy."

The bitterness that soured my words caused her to pause thoughtfully. "And that was because of Fr. Kavanaugh?"

I nodded.

"What an unexpected and ghastly way for him to die," she said quietly, removing the red mittens. "Falling down those stairs in the dark and breaking his neck."

When I didn't say anything, she closed her eyes and touched her nose with the tips of praying fingers. "May his soul rest in peace."

I could have added an Amen, but it would have been a lie.

Patricia sat down in the chair that no one except Fr. Kavanaugh had ever used, placing the knitted mittens, one on top of the other, on the table. "Russell, why do you think you came back here?" The directness of her question caught me off guard.

"What do you mean?" I managed to say.

"Why did you go to all the trouble of flying back here at Christmastime when we both know you could have made arrangements to dispose of this house without leaving Boston?"

The best I could do was shrug.

She looked straight at me. "I think you may well be in the midst of the same journey I took some time ago." Her from-the-heart sincerity was a weapon that made me nervous. "I think," she continued, "that when we were young, you and I were the type of people who weren't content to accept the things we were told not to question."

The furnace in the cellar grunted again, either coming to life or getting ready to blow Patricia and me to kingdom come. She didn't seem to notice.

"I think we both rebelled, in all probability for very different reasons, and took paths that soared in earthly terms beyond anything we had ever experienced or expected. We lived lives that many people would consider ideal." She smiled. "From Harrisville to the moon." The smile faded as she became thoughtful. "But as years went by, we grew increasingly unsatisfied, each new year demanding more work, more accomplishments, more trappings of the good life to mask the absence of truly meaningful accomplishments." She laughed quietly. "Or in your case, judging by the shopping habits I observed this afternoon at Mr. Kim's, requiring more women to distract you from the lack of real values in your life."

I couldn't help picturing Dr. Kite sitting in the corner of the kitchen, scribbling down every word of our conversation.

"In my case, the great wake-up call was the loss of my family. Because I had no spiritual foundation, I lost my bearings completely. For years..." She was suddenly silent, taking her time to back out of the road she had started down. A minute passed before she stood and walked over to the kitchen windows where she seemed to contemplate the stained-glass windows glowing on the other side of the driveway. "Forgive me for being judgmental, Russell. I know I have no right to make such an assumption about your life. I only know that the trajectory of my own life before now reminded me of those Fourth of July fireworks they set off at McKinley Park when we were kids. They rocket into an empty sky, explode in spectacular brilliance, and then nothing but empty sky again."

She came back to the table and picked up the mittens. "Over in the church, as I contemplated the peaceful expectation of Christmas, it came to me that your return today was no accident. Whether you know it or not, you came back here to meet me and meet Vinnie and revisit the place where you first met God."

Patricia pushed back the heavy sleeve of her coat and checked her watch, clearly embarrassed by the weight of the message she had just delivered. "There are some last-minute things I have to do over at the church." She struggled with the top button of her coat but finally got it. "Please try to come over to the Mass. I think you'll find that St. Lawrence's is an entirely different place than you remember." To my complete surprise, she gave me a hug. "God bless you, Russell."

I let her out and turned to face a living room that could have been the stage setting for a 1950s television program, complete with a stack of *Collier's* magazines on the coffee table and the dull-gray eye of a Zenith television staring blankly from the corner near the fireplace. The old sofa, yellowing doilies pinned to its wide arms, was much too tempting to resist. I sat heavily and closed my eyes for the first time since waking up in a Boston hotel with a woman I hardly knew. The bells atop the church next door seemed to ask what kind of a person behaved like that on Christmas Eve. I smiled weakly and raised my hand. "Guilty," I said aloud. Not that I felt good about it, but not that I felt bad about it either. I opened my eyes and focused on the stairway across the room. My bedroom was on the right side of the landing at the top of those stairs. My mother's big bedroom, scene of the sinning that took place while Catholicism was drummed into my head in classrooms a stone's throw away, was at the end of the hallway. They were both dead now, my mindless mother and the snake who came slithering out from under a rock when my father died.

The thought of trudging all the way up to the cavernous attic and working my way back down, searching for God knows what, seemed more senseless than ever. It wasn't like there was some beloved reminder of my childhood waiting to be rediscovered. Such treasures belonged to boys with normal lives, not a slave who Fr. Kavanaugh kept far too busy to play baseball or football or join the Boy Scouts. I dozed long enough and deeply enough to awake with a start. The dream had been no more than a snapshot of his twisted body at the bottom of the church stairs. I closed my eyes again, struggling for the thousandth time to decide whether I actually meant to kill him. As incensed as I was about what he had done to Butchie, I probably did. What I knew for sure was that I didn't do a damn thing to keep him from falling and had never for one minute wished I had.

It might have been my imagination, but it seemed like the old furnace was finally pushing a little heat up into the house, warmth that felt so good I closed my eyes again.

Chapter Sixteen

My mother looked over her shoulder and told me she had called someone about the furnace but was told they couldn't send anyone until after Christmas. Even with my eyes closed, I knew she was fixing pork chops and sauerkraut, a dish, Fr. Kavanaugh regularly complained, she had never learned to prepare anywhere near as well as his dear, departed mother. Smoke rose from the snapping frying pan, forming a pungent cloud that spread slowly across the kitchen ceiling. "He's late," she declared nervously, glancing at the clock above the refrigerator.

"He's dead," I told her.

She shook her head. "Such nonsense."

Dr. Kite dragged his big swivel chair in from the dining room and sat down. He flipped open his notepad and carefully placed it on the top knee of his tightly crossed legs. "Now maybe we will finally get somewhere. Mr. Flynn, please tell me who these people are."

There were four people in the kitchen besides Dr. Kite

and me, but I only knew three of them. "My mother, Rose Marie Flynn," I began, nodding toward the stove.

Dr. Kite clicked open his Montblanc, stating he had assumed as much.

"My father, Dennis Flynn," I told him, gesturing toward the man sitting next to me, his back to the stove. It was my mother's chair, not that she ever sat down much when Fr. Kavanaugh was here. My father looked exactly like he did in the photographs. The sleeves of his army uniform were rolled halfway up his thick forearms just like they were in the great picture taken when I was a baby, and he was cradling me like a football. The bright sunlight of that long-ago afternoon chiseled his face in dark shadows that made no sense indoors.

"His *dead* father," my mother hissed, stabbing the pork chops out of the frying pan and arranging them on a platter lined with folded paper towels.

"Excuse me for dying, Rose Marie." My father winked at me, pushed his chair back from the table, and strolled over to the refrigerator. "Is my beer still in here, Rose Marie?"

Dr. Kite scribbled away. "The exact date and cause of your death, Mr. Flynn?"

"August 17, 1941, heart attack."

"Struck dead by God is more like it," my mother interjected. "While you're making all those notes, ask him what he was doing when God struck him dead. Ask him exactly what he was doing."

My father laughed, stooping to get a better look at the bottom shelves of the refrigerator. "Playing golf at Hamilton

Country Club. Third hole. Par three. Blacked out bending over to tee up my ball. No pain. No nothing. Just lights out."

That wasn't good enough for my mother. "Tell him what day of the week it was, Dennis Ignatius Flynn. Go ahead and tell him it was a Sunday," she persisted. "A Sunday morning when any decent Catholic man would have been at Mass. God struck you down for your sins, Dennis Flynn! Fr. Kavanaugh assured me he did!"

"I tend to doubt that, Rose Marie." My father had somehow found a beer that had never been in the refrigerator in my lifetime. He opened it, and took a long swig, then smiled at my mother. "Anyway, you better hope he didn't, because if God strikes men dead for playing golf on Sunday morning, just imagine what he has in store for a woman who spent her days diddling her pastor while her little boy was in religion class with the good nuns next door."

He winked at me again as he came back to the table and sat down with his beer. My mother's habitually pale face glowed like a neon beet.

"We are finally getting somewhere," Dr. Kite mused, clicking his pen rapidly while reviewing his notes. "Indeed we are." He looked at me quizzically and nodded toward the woman sitting directly across the table from me.

Shade cast by The French Lady's broad-brimmed hat obscured all but her bright-red lips and the small beauty mark at the corner of her mouth. She removed a speck of tobacco from the tip of her tongue, studied it, and flicked it away with the same hand scissoring a lipstick-stained cigarette between two very long fingers. When I told Dr. Kite that her name was Mrs. DeSimone, she nodded as though she had just been introduced as a guest on a TV talk show.

My father raised his beer and said he was pleased to meet her.

"Harlot!" my mother hissed.

Dr. Kite spelled the name out loud as he made a note of it. "Capital D, capital S?" he inquired, raising an eyebrow in her direction.

The French Lady took a long drag on her cigarette and bowed her head so slightly that the brim of her hat barely moved. Dr. Kite pointed his pen at each of them, apparently making sure he had all the characters straight.

"Mr. Flynn, Mrs. Flynn, Mrs. DeSimone," he mumbled, making three checks in his notebook. "And," he announced dramatically, turning toward the mysterious person sitting in the chair that had always been reserved for Fr. Kavanaugh, "I have asked God to be here."

Nobody except me seemed to think that what Dr. Kite had just said was any big deal. My mother glanced at the clock again, apparently wondering why Fr. Kavanaugh was late. My father took a swallow of his beer and stifled a burp, and Mrs. DeSimone studied her long, red fingernails. I had the uneasy feeling that all of us should do something before God got mad, but I had no idea what. We had been taught at St. Lawrence's to call a bishop Your Excellency and a cardinal Your Eminence, but the subject of meeting God had never come up. For His part, God did nothing except stare into the palms of his cupped hands as though there were something in them that only He could see. His hair and beard were a little wild, like He had just been outside on a windy day, but they were very clean and shampooed-looking. There were no little angels flying around his head or anything like that, but I couldn't help but notice that his white robe seemed to glow the way a lampshade glows. He was wearing a wristwatch.

I had seen enough Holy Cards in my day to know that He had to be God the Father. Number one, he didn't look like any picture of Jesus that I had ever seen, and number two, it was a pretty good bet that he wasn't the Holy Ghost, because the only ways I had ever seen the Holy Ghost pictured was as tongues of fire or as a dove.

Butchie McDevitt came into the kitchen from the direction of the living room and dragged a chair up to the table. "My old man couldn't make it. He's playing cards at the Moose." When he offered my mother a Lucky Strike, she recoiled as though it were a thing vile and disgusting. Butchie shrugged and looked across the table at me. "Hey, Peckerhead, where you been?"

"Who is this creature?" Dr. Kite inquired, pointing his pen in the direction of Butchie, who flipped him the bird and said he was Santa Claus.

Dr. Kite cleared his throat. "As you all know, this is Christmas Eve, a special night for God when He is, shall we say, wearing his Christian hat." I could tell by his smug smile that Dr. Kite was quite pleased with his theological witticism, but making a wisecrack about God with Him sitting right there made me very nervous. God just kept staring into his upturned palms. Either He didn't mind Dr. Kite's little joke or He knew that He was going to have the last laugh anyway, so there was no rush dealing with smug psychiatrists with tasseled loafers. "Mrs. Flynn, is there anything you would like to ask God?" Dr. Kite continued.

She was so busy scrubbing the frying pan with SOS that she didn't even turn around as she shook her head. "Oh, wait a minute," she suddenly shrieked, spinning around and wiping her hands on her apron. "I certainly do have a question for Him. Why on earth would Fr. Kavanaugh take up with a woman like that?" Her finger shook with anger as she pointed at Mrs. DeSimone.

"Why would he ever have anything to do with a woman like you? That is the question," shot back Mrs. DeSimone, jabbing the air with her cigarette as she fired the words at my mother.

My mother glanced nervously at God before answering. "Because of the rule."

"What rule?" Mrs. DeSimone scoffed.

"As God would tell you," my mother started, apparently assuming that God was going to back her up, "priests who are specially selected by God are permitted to partake of the comforts of chosen women, women who will be rewarded in heaven for the good work they do." She recited the words as though she had been asked a catechism question. "Women such as myself are revealed to holy men like Fr. Kavanaugh in spiritual dreams."

Mrs. DeSimone laughed out loud, startling my mother to the point where she had to gather herself before continuing.

"I was the woman chosen by God to comfort Fr. Kavanaugh—*to renew his spirit* was the way he put it—so he would be able to carry on the exhausting work of tending to a parish consisting of all manner of sinners."

My father shook his head. "You were always gullible as hell when it came to religion, Rose Marie, but that is one for the books."

Mrs. DeSimone stood up and walked slowly across the floor, waving my mother away from the sink. "If you believe those things, Mrs. Flynn, you are crazy. Fr. Kavanaugh and me, we did what men and women do. He tried to tell me all that crap he told you. One time he brought his dirty laundry to my house, and I threw it out into the front yard. One time he told me what he wanted for dinner, and I told him to go see you." She crushed out her cigarette in the sink.

Disbelief and confusion registered on my mother's face. She looked at God, twisting her apron into tight knots with her nervous hands. "Tell her, God, tell all of them that you told Fr. Kavanaugh in a dream that I was the one chosen to comfort him. Tell them that it was a way for me to gain a higher place in heaven."

My father tapped his empty beer bottle lightly on the table. "Rose Marie, you must be an idiot." He sounded much more sad than angry.

God rose to his feet and spread his arms. His hands were large, but unlike Fr. Kavanaugh's, his fingers were thin. His nose was also thin and a little long but not nearly as long as Vinnie Rinaldi's nose. His eyes were either green or blue, it was hard to tell, and they were fixed on me. The strange thing was that I could read his mind even though ever since I was a kid, I had been taught that God was the one who knew what everyone else was thinking. *At some point in their life,* He was thinking now, *everyone receives the word. You, Russell, received it one spring afternoon in the seventh grade when Patricia Delsey stood up and spoke words wise beyond her years. Words I intended for you. I am Catholic, I am Lutheran, I am Baptist and Buddhist and Hindu. I am no religion, and I am all religions.*

Dr. Kite jotted away furiously, no doubt in anticipation of the bestseller he would start working on the second he got back to Boston.

God cleared his throat and looked at me hard. *Keep using Kavanaugh as an excuse for your actions, and you will end up where he is.* His bushy eyebrows flicked a time or two, the green-blue eyes softened, and e left. It wasn't clear just how he left, but suddenly he was gone. They were all gone.

⊶∞∞⊷

The resounding peal of St. Lawrence's steeple bells shook the bones of the house gently but persistently, prodding me into a confused state of wakefulness. "Angels we have heard on high," they called into the winter air, "sweetly singing o'er the plains." Brainwashed to the point of lunacy, I knew the words to more hymns than the average monk.

Downstairs in the cellar, the furnace reacted to the bells by launching a series of ominous groans. I buttoned my coat and put on my gloves, wondering if Dr. Kite would conclude that such a bizarre dream was a sign that my mind was trying to let go of the baggage of my sorry childhood or a warning that coming back to Harrisville was the worst thing I could have possibly done. I turned off the lights and locked the door behind me.

CHAPTER SEVENTEEN

The light snow had turned to sleet, producing a torrent of tiny ice pellets that danced crazily on the sidewalk in front of the house. Up and down Prospect Street, strings of miniature lights continued to cast a spell on the cold night, a yearly transformation of the ordinary into the bewitching perpetuated by Catholics and Protestants and by those of no particular religious connection who simply took joy in the peaceful beauty of Christmas.

Unimpressed by the magic of it all, a man slumped on the front porch steps, his head between his knees and an empty whiskey bottle at his feet. He awoke with a start and growled incoherently when I touched his shoulder.

"Do you have some place to go? You're going to freeze to death out here."

"Fuck you," he mumbled as his head dropped back between his knees.

"Is your name McDevitt?" I asked. The crazy thought that he might be Butchie's father had stayed with me since

Patricia and I crossed paths with him at Mr. Kim's.

"What?" the drunk slurred, wiping his mouth with the back of his hand.

"There used to be a man named McDevitt who ran a gas station next door. He had a son named Butchie."

The old man tried to focus on my face but gave up and reached for the bottle. After tilting his head back and sucking nothing but air, he flung the bottle out into Prospect Street.

"I used to live here," I attempted to explain, pointing at the empty house behind him, "with my mother, Mrs. Flynn. Do you remember us?"

He made a half-assed effort to turn and look at the house. The tirade that followed was a confetti of incomprehensible words.

Something had to be done with him, whatever his name was. No one with a lick of sense would leave the family dog outside in this weather, much less a human being with no protection against the freezing night but a torn sweatshirt. Beyond Mr. Kim's gas pumps, a telephone booth signaled like a lantern through the blowing snow. Making a phone call to the police struck me as a reasonable idea until I remembered Patricia saying that no one had ever been able to keep the man at my feet in a homeless shelter. The lusty voice of St. Lawrence's old pipe organ escaped into the night as the heavy doors opened to welcome flocks of parents and children hurrying to Mass. *Why not*, I responded to the solution the inviting doors suggested. The Fr. Kavanaugh I knew would have had a shit fit if anyone had dragged a freezing drunk into his church. That thought alone was reason enough to do it.

"Come on, Buddy, let's get you into a nice warm back pew."

He came awake, cursing when I tried to lift him. "Get the fuck off me, you bastard!" he slurred. The man was too drunk to do any damage with his fists but that didn't keep him from trying. There may have been creatures on earth with worse-smelling breath, but my guess was that most of them were housed safely in zoos. His clothes reeked with the smell of urine. I backed off and let him slump back onto the steps. It would take a better man than me to drag him over to the church and up all those granite stairs. Plan B was the answer: I'd drag him into the house and lift him onto the living room sofa. If I couldn't manage that, I'd leave him sleeping on the carpet. Either way, he wouldn't freeze to death.

A weird thought occurred to me as I lugged the half-snoring, half-cursing body across the porch. If it was true that the dead can see us from wherever they end up after their days on earth are through, my mother would surely let me know if the man being dragged into her beloved house was Butchie's father, a man she regarded as a disciple of the devil himself. After I got him as far as the living room carpet, I let him down gently and listened. There was no rumble of winter thunder, no rattling of chains high in the attic, and no unworldly moans from the furnace in the cellar. Either he wasn't Mr. McDevitt or all that business about the dead being able to see us from the hereafter was no more true than the rumor that there was a spanking machine in Sr. Superior's office.

Now what, Mr. Good Samaritan? I asked myself. *What is this guy going to do when he wakes up, half sober and totally confused? Ransack the house looking for booze? Burn it to the ground when he doesn't find any?* My fingers turned the house key over in my pocket until, as though I had rubbed the genie lantern, a startling idea came to me. There was no real need for me to sell the house. I wanted to get rid of it and sever the last tie to my hellish childhood, but I didn't need the money. I didn't even *want* the money. Whatever I spent it on or invested it in would continue to tie me to the nightmare of my childhood. One thought led to another as I rolled the key around in my pocket. Maybe Patricia and her order of nuns could use the house for one of their programs. The location couldn't be any better; the only thing separating it from the church property was the remains of a hedge that may as well have never existed.

The metallic finality of the door latch catching behind me seemed to sound an emphatic Amen to everything that had ever happened behind the walls of one very large and very tired Victorian house. The only thing left to do was find Patricia, tell her about the old man sleeping in the living room—her living room—and give her the key.

It was the first time I ever made the short walk to St. Lawrence's without wishing I was somewhere else. I might even admit to feeling merry about it.

CHAPTER EIGHTEEN

On the landing atop St. Lawrence's worn granite steps, a mother struggled to keep her umbrella centered over two small children cradling plastic angel wings against their snow-covered coats. When I reached around them to open the heavy door, angelic sounds of children rehearsing the sacred sound of Christmas greeted the wintry night.

"Just look at how beautiful everything is!" the woman exclaimed to her children.

And it was. At the front of the church, thousands of star-like lights nestled in the forest of cut pines and poinsettias surrounding the white marble altar. To the left of the altar, in front of the straw-roofed manger it had been my unwanted responsibility to set up every Advent, Patricia whispered last-minute instructions to Jesus and Mary and began straightening wings and halos on an assortment of excited angels and saints. It was obvious that she would not have traded being with those kids on this special night for a pile of gold.

Without thinking, I dipped my fingers into the holy water font and blessed myself as I moved into the church to make way for families flooding through the door and children darting down the aisle to join a growing huddle of their classmates surrounding Patricia. An usher held up one finger and signaled for me to follow him to a seat he had located halfway down a side aisle. I had not planned to actually attend Mass; all I wanted to do was find Patricia and tell her about the house. Unable to devise a signal to convey such a message, I gave up and found myself genuflecting and sliding into a pew as naturally as I had blessed myself with holy water. Before I knew what I was doing, I had lowered the hinged kneeler and was halfway through a Hail Mary. Startled at the ease with which I had been swept along like a leaf in a stream, I sat down, my long-ago conclusion that there was nothing real about religion threatened by the devious fragrance of pine trees and candle wax.

I felt like a trespasser, an interloper who, at any minute, could be asked for his ticket and shown the door when he couldn't produce one. Communion would be a dead giveaway. Unless there was another unconfessed womanizerslash-pastor killer in the congregation, I would be the only person who didn't stand up and get in line when the time came. People in my pew would be forced to stumble over me, their Christmas liturgy defiled by wild speculation about the state of my soul. If I faked it and made my way up the aisle with the rest of them, no one would be the wiser. The more I thought about that option, the more uncomfortable I became, a reaction no doubt reinforced by the eyes trained on me like a pair of security cameras from the huge crucifix suspended above the altar. There was only one way for a person whose milk bottle soul had run dry to get back in the game.

Only one person remained in line at the confessional nearest to me: a woman fingering a rosary who looked too old to commit any sins worth worrying about. Above the carved wood door of the priest's compartment, the name Father Rinaldi explained why I had not yet spotted Vinnie. I smiled. I couldn't help it. After listening to that old lady, my sins, especially the big one, would blow his mind. It wasn't the classic reason for going to confession, maybe it was even a sinful one, but after the things I had done, a little sin like that would barely register. With the stupid feeling that the plaster eyes of the crucifix were following my every move, I squeezed my way out of the pew and took my place in line.

"Do you have much to tell?" the lady with the rosary turned and whispered.

"Only one murder," I whispered back.

The look of shock that contorted her face vanished as fast as it appeared. "Such a jokester," she replied.

A wave of excitement swept through the packed church as Patricia's cast of Nativity characters made their way to the rear of the church and lined up for the start of Mass. Necks craned as families tried to locate a particular shepherd, angel, or Wise Man. Like a movie director, Patricia readied her charges for action and signaled to the front of the church where a bell rang, bringing the congregation to its feet. The huge pipe organ high in the loft ignited, the choir cut loose with the wonderful Latin sounds of "Adeste Fideles," and St. Lawrence's Church awoke in a way it never had in my childhood. The face of an angel turned red as a holly berry when a young child squealed, "There's Sarah!" Christmas or no Christmas, the laughter that erupted would have blown Fr. Kavanaugh's mind.

I pushed back the heavy curtain and lowered myself onto the kneeler in the cramped darkness of Vinnie's confessional, filled with the odd feeling that I was watching this happen to someone else.

From the other side of the confessional, the murmur of the old woman's confession droned like a distant insect, too faintly to betray actual words but clearly enough to reveal the hesitancy in her voice and the prodding tone of Vinnie's nasally interruptions. As a boy, I had dreaded the moment when the singsong cadence of absolution signaled that at any second, it would be my turn to take a stab at making vivid daydreams of the naked women on Mr. McDevitt's calendars sound no more serious than falling asleep before finishing my night prayers. The small window scraped open, making the exact wood-against-wood sound I remembered. I sensed Vinnie tilting his head toward me in the darkness, his big nose almost touching the perforated plastic screen.

"Bless me, Father, for I have sinned." I had no idea if Catholics still started confessions that way, but those were the words that had been chiseled into my brain, as were the next ones. "It has been many years since my last confession."

"How many years?"

"However many years it's been since I left Harrisville, Vinnie. What was that, thirty-five, almost forty years ago?"

"Russell? Praise be to the Lord on this holy night," he extolled after I assured him it was me. "This is no less than a Christmas miracle." He cleared his throat and lowered his voice, which had risen several octaves above the hoarse whisper normally employed by priests in the confessional. "Please proceed with your confession."

I breathed deeply like a basketball player at the foul line. "Where should I start?"

"Start with the most serious sin you have committed since your last confession."

I decided to save that one for last and opened with, "I have had sex many times with many women."

"You must be more specific. How many women and how many times?"

"I have no idea, Vinnie."

"Please call me Father Rinaldi in the confessional."

I took another deep breath. "I'll try."

"Thank you. Now think hard. Roughly how many times have you committed this particular sin?"

"Honestly, I have no idea. Hundreds of times, maybe thousands."

A sigh passed through the thin plastic screen. "Let's try another approach. How many different partners did these sins of fornication involve?"

The term he substituted for having sex sounded so biblical. I never thought of any of them as *fornication* partners. They were just women I had screwed, every one of them willing, and most of them very able. Extremely enjoyable memories fought for my attention, but I fought them off, remembering where I was.

"I'm sure you want this to be a good confession, Russell," Vinnie prodded, "a cleansing of the soul at Christmastime so to speak. Try your best to quantify these transgressions."

Without much hope of success, I did a quick calculation. The first time was freshman year of college with a girl named Brenda who was in my introduction to economics class, but I didn't get really rolling in the sex department until I finished law school and moved to Boston. Taking the number of years that had passed since then, multiplying that number by twelve to determine the number of months, and multiplying that answer by eight to arrive at the number of weekend nights, I came up with a subtotal to which I added something for occasional scores made during the work week, subtracted the two weeks when I was recovering from an appendectomy, and came up with a number that surprised even me. "Between one hundred and ninety and two hundred women," I told him.

"Good heavens" came the delayed reply through the screen.

"Vinnie, I'm fifty-one years old. It's kind of been my hobby."

There was a pause before he said, "Let's move into another area. How many times in your years away from the sacraments have you missed Mass on Sundays and holy days of obligation?"

"All of them, Vinnie. Except for weddings and funerals this is the first time I've been inside a church since we were kids." At the last second, I remembered the one Sunday when I had gone to Mass with the woman I had had sex with the night before, but I decided against getting off on a tangent.

"Could you at least address me as Father Vinnie?" Beyond the cramped darkness of the confessional, the choir had begun singing "Oh Little Town of Bethlehem."

"Look, Father Vinnie, there might be other people waiting to go to confession, so I might as well get to the point. I didn't come in here to talk about sex, or missing Mass on Sunday, or how many times I ate steak on Friday when that was still a sin. Those kinds of things have never bothered me."

"I don't quite understand. Those are all grievous sins..."

"Vinnie—excuse me, Father Vinnie—before we go any further, I need for you to assure me that the seal of the confessional is still in force. I know you said something about it on the airplane, but I need you to confirm that point. "

"Of course it is."

"No matter what I tell you?"

"Russell, the seal of the confessional is an essential aspect of the Sacrament of Penance. It is a sacred trust. I would be excommunicated if I ever revealed something that was told to me in the confessional."

"OK, fine. I just wanted to make sure."

"You have nothing to worry about. Please proceed with your confession."

"I committed the sin of murder. Once."

After he partially regained the gift of speech, Vinnie uttered a sound that was apparently made by rolling the words who, what, and when into a ball and delivering them with a gasp.

"I killed Fr. Kavanaugh."

"Oh dear God!"

There was a creaking sound as though Vinnie had fallen out of his chair. Minutes passed before the creaking repeated, and Vinnie whispered, "Fr. Kavanaugh fell down the stairs behind the church and broke his neck."

"I pushed him. Kind of."

"Dear God!"

"But why? He was a wonderful priest. He was my idol. Why on earth would you want to harm him?"

"Because he killed Butchie McDevitt."

The silence that followed made it clear that Vinnie was trying hard to sort things out. "You mean that hoodlum who lived at the gas station?" he finally asked. "What reason would Fr. Kavanaugh have for doing a thing like that?"

"Because he knew that Butchie had seen him screwing Mrs. DeSimone."

"Mrs. DeSimone?"

"The French Lady. The woman who always wore those big, black hats to Mass."

I took the incoherent mumbling that followed for absolution, blessed myself, and went back out into the church.

Chapter Nineteen

Delivered with an unmistakable sense of joy and expectation by a young priest with a clip-on microphone, the gospel retold the familiar story of Mary and Joseph arriving in Bethlehem and finding no place to stay except for a stable. Some of Saint Luke's words had been meddled with over the years, but the heart of the account remained unchanged from my youth and from long before that. When I was a boy, the part about the angel of the Lord appearing to the shepherds in the field never failed to create in my mind the image of an endless sky in which a million diamond-like stars formed the background for one huge star that looked like a dazzling, silver sun. My experience tonight was the same in every detail.

After the reading, Patricia's kids poured out of the front pews and took their places in front of the altar while two of the oldest shepherds placed a crib and a plastic Baby Jesus with stiff outstretched arms between Mary and Joseph. One of the smallest angels, apparently seized by panic when she looked up and saw the packed church, screamed for her mother, bringing Patricia out of the wings to give her a hug and hand her to a woman who had hurried down the aisle. As many in the congregation stood to get a better look, the Three Wise Men appeared from behind the lighted pine trees and placed what appeared to be cigar boxes wrapped in tinfoil next to the crib. The Blessed Mother said something to Saint Joseph that I could not hear, breaking up the people in the front pews and causing the mortified girl to drop her face into her hands. The sound of an unseen pitch pipe refocused the cast and generated a surprisingly good rendition of "Little Drummer Boy." Seized by a very un-Christmas-like thought, I hoped that, miles away in snow-covered Mt. Olivet Cemetery, Fr. Kavanaugh turned over in his grave when he heard the huge round of applause that followed Patricia's kids back to their seats.

As the church quieted in anticipation of the Christmas sermon, throats cleared, men coughed, and butts squirmed in the centuries-old quest to find comfort in hardwood pews. Missing from my days at St. Lawrence's was the collective cringe as Fr. Kavanaugh gripped both sides of the pulpit in his bear-like hands and strafed the sinners collected before him with a withering beam of disapproval. Tonight the cringe was missing, replaced by the sense of quiet expectation that accompanies the opening curtain of a play or the lowering of the lights in a movie theatre.

The priest with the clip-on microphone spread his hands and cried out in a voice worthy of Santa Claus, "Welcome to each and every one of you, and a very merry Christmas!"

He pushed back the fabric of his gold-trimmed vestments and dramatically studied his wristwatch. He held the watch up to his ear as though he were checking to see if it was working. Quiet laughter swept the church.

"I see that it's not quite Christmas yet. About four and a half hours to go." The watch disappeared under the wide fold of his alb. "But let's say it again anyway. Merry Christmas!"

It was obvious that the kids knew him and were completely comfortable in his presence because without hesitation, they responded with glee. "Merry Christmas, Father Bailey!"

Smiling, almost laughing, Fr. Bailey held up his hands. "Tonight I'm going to tell you a Christmas story. A true Christmas story." The kids grew still as did their parents and grandparents and, as much as could be expected, their little brothers and sisters. "I know it's a true story because it happened to me one Christmas morning when I was a little boy." He made a show of looking up into the vaulted structure of the cavernous church and pretended to think very hard. "Let me see, I was—yes—I was seven years old."

The woman at my side listened in open-mouthed wonder, a well-worn rosary frozen in her blue-veined hands. "Isn't he wonderful," she sighed, patting my knee and repeating her words, this time loud enough to cause a couple sitting in front of us to turn and nod emphatically. "In the old days," she continued, lowering her voice, "we had a pastor who was so terrible that I stopped going to Mass. God forgive me." She patted my knee again and leaned closer. "They say he fell down the stairs behind the church, but I believe what happened to him was God's work, if you know what I mean."

Perhaps a theological whiz like Saint Thomas Aquinas would have had an intelligent comment to make about the role played by God on that long-ago night, but I didn't. I smiled and was about to turn my attention back to the priest telling the Christmas story when a bewildered-looking Vinnie exited his confessional, rubbing his temples the way people with terrible headaches do. He surveyed the vast sea of faces in the packed church, thinking, perhaps, that if he didn't spot me, he might succeed in convincing himself that my confession never happened. When our eyes met, his shoulders slumped under the weight of knowing that he had not fallen asleep in the confessional and had a night-mare. He shook his head slowly and staggered toward the sacristy, dragging with him the weight of a terrible truth he would never be able to share with anyone.

"Isn't he wonderful," the woman sitting beside me repeated, referring to the priest in the pulpit, not Vinnie. "I love the stories he tells as much as the kids do."

I had to admit that he had everyone's attention, a feat accomplished without Fr. Kavanaugh's bullhorn delivery or the threat of eternal damnation. This priest—Fr. Bailey—did it with the skill of a storyteller, lowering his voice just enough to bring the kids to the edge of their seats before revealing that as the long-ago Christmas approached, he wanted a particular gift very badly. Smiling as his eyes swept the faces of the mesmerized children, he raised his voice again and baited them. "You will never, ever guess what I wanted."

"I know! I know!" Dozens of kids waved their hands wildly, begging for him to call on them. Others, completely carried away with excitement, shouted answers. "A bicycle! Rollerblades! A football!" Fr. Bailey, his smile blossoming into laughter, shook his head at every shouted guess. "A baby doll!" That one brought down the house.

Fr. Bailey held up his hands and patiently waited for the church to quiet. "You will never guess, not in a hundred years." Hands flew up again, more guesses filled the vast interior of St. Lawrence's. "A piano! A dog!"

Once again, the priest raised his hands. "No, none of those things. What I wanted for Christmas that year, what I wished for with my whole heart and prayed for every day of Advent was, was..." The kids were spellbound, some rising halfway out of the pews. He teased them again. "What I wanted for Christmas that year *was*...." I could almost hear a drumroll as Fr. Bailey prepared to put out the fire of their curiosity.

"I wasn't much older than some of you, and I remember thinking how cool it would be to have my very own *monkey*, a monkey with a red jacket and a little hat who would ride on the handlebars of my bicycle, who would sit in his own little chair while our family watched television. I even planned to bring him to school with me."

As the kids howled with glee, my heart leaped at the certainty that if he wasn't doing it already, Fr. Kavanaugh was spinning in his grave like a rotisserie chicken.

"Oh gracious, a monkey!" the woman beside me exclaimed, wiping laughter tears from the corners of her eyes. "A monkey for Christmas!"

The only person not caught up in the joy of the moment was Vinnie, who had stumbled out of the sacristy in a trance and taken a seat at the side of the altar. His face registered no more life than the plaster statue of St. Lawrence while Fr. Bailey described the tear-filled Christmas morning, his father's kindly explanation of why a monkey would not have been happy living in a split-level house with five children and two dogs, and his discovery of a gasoline-powered model airplane that made him forget all about the monkey.

"I'm telling you all of this because tomorrow morning under the Christmas tree, you probably won't find everything you wished for, and that's OK because your presents, no matter how exciting they are on Christmas morning, will soon become old and be set aside. What will last throughout the year, if you open your hearts and hold it there, will be the peace of this night, the wonderful sense of expectation that settles over the world on Christmas Eve and prepares us for the coming of Jesus Christ. May the peace of Christmas be with you all through the year and all through your lives." He closed his eyes for a few seconds, then raised his right hand and blessed us all, and as simpleminded as it made me feel to think such a thought, it felt good to be included within the sweep of his hand and to understand what every Sunday of my young life could have been like.

Chapter Twenty

Patricia was busy consoling a sobbing Blessed Mother when I caught up with her after Mass.

"You corrected yourself very quickly. I'm sure no one noticed."

"One of the shepherds laughed at me."

"I didn't see anyone laugh, and I was right over there in the first pew."

"Stanley Koloski did. I heard him."

Patricia was in the midst of assuring the Blessed Mother that she would be sure to speak with Stanley Koloski when one of the Wise Men scampered down the aisle. "Mom and Dad are waiting for you in the car!"

After watching the two of them disappear into the night, Patricia looked upward and blessed herself, perhaps thanking God that the Mass had gone smoothly and asking Him to give the Holy Family, the assorted Nativity visitors, and the holy host of angels a safe ride home with their parents.

"What was that all about? I didn't think even Fr. Kavanaugh could make the Blessed Mother cry," I teased.

She laughed. "I don't know if you noticed, but when she was reciting her lines, she addressed Saint Joseph as Kevin, which is the boy's real name."

I shook my head. "It must have happened when I was in the confessional."

If there were any way to take back the admission I had just so carelessly made, I would have done so. Patricia appeared to be stunned.

"Russell Flynn! Praise the Lord!" she exclaimed loud enough for the words to bounce around the emptying church.

"OK, OK. Don't get weird on me."

A small angel appeared out of nowhere and put both arms around Patricia, whose eyes closed for a moment before she gave the little girl a bear hug and sent her on her way.

"Is that difficult for you?" I wondered aloud.

Patricia wiped a tear from her cheek with the heel of her hand. "Is what difficult?"

"To be so close to these children after the way you lost your own."

She noticed a child's glove on the floor and stooped to pick it up. "It's the only thing that keeps me from losing my mind. My children live on in every child I teach. I see them grow and change, and I feel their love." She studied the small glove before folding it carefully and pushing it deep into the pocket of her wool skirt. "And someday I will see my own children and my husband again."

She didn't need anyone like me asking her if she really believed that was going to happen. Not tonight. Not ever.

An altar boy hurried out of the sacristy and bounded up the marble stairs to extinguish the stately candles, taking the last two steps with a leap that would have cost him dearly in Fr. Kavanaugh's day. Patricia seemed to read my mind. "Things have changed since you lived in the house next door," she said, smiling.

Her mention of the house jarred my memory. "By the way, this is the reason I came over to the church in the first place." I fished for the key in my coat pocket and handed it to her. "Merry Christmas."

I had to explain to her twice that I was giving her the house.

"But why?" she asked when she understood that I was serious.

"Why not? I don't want it. I don't need it. Life has been good to me, at least the part of life that started after I got the hell out of Harrisville."

"Russell…"

"Besides," I interrupted, " you may or may not know this, but my Grandfather Cornell donated the land for this church and most of the money to build it. I never knew him or my grandmother, but I'm guessing my doing this would make the two of them very happy."

Patricia looked toward the altar and then at me. "We do have a growing daycare program that is currently housed in the convent basement." She folded her hands and closed her eyes as if she were receiving a message only she could hear. When she opened her eyes again, she relayed the information to me. "The house will have to be deeded to the Sisters of Notre Dame de Namur, not to me."

I nodded, taking a business card from my wallet. "Send me a note telling me who I have to deal with, and I'll get the legal part of it rolling after the New Year."

"Flynn and Sinclair, Attorneys at Law," she read, studying the card.

"At your service."

"I remember enough about Boston to know this address is in the high-rent district."

I didn't deny it.

She turned and studied the manger scene. "What a night of wonders Christmas Eve is, Russell, so filled with peace and hope, and now the joy of your incredible gift." She held out her hand. "Will you join me in a Christmas prayer before you leave?"

She continued to hold my hand as we knelt together at the altar rail. "Lord Jesus," she prayed, "please bring Russell home as you brought me home. Straighten the difficult path he has traveled, and have him see the promise of this holy night."

The experience of holding her hand was unlike anything I had ever experienced with a woman. After I managed an awkward Amen, she released my hand, blessed herself, and stared at the plaster figurines. "When I was a little girl, I used to kneel here before the manger and pray that they would come to life."

I once knew their number by heart, down to the four lambs so small they sometimes became lost in the straw. They were all still there: the angel attached by a wire hook between its wings to the peak of the stable roof, the sheep, the camels, and the Three Wise Men whose names were among the rare items of religious dogma and detail I had managed to forget. An unintended edge soured my words as I began to recount out loud how I had been sentenced to jobs like putting together the manger scene when other kids were outside sleigh riding and throwing snowballs.

"Russell." Patricia stopped me softly. "It's time for you to forget all of those things. Fr. Kavanaugh died when we were still in grade school. How long are you going to allow your anger toward him to make you spiritually blind?"

The altar boy, who had finally finished putting out the candles, exited the altar as though bounding down marble steps was an Olympic event. His starched, white surplus was halfway over his head before he reached the sacristy door.

"There is joy in this parish now," Patricia said, smiling. "I am truly sorry there was no joy here when you were that boy's age, but it's not too late to open your heart to the strength and peace of God's love."

If someone like Vinnie had spoken those words, I would have written them off as a naive repetition of the things that had been pounded into our heads in religion class, but this wasn't Vinnie. It was an intelligent woman with life experiences that would have soured most people on the concept of a good God.

"You really believe there is something to religion, don't you?" I asked with as much sincerity as I had ever asked a question.

She looked at me for a minute, choosing her words carefully. "Russell, what I believe is that we all need an anchor, something solid to tie our lifeline to, because sooner or later, things get rough for most of us, and we need something to hold on to."

"And you think Catholicism is that anchor?"

"For people like us."

"Like us?"

"People who grew up as Catholics. It's just so much less complicated to embrace what you already know." She took me by the arm, and together we walked slowly toward the back of the church. "For someone who grew up as a Methodist or a Baptist or whatever, unless there are special circumstances, they are probably better off staying with what they know. That's not the company line. It just seems to make sense."

"Patricia, you have no idea what he did to my mother. You have no idea what he did to..."

"Forget Fr. Kavanaugh, Russell. He wasn't the Catholic Church. He was just a man, an overbearing, intolerant human being who had no concept of the peace religion can bring to a person's life."

"But the archbishop and the other people in power must have known what kind of man he was, and yet they continued to allow him to function as the pastor of St. Lawrence's."

"Russell, I don't know what those people knew and what

they didn't know, but think how long ago all of that was. Isn't it time to move on? Isn't it time to stop letting your experience with one dreadful person distort your vision of what life can be?"

We had reached the vestibule. I didn't want to leave her, but I had to get to the airport in time to see about flying back to Boston tonight instead of tomorrow.

"You would have made a damn good priest," I told her as I buttoned up my coat and put on my gloves.

She laughed. "It's against the rules."

"Still? What a shame. Oh, by the way, there's a man passed out in the living room next door."

She looked at me quizzically. "Who?"

Because it didn't feel right to refer to anyone as a drunk on Christmas Eve, I told her it was the homeless person we had seen at Mr. Kim's that afternoon. A safe guess was that her brief silence was filled with a silent prayer for the man.

"I'll take one of the priests with me and check on him in the morning. Do you think he will be all right until then?"

"With you praying for him, I know he will be."

She blushed. "Russell, whether you like it or not, I will be praying for you too. Every day."

I pushed open the heavy door. "Thank you, Patricia. If I ever reach the point where I think God isn't mad at me, I'll say some prayers for you."

"He isn't mad at you, Russell."

From the top of the church steps, I took a last look up and down Prospect Street and at the beds of star-like Christmas lights transforming the night in a way I had never recognized in all the years I lived here. There was something about Christmas Eve, "a wonderful sense of expectation that settles over the world," the priest who gave the sermon about the monkey had said. How incredibly wealthy were the people who experienced that feeling throughout their childhood. It was like a wonderful present they opened year after year. The bells in the steeple high above Prospect Street chimed the last notes of the beautiful hymn whose richness Fr. Kavanaugh's years of cruel domination had never tarnished.

The dark night wakes, the glory breaks,
And Christmas comes once more.

Attracted by pale-yellow light spilling through the living room window of the house next door, I climbed the snow-covered steps and wiped an oval in the thin layer of frost coating the glass. The man I had dragged into the house had not moved a muscle. If I still had the house key, I would have gone inside and slipped a twenty into his coat pocket. It was stupid to think he would use it for anything except to buy more booze, but what did it matter. It wasn't like he was training for the next Olympics.

Butchie McDevitt claimed that Christmas was for pecker-heads. It wasn't the stupidest thing he ever said, not by a long shot, and I had never argued with him about it. For one thing, the price of disagreeing with Butchie was almost always an arm-numbing punch in the shoulder, and to tell the truth, with Fr. Kavanaugh around, Christmas was no more fun for me than any other day of the year. He never let up, not at midnight Mass, not when the Ladies' Sodality decorated the church so beautifully, never. I cut that well-worn thought short. Forget the bastard. Patricia had not used those exact words, but she was right. Forget the bastard.

Sitting in the rental car, waiting for the defroster to do its thing, I remembered the book I discovered on a special shelf Sr. Ann Joseph set up in the school library one Advent. It was called *The Magic Window* or *The Christmas Window* or something like that, and it was about how every Christmas, a special window opened, and if you looked through it, God let you see how wonderful things in this world would be if everybody believed in Jesus.

I pulled out onto Prospect Street and headed for the airport, embarrassed to find myself wondering if that window had opened for me this evening and if what I saw was Patricia Delsey who, after everything she had been through, had embraced the things I had always believed were a load of crap. It wasn't like I was going to run out and join the Knights of Columbus or sign up for Vinnie's annual clothing drive at Boston College. I might—*might*—go to Mass every once in a while, and now that I had a clean slate, I might even stop trying to score with every good-looking woman I met.

The light at Thirty-Eighth Avenue turned red. Who the hell was I kidding? Maybe I would start slowly and climinate the married ones and, after that, any woman under the age of forty. It was still Christmas Eve, and I was already backsliding. I could picture Dr. Kite listening to all of this, his legs tightly crossed, his tasseled loafers twitching, and his Montblanc poised. "Mr. Flynn," he would conclude smugly, "do you actually believe there is a glimmer of hope for a man who just spent Christmas Eve falling in love with a nun?"

CPSIA information can be obtained
at www.ICGtesting.com
Printed in the USA
BVHW031931110820
586132BV00001B/133

9 781643 884011